Best wish...

THE CURSE OF MALENFER MANOR

Iain McChesney

WAYZGOOSE PRESS
Publisher of quality genre fiction and literary non-fiction

THE CURSE OF MALENFER MANOR

Copyright © 2013 by Iain McChesney

Published in the United States by Wayzgoose Press.
Edited by Dorothy E. Zemach.
Cover design by DJ Rogers.

Printed in the United States.

ISBN-10: 1938757106
ISBN-13: 978-1-938757-10-5

DEDICATION

for Adrienne
Ben *and* Aidan

Contents

Prologue
Haute-Marne, France (1794)

SUCH HEAT! THE GIRL TURNED HER FACE AWAY. THE HORSE SHIFTED roughly between her legs as if trying to escape. She heard the order given and the snap of the whip that caused the animal to lurch beneath her. There was a sensation of space in the hot breezy air before the branch took the strain to catch her; it creaked as the rope bit into her neck, and then she kicked with the panic of drowning.

Leaves curled brown before her eyes already trembling from the trauma, but she could make out a glow like a blacksmith's altar through the limbs of the sylvan tower. Far off flames engulfed the lofty chapel roof, and from beneath came the shrieks and cries of the damned locked up within. Their anguish blew low on a mistral of woe, and her tears were for their torment.

Help them! Help them, please! She tried to speak, but her swollen tongue was silent, her last earthly words already lost as she choked for breath not coming. The sound of the men as they galloped away accompanied the pleas of the pitiful.

The world turned about her, slow and patient, while she flailed in the air quite helpless, and then he came into view – old Malenfer himself – staying with her till it was over. Her eyes rolled up past the twisting rope to the thick sooty sky beyond the branches, then gone was the feel of her heavy legs as she drifted hollow and freely; but the strong taste of iron, blood in her mouth, stayed with her for the last seconds.

Then all was cast into the void and at last she knew true silence; though the pungent scent of fast-cooking meat and the tannins of wood smoke lingered.

And something, somewhere, was burning.

Chapter 1
Dermot Ward (Paris 1919)

ON THE WAY TO MONTMARTRE, HALFWAY UP THE RUE DES TROIS FRÈRES, is a small tight lane to the left. It is poorly lit and uninviting and not obvious to the passerby. If you did manage upon it, you would have to follow it trustingly, for it gives no hint of a thoroughfare, but it would soon reward you and open out, delivering you into a pleasant courtyard.

This cobbled, treed oasis was the home of an old long-established brasserie – Le Jardin des Cygnes. When the weather was good, life took place under the shading poplar branches around the white painted tables of this garden of swans, but in February its patrons stayed huddled and bundled, comfortable behind stained glass doors. There they nested, warm and dry, waiting for spring's migration.

In the center of the café window hung a large cured ham, smoked in acorns. Propped against it, a dusty chalkboard showed the day's menu written out large. There were gaps in it, like missing teeth, where popular fare had sold out. And there were two flags, both tricolors, hanging limp in the absence of a breeze. One was most familiar: the blue, white, and red of the French republic, though this specimen had its colors washed soft by time, its cloth worn nightdress-thin. The other flag was new and bright, its fresh dyes almost wet: an independence flag for a pregnant nation, one conceived but not yet delivered. The green, white, and gold of an Irish Free State hung presumptuously from its lanyard.

A local would have noticed Paris was suddenly full of such adornments, totems of petitioners to the battered colonial powers. This new trade in patriotism could be seen almost everywhere; it had arrived in the night only weeks before as the delegations drew nearer. It had started before the appearance of David Lloyd George, Britain's Prime Minister, who was soon joined by President Thomas Woodrow Wilson, who had sailed from his native Virginia. France's Clemenceau, the host of the Peace Conference, was flanked by a sizeable contingent, as if in scale he might overawe the charisma of Orlando the Italian. The victors were all now settled in town and eager to slice up the cake.

Why was he so sure, Arthur asked of himself, that Dermot was somewhere near? But was this not Paris and 1919, was the world not gathered today? Everyone to see empires carved up as the treaty was inked at Versailles. History was being made, Arthur conjectured, and Dermot would surely be drawn. He'd fly like a moth to the radiant flame of intrigue and prospect and hope.

Arthur pressed forward in his search for Dermot, now in its fourth day since his arrival, his own sobriety increasingly at odds with the scenes he encountered. Things had gotten worse as his route climbed into the hill that was Montmartre. With each step he fought the despondency that grew with the prospect of failure. He had been walking for almost fourteen hours, and the confidence of a noonday sun had dipped with the fading light – doubt had long been plaguing him; it gnawed like a boneyard dog.

What if Dermot died in the war, one amongst the many? Maybe he was wounded and sent home, or he languishes still in a hospital. He could have stayed on with the regiment? It's not a far-flung idea. He could be anywhere, even gone home, so why am I searching today? Am I wasting time and hope on a friend I don't know even lives?

But no, Arthur decided. If Dermot was still alive, then he would be here, somewhere, right now. The friend he remembered was a man who could not settle down, a man in search of an elusive peace beyond the conflict of nations. Paris was an island where the flotsam and jetsam of humanity washed ashore. Where a man like Dermot would surface.

Arthur turned left into a narrow alleyway to avoid a ribald group. Drawn onwards by the lilt of music, he continued up the lane. At the sight of a pair of hanging flags and the sign of the hissing swan, Arthur felt as fresh and hopeful as when he'd stepped down from the train.

Dermot, as usual, had come alone. He shoehorned himself into a horseshoe booth across from a boisterous group. Two men of disparate age were pressed around a painted Mademoiselle. The older man was either doing all right, or the younger could be doing much better. The trio were partners in libation, however else things sat; there were a dozen empty glasses on the table.

The Swan was a mixed crowd, popular with the working poor – the porters and the tradesmen. There were students too, and a gaggle of artists, and a diversity of conversations. Only a few of the patrons were in uniform compared to the other bars in the neighborhood. That was another reason Dermot liked the place – that it helped with the forgetting. Dermot was a man on a mission, a one-track mind: he intended to get drunk before sleeping.

"Your best health, father," he toasted his tablemates, loud enough to be heard above the din. He raised the glass he'd acquired at the bar and saluted their momentary attention. He had been thinking of the letch in *La Cousine Bette*, but the name of Balzac's old man escaped him.

"Father?" the woman repeated and broke into a hysterical cackle. Her amusement redoubled as the younger man made predictable jest of his accent. Dermot's labored pronunciation always got a comment from the locals, but he took their fun in good stride.

Dermot felt the older man eye him warily. Judging him, perhaps. Deciding for himself whether or not the foreigner was harmless. And what did he see, Dermot wondered to himself, how did he look through those eyes?

Dermot Ward was not yet thirty, but the boy had long since left him. Nearly five years in France had gifted him the language and nightmares to last a lifetime. His arms and legs, once long and awkward, were knitted hard with sinew and muscle. He was animate when he spoke and agitated at rest, which sent his piles of curled hair to bouncing – blond streaked with red, or red bleached by the sun, but already when he shaved he saw gray. His fair complexion, as much as his accent, marked him as different to the natives.

Annoyed, perhaps, by his interruption, the man begrudgingly returned his salute. The collection on the table grew larger. Dermot cast a look about for the waiter, his mouth already grown dry.

"English?" The older man asked him, uncomfortable in the tongue of that country.

Dermot's mind was wandering off by itself, as it was wont to do. *Two hundred feet in a standard spool. Grade two has one hundred fifty. Continent wire is always in meters: fifty meters to a French blasting spool. Three feet, three and four-tenths inches in every meter is three point two-eight feet. One hundred sixty-four feet – and a hair – in a spool of Frenchy's best blasting cord.* The mathematics gave him comfort. There was a certainty to it he could cling to.

"No, I'm not English, father." He answered the question in passable French.

Two spools of anyone's gives you three hundred feet, at least three hundred feet; ninety-one point four four meters. You don't want to be closer than that.

"I'm from nowhere really, father. Not anymore. This is home now; good as any."

"But you served?" the older man persisted. He stroked his stiff right arm, as if from habit, and Dermot saw it was unwieldy. A memento, he thought, a souvenir from the war. *Such a lot of men carrying those.*

Dermot momentarily seemed not to hear the question, his mind once more whirling away.

Treat glycerine with sulfuric acids and nitric and you have yourself nitroglycerine – Alfred Nobel's precious gift to engineers and warmongers everywhere. Characteristics (remember the manual): high detonation velocity; shattering action; high grades resist water well. Poor fume quality – take extra care underground – sensitive to shock and friction. "You only drop the box once, boys." Lesson number one well learned.

Where was that short-assed waiter to be found?

"Oh, I served, father. I saw my share. More than I'd care to remember." The older man waited for more. "I served for France. In the Legion. I was a mining engineer."

Dermot had eyes like shallow water that you find in warmer seas, an effect enhanced by coral eyebrows that sat high upon his face. Usually they bore a look of incredulity at what the world sent his way. But not always. Sometimes, when the memories returned and he was forced to revisit those days, his eyes would darken, as beneath a hurricane sky, and his eyebrows would draw in tight. The older man caught something of this now and let the topic be. He followed another string.

"So where were you from before the Legion took you? Not American, I don't think. Australia perhaps? Ireland?" Inspired, he dipped his head to the flag in the window.

Where do you start? What is a nation? How do you define a people? Is it a matter of resistance; is it who you are not? Is it a matter of what you fight against?

"You're right there, father. I was born in Donegal. It's a small enough town in Ireland, so it is, if that is important to anyone."

"Irish. I told you so!" The older man cheerily claimed a victory, but no one save he seemed to care.

Everyone wants a label: "Irish"; "Foreigner." How do you define a nation? Do you go back before the plantations and the colonization of a country, when the new world was barely discovered? Or does Ireland really start with

Oliver Cromwell and his war that killed half of the people? Is it slaughter and famine on an apocalyptic scale that is required to cement an identity? We grew potatoes for an English economy and a million of us died from starvation.

"What did you give your arm for, father? Was it France, perhaps? Or Liberty?" The older man's interest was sliding away. "Do you have a job yet, father? Are they giving you a pension? How many friends did you lose these past years?" No one liked this sort of talking. "I'm from the same place you are, father. All of us are bloodied together."

Dermot could see he had lost his attention, and why not, with a handful like her beside him? The bars and streets were full of men being demobilized – carousing before being sent home. Dermot didn't mind, he bore him no ill will, but he knew the man's suspicions were wrong. He wasn't crazy or grinding an axe; he only wanted to forget. But he wasn't drunk enough to sleep. Not nearly drunk enough. The war would be waiting if he tried too soon, and the tunnel would beckon him under.

Their waiter was an Anjou dwarf whom the patrons called Maximilian.

"My name's Henri!" He'd get annoyed, and somehow that was funnier.

"Two more, Maximilian!" Dermot waved his empty glass as the little man scuttled by.

"Odd nut," said Dermot. "Hey, you want something else?" The table declined him politely.

A long wooden counter along one wall served up drink to the crowd in the brasserie; here, upstairs, they had the seclusion to indulge in the forbidden drink despite its recent prohibition. Wine and beer could be had in the main room, spirits too, or coffee. But if you were known or invited and vouched for, the Swan would admit you back here. A museum of bottles terraced the back, stacked from the till to the ceiling. At its apex hung a tarnished silver tray, nailed securely to the beam to fend off boisterous pilferers. It bore an inscription in painted rhyme that Dermot had committed to memory:

Here can be found the men serving absinthe;
Alchemists pour the green into tumblers;
Crowned with a spoon, plated in silver;
One cube of sugar suspended o'er each.

Queued aproned waiters hoist jugs of iced water;
Assemble their trays of lime-colored cordial.
Ethereal creatures, procurers of promise;
Melt round their patrons; together the host!

Dermot loved the enthusiasm of it – *Together the host!* His people. Exactly. Why would they ban something so good? Not that their efforts had met with success.

The dwarf returned. Dermot took two glasses from the attendant Maximilian and settled his account with loose change. Each tumbler held a single finger of absinthe, the color of a rank algae bloom. With a practiced hand Dermot emptied one into the other – *the twixt into the twain* – and returned one empty glass to the tray. The Anjou waiter knew his customer's habits and departed following this exchange.

Dermot reached for the jug that bore the ice and topped up his glass with chilled water. The next part he did very slowly. It was the drip, drip, drip he liked the most – a hypnotic dissolution – the sugar cube crumbled and ran through the holed spoon and mixed in the bottom of the solution. It was sheer chemistry. A science of the impossible. Numerology and divination. The mystery of relative gravities. The Philosopher's Stone in a glass. The color now swirled, thickened and clouded, and spun milky and turgid before him; he watched while the louche effect gradually evened and the potion he'd brewed came to settle. For Dermot, it was like watching a mind churn an infinite computation and decide on a definitive answer. Here was the certainty and the peace of escape. His mouth began to salivate.

"To alchemy." He raised his glass in a toast to the Fates, and then put his lips to the welcome cold rim.

The cut of alcohol kicked in sharply, a punch behind his ear. The ice water and sweetener was an antidote, and enabled his palate to take the aniseed. A rush of blood surged through his limbs, and his mind slipped from its leash. With the tremulous pleasure of anticipation served, the café faded away. Dermot's head flopped to the side and he gazed through the colored glass window.

How long had he sat that way? When he looked back on it he could not say. The light at first drew his attention because it appeared strange, clustered as it was around the tree. Dermot pressed his face to the window and squinted to make his view clearer. It was there, all right, sharper than before, and the figure began to take shape.

"Jesus Christ!" he exploded, startling the table from its nuptials.

A dish of oily fish was knocked and spilled. It soiled the laughing woman. "What the hell's the matter with you?" The two men helped to brush her down, which led to lots of slapping.

"I just saw someone," Dermot explained, putting his hand to his head and wiping a clammy brow.

The drinkers, recovered, laughed at him then, the three of them joined in the joke.

"Feeling all right over there?"

"Back with us, Irish?"

"Want to cut that green stuff out."

Dermot felt a pall of fear, but he chanced another glance. The man he had seen was nowhere in sight. The tree in the courtyard was alone.

"What's the fairy brought you tonight, then? What's hiding there out in the shadows?"

The green fairy. The gift of the absinthe. A foot into another world. Dermot had heard of hallucinations before, but nothing like this had happened– yet the vision had looked so real. Dermot drew his hands to his lap, conscious that they were shaking.

"I just saw a man," Dermot confessed. "He was a friend from long ago."

"Then bring him in. What's all the noise for, Irish?"

"The man I saw died in the war."

Chapter 2
The Last of the Malenfers

THE DOCTOR DROVE CAREFULLY THROUGH THE BLACK AND RAINING night. The unpaved road rattled the suspension and kept his speed down low. The tires bounced through puddles in the ill-kept potholed road, little more than a grooved track scoured by centuries of carts.

He knew he was getting close.

In his headlights, he saw the barrier gate and then the flag of the approaching man.

"Quarantine!"

He made out the one shouted word, but the rest he could not hear. He shifted the car into neutral and stood firmly on the brake.

The young man wore a damp flat cap beneath a long waxed sealskin cape. "Oh, doctor, it's you. I couldn't see. I'm sorry, go on through."

For a second, a square splash of vivid color stood out in the headlight. It was the gateman's yellow flag to warn of plague, a signal to keep the unwary away. The doctor rolled his window up and slid the car back into gear. The gate hinged open before him, and he drove on through. Once past the outbuildings, the courtyard was lit up from the manor. He rolled his car to a rest and lifted his bag from the seat. A stooped man met him with an umbrella – he had emerged when the car drew near.

"Any change?" the doctor asked.

"Not that I hear, sir," answered the figure, and then they were both indoors. They shook the rain onto the floor; the wind had rendered the umbrella symbolic.

The doctor didn't wait. He headed for a wide grand staircase, all too familiar with the way.

"Any others with new symptoms?" he asked, quickly mounting the steps, ascending above the servant.

"No more, sir. None come down with anything new, just the

young master as before." The man's voice trailed behind him; the doctor was in a hurry. "Madame is up there with him now."

At mention of that name, the doctor stopped cold, one foot left hovering an inch above the tread, suspended as if frozen. Without turning or answering, the doctor recovered. He slowly lowered his foot back down and continued his ascent.

Michel Malenfer was grievously ill. He was all of sixteen years old. Two weeks before, he'd been robust of frame and full of strength, befitting a boy on his way to being a man. Two weeks had changed everything for him. The Spanish Flu had returned.

The disease had run its first course through the Ardennes countryside nine months before, in May of 1918. "La Grippe," they had called it then. With vast armies squared off, with millions of troops on French soil, who was concerned about a simple disease? Who had the time for a cold? But La Grippe was no ordinary flu, and it would not be ignored. It fell on the land like a judgment; it fell like the hand of God.

The war had raged for four long years, and the government sensed its closure. A plague, of course, would be bad for morale, so the local news was censored. But Spain next door was neutral, and so didn't have such restrictions. Spain was the first to report widely on La Grippe, and the doctor had read the newspapers. Born in the Pyrénées, his father had taught him the language. Madrid said that one patient in five was dying, if such a number could be believed – that the young and healthy were succumbing the most, that the old were left to live. It was a conscription engineered by Satan himself in tribute to Europe's great powers.

Then on November 11th, 1918, the Great War ended with an armistice. Ten million soldiers had died to bring the peace. Ten million dead. Such a number.

An armistice may stop a war, but a plague respects no treaties. The Spanish Flu was contagious; one in four came down with it everywhere. And it spread, and it spread, and it spread. Five hundred million around the world might eventually be contaminated, and fifty million of those might perish. *Fifty million dead!* Such a number. Impossible perhaps to imagine such a thing, but the troops coming home to their families brought more than their love, their scars, and their stories. Some of them brought a temperature that soon turned into a cough. No, La Grippe was no ordinary cold, and one month ago it had returned. As if France had not suffered enough, the Flu's second coming proved worse than the first, and the doctor was kept very busy.

The Malenfer farm was miles away from the town. It was distrustful of strangers; its inhabitants kept to themselves. Yet eventually, perhaps inevitably, it too had finally succumbed. Michel Malenfer had taken ill, and his physician had been summoned.

The doctor's stride resounded confidently against the polished floor – his walk, at least, was more assured than what he felt inside. His leather bag of balms and tools knocked rhythmically against his leg.

His patient was fortunate enough to be afforded every conceivable comfort. Every remedy against the plague had been put at his disposal. He was attended round the clock – staff and family shared the burden – and three nurses had been brought up from town to sit shifts inside his chamber. Constant care was therefore given to Michel's precarious state. This personal attention might have been called an indulgence, when others went so stretched, but to the doctor's mind Michel's prospects looked grave, and he cautioned against anything less. His patient enjoyed his own rooms in which to suffer and linger, and a large bed with pillows aplenty where he might sweat and waste away. Good light if the doctor ordered, and thick drapes if dark was best. There was a fine chair for lucid moments if he managed to sit up, and most handsome of all was a prize view to the rolling fields beyond.

If the patient needed reason to live beyond the indomitability of youth, then he might dwell on his inheritance: Michel was the last male in the Malenfer line and heir to the vast estate. The doctor considered the possibility of a wealthy grateful patron. It never did a gentleman harm to have friends among the gentry.

Madame is up there. That's what the help had said. The doctor wiped his forehead on his sleeve and tucked his damp hat under his arm. He pulled his shoulders back and squared his chin, and then pressed down on the bedroom handle. It opened. The doctor walked stiffly within.

"Madame?" The doctor didn't immediately see her. Shadows filled the place from a smoking oil lamp and the glow from the warming fire. He wasn't sure if she was there. He closed the thick door behind him. It swung easily on silent hinges and clicked loudly when it shut. The nurse's chair was vacant.

The wood fire was reduced to a crackling husk of radiating embers; unlike his own small house in town, the manor had no need for coal. The fireplace threw a dancing light across the bedroom floor, and Michel, his patient, he could just make out, half-hidden amongst his covers. The doctor saw her then: She stood still beside the tall drawn drapes, black like ancient sorrow.

"Do whatever you came for, doctor, but I know that he's no better." She didn't look at him as she spoke. She stared beyond the high bay window as if able to see through the blackness.

The doctor drew up short, startled for a moment. "It might be better to turn up the lamp?" he suggested.

"No. Leave it. Things are fine just as they are."

She was petite. Her gray hair was pinned severely back, and she wore a conservative gown of black silk. Everyone knew Madame habitually wore mourning and had done since she was widowed. The doctor found her disturbingly appealing. He was of an age with her and a widower himself. He thought her beauty crystalline: too cut, too sharp, too clear. He thought of such things when he was lonely, late at night, or had the company of a drink, but to Madame he never presumed, and to the world he said no such thing.

The doctor left the lamp as it was and took his patient's signs. He lifted back the quilt and prodded around his neck. He took a pulse from the boy's limp arm. Michel lolled. He looked emaciated, black hair damp with perspiration. The doctor withdrew his thermometer from the armpit and noted the boy's temperature had not changed. Michel managed one lucid glance and then nodded off again. *Gray eyes. Such clear gray eyes.* The doctor made some further notes and flipped back through his book.

"He hasn't gotten worse, Madame," he ventured to please. "That is fortunate."

"Hasn't gotten worse. What do *you people* know?"

"Excuse me?" Ever wary in Madame's presence, he was still taken aback by her tone.

"What do you *know* about anything?" This time he didn't deign to answer; he sensed there wasn't a point. "I've had six children, doctor, six of them! And this one my baby boy." She was stiff, rigid with antagonism, her shoulders tense like a striking clock just before the hour.

"He's stable for now," the doctor said cautiously. "We need to make sure that he drinks."

"What good are you doing here? Only two I've got left. Only two of my babies are left me."

"We're all doing our best for him, Madame."

"You can't help. None of us can. It was the Curse that did for all of them. It's the Curse that will have us all."

The doctor stalled. He knew the talk, but he'd never heard *her* say it.

"It's a disease, a flu, Madame. A..." – he struggled for the words – "...a terrible thing. But, Madame, we know how it works..."

"Knowing doesn't help anything!" she cut him off.

They both stood quiet and unmoving, but he did so because he was lost. The fire danced low, and the rain tapped on the window-panes. The doctor wondered if he should go.

"Knowing won't make anything better, doctor. I know already how this ends."

The doctor closed his bag.

"One by one I've lost them all. It took all the rest of my children from me, and it will have Michel yet. And when they're all gone, I'm not too proud to think that somehow I'll escape. Oh, no. There's no escaping fate. So why do I bother sending for you? Why do we fight it at all?"

"He isn't getting any worse," he tried once again. "Fluids, he needs fluids. Soup is good if he'll take it."

"Go home, Doctor." Her back was to him still, her long neck pale and thin. "Close the door behind you, doctor, go and prepare your bill. Science will be proud of you; you've done an excellent job. All you could do and more, I'm certain, and still not nearly enough."

He took a last look at her, fighting his temper, baited by her dis-paraging tone. He swallowed his tongue, picked up his hat, and left with no final word.

The kitchen at Malenfer Manor was snug and low and warm. Its ov-ens were always on early for bread and worked hard till dinner was served; they boiled water for drinks at all hours of the day and heated milk when the sun had gone down. A vegetable broth could normally be found simmering and ready. Catacomb pillars buttressed its ceil-ing and the stone floor gleamed polished and gray; it glowed with the sheen of lifetimes of service that had worn the hard surfaces down.

At difficult times, the kitchen was a refuge on the estate: It gave heat, which was in short supply; companionship to those in search of it; and protection from the family above that rarely ventured down-stairs to see it.

The kitchen was, as usual, occupied.

"You think he's getting better?" The young man sat on a thick scratched table over which he dangled his legs.

"No, I don't. I don't. I think he's just the same," a doughy, white-haired lady answered with sincere concern. She wore a pinstriped apron of office and her hair up in a clasp off her neck.

"And what happens if he gets worse?" continued the young man, looking down upon the housekeeper, who sipped slowly from her cup as she talked.

"Émile, don't say such things! You'll bring the boy bad luck." She spoke with a maternal care; indeed, she had seen them all grow up.

Émile put a boot upon an empty chair and rested a hand on his chin, the habit of a thoughtful child that looked dim-witted on a man. He was robust, barely twenty, blessed with waves of chestnut hair long enough to tie back in a ribbon. He wore it loose and with his wildling's eyebrows he looked ever ready to dash about. "Berthe, dearest. There's no use hiding from these things. As bad as it is for them upstairs, what's it going to mean for us? You know how it is. What happens next? It's no sure thing if the worst should happen. That's all I'm trying to say."

"It's not right to think of ill coming to him, the young master," Berthe chided. "It don't help any," she persisted in her defense, and retreated again to her cup.

"You've worked for them all your life," Émile pressed. "He's the last of the line. No more Malenfers after Michel."

Berthe refused to be drawn.

"Who'll you end up working for if he's gone? You see Sophie going to run this place? Or maybe you think Madame will skip a generation, and give it all to Simonne? How do you see that working, then?"

The housekeeper gave a snort of derision.

"Well, exactly! That's just my point."

There was a draft and a door slammed, followed by stamping feet. They both broke off and looked up expectantly to catch sight of who had come in.

"Don't stop for me." The voice preceded the appearance of the hunched older man.

"Where have you been?" Berthe asked him, rising to fetch him a bowl of soup. Émile pushed back the chair his foot had been on to give the arrival a seat. The old man shook himself, throwing rain around, and hung his overcoat up. He moved quickly to join them, belying his advanced years and despite a stiff left leg.

"I just saw the doctor leave," he informed them with a grin. "He was right put out, I tell you. He'd barely even been!"

"What was the matter with the doctor?" Émile asked.

Berthe put the bowl in front of the Malenfer footman and passed him the wine and a glass. "Madame's been loitering all day," she put in, while the footman took a sip.

"Well, that explains that. I'm sure she had a few choice words for him." Émile was amused. "Bet she tore right into him!"

"Better him than us," said the sage footman.

"Did he make mention of the young master?" asked Berthe.

"Like I said, not a word. Face like fizz was all. I think he's got a shine for Madame."

"Get away!"

"Dirty old man."

"No, I do. Can't see's why. Can you imagine that pair? But what were you all talking about before I got in?" The twisted man used both of his hands to steady his shaking glass, his fingers struggling to manage.

"We were talking about What Happens Next, to them upstairs," said Émile.

"Ah..." said the old footman, a disfiguring scar twisted across his cheek as he smiled at the revelation. "We're back to the Curse again."

"Gustave!" Berthe chastised, as if she'd heard something vulgar. Émile looked about to speak.

"If you're not actually talking about it, then you're thinking it," Gustave challenged them. He appeared to take a measure of pleasure in watching the housekeeper squirm. "The Curse will get them all!" he cackled.

"Gustave!" Berthe repeated, paling, which brought a laugh from the grinning old man.

"Well, it's done a pretty good job up till now." He turned the soup bowl around with his hands as if to chase its heat.

"How much money do you think there is?" Émile put in; he looked guilty for imagining.

"Christ! Who the hell knows? What a question, lad." Gustave shook his head as if considering. "Heaps," he mumbled, the answer bubbling out of the side of his mouth. His head looked to be working to do the sums but in the end didn't quite get there. "A serious pile, anyway."

"So if Michel doesn't make it, flu or curse or whatever, what's your best guess then? Sophie or Simonne for the inheritance?"

"God, I did miss it, didn't I! Have you two been talking about this all night?"

Berthe looked away, slightly ashamed of the answer, but didn't make a move to go.

"Sophie should get it," Émile pronounced. "She's Madame's daughter. She'd be the only one left after Michel."

"But then what?" Berthe couldn't resist. "You know what Madame's thinking. Will she marry again? Who would she marry? Might she have any more children?"

"God almighty, you lot have been talking. I don't know! She might, obviously. Why not? She could do whatever the hell she wants."

"Madame's always so hard on her, though," Berthe joined in, pointing out the obvious.

"So... you think she's not worthy? Would that matter? Simonne might get it, instead?" Émile was officiating, not backing sides. "That's what you're saying, is it then?"

Gustave let out a roar of glee, his split face lighting up. "Can you imagine? This place run by her. The nutcase granddaughter getting it all? She'd give it away to the cats."

"I don't know." Émile shook his head. "How bad could it be? How much worse could it be than now?"

"You'd just better watch your tongues. That's all I'll say." Berthe got up and waddled back to the stove. "Madame's likely around for a good long time yet, and God help you if she hears you talking like that – you'll be lucky to stay on the farm." The kettle went back on with a clatter. It took its treatment stoically, as one familiar with such handling.

The young servant and the old servant traded glances, sharing the image that went with the thought of Madame overhearing their gossiping. Both recoiled in horror.

"Well, I for one hope he pulls through," Émile pronounced patriotically.

"And so do I! God bring him health, and save us from the consequences. Better the master you know than the one you don't." The old man was a pragmatist.

Another head popped in and shut them all up for a second. It was only the scullery maid. "Émile, your brother's outside looking for you."

"What for?" But she had gone. "It's not my turn at the gate yet!" he called after. "All right," he said resignedly, making an effort in getting up. "See you lot later then."

"Yes, my boy. Good night."

As soon as he was out the door, the cold and draft set in. Émile made his way down the cluttered hallway with his head turned low, not looking. He fumbled at his buttons while trying to put his jacket on.

"Hello, Émile." He startled and pulled up, surprised. It was a girl's voice from the shadow, a voice he couldn't mistake.

"Simonne? What... I mean... what are you doing down here?"

She was dark and slim and pale of skin with long straight raven hair.

"I was following someone." She paused, flustered, but didn't elaborate. "She's gone now. It doesn't matter."

"Berthe?" he suggested, trying to be helpful. "Berthe's in the kitchen." Simonne shook her head no. Émile was left unsure what she was talking about, but that was sometimes the case with Simonne.

"Well... can I help you? ...with anything?" He felt the need to clarify. "With anything you might need... down here?"

Her lips were flush and open a touch so he could see her tongue behind them. Émile always felt uncomfortable beside her, and the knowledge only agitated him further.

"I know what's going to happen, Émile, I know." She whispered it, and there was anguish to her voice. She tried retreating back into the shadow.

"Know?" He didn't understand. He took a step towards her. "Simonne? What do you mean? Tell me," he said, concerned. "Know what?"

"It's Michel, Émile, it's about Michel." Simonne was trembling.

"What are you talking about?" He was getting annoyed. *Why is she always like this?*

She shared it like a sticky sweet: "Michel is going to die."

"What did you say?" he was incredulous. "What are you saying? Simonne? Simonne, stay!" Émile appealed to her without reply, for Simonne had turned and fled. Her long thin nightgown billowed behind her; her small slippered feet carrying her away.

Michel Malenfer shook awake. He felt a disturbance, although there was no one visible in the room, nothing to occasion his surprise. It was the middle of the night, ten minutes to two by the carriage clock on the mantle. The fire was burnt down, an occasional lick of flame from the last of the logs the only light to be had. He looked around. There was no nurse, her usual chair unoccupied. Likely she had gone to fetch something to eat, and that was what he'd heard. The patient lifted a glass from his bedside table and managed a few sips of water. He returned it with a trembling hand, knocking a spoon from a bowl. Cook had been sending up a distillation of broths that he couldn't stand the taste of. He reached over to try to pick it up but gave up from the effort. Mother had even sent for oranges – in winter, and with food being rationed. But the taste of them burned his chapped lips, and Michel had refused them.

It could wait. All of it could wait. Tomorrow he'd make himself eat again. Tomorrow.

He was just settling down when the door opened quietly. Michel looked around, expecting his caregiver, and was surprised to see the visitor.

"Oh, hello," he said. "What are you doing up at this time? Is there something going on downstairs?" But he got no answer. "What are you doing?... Now wait!..."

The muffled sounds of the short struggle went no further than the bedroom walls. Michel was a puppy in his weakened state and weighed down under lamb's wool blankets; his arms were constricted beneath tight linen sheets that cost a month's wages for some. The goose down pillow fit snuggly to his face; a mask he wore for a minute. His animal thrashing stalled and subsided, and he finally lay quiet.

The pillow was fluffed and placed back on the bed. The blankets were straightened a little. Michel's head was turned, his tussled hair petted down, and his open, gasping mouth gently closed. He looked in the end like a boy at peace. The visitor left the room.

It was Michel's nurse that found him. Despite what she'd witnessed in the war and through the Flu, she was not inured to grief. She was saddened by what she discovered in the bedroom – the young ones upset her the most. She sent, quite unnecessarily, for the doctor, who paid his patient a final visit. A death certificate was issued, along with an invoice, before the sun had dried the dew on the windows.

Master Michel Malenfer, the last of his line, had passed away February 9th, 1919, "from complications of influenza."

Chapter 3
The Western Front (1916)

THE BIG SHELL FELL SHORT. FIFTY YARDS TOO SOON IT DROPPED, WHILE the men in the tunnel still labored. On the surface of the earth, the soldiers scurried, hunkering down in their trenches. They whispered prayers to their Christian God in muffled Prussian accents, while those deep below heard nothing at all as the noise from the shell whistled closer. One hundred feet before Fort Vaux, the shell landed above their tunnel.

The shock shattered the timbers. The bracing that supported the excavated run blew out all around them. The ceiling caved in and the dirt moved quickly, keen to reclaim what had been stolen. The surge pummeled the breath from the miners' lungs and cracked ribs with its force and pressure. Men and rock were cast about; the hard air stove in eardrums. In a moment all was black and tight, and the earth was close and settled. The sappers' tunnel was as quiet as a tomb, for that was what the big shell had made it.

Dermot awoke in a black grip that held him, unaware of which way was up. There was dirt in his mouth; he spat it half clear, feeling it run off his lips. His breath seemed to come from close by. There was a weight pressing down on his chest.

"Hello?" He spoke into the pitch. His voice was soft, respectful almost; he had to think about where he was.

"Have you ever seen such a darkness as this, Sergeant?" The familiar voice was close at hand.

"Arthur?" Dermot tried to move a little. He wiggled his fingers and toes. "Are you hurt?"

"No. I'm all right. It's been about an hour, I reckon, though I think I was out for a while. Welcome back, Sergeant. I wasn't sure you'd make it."

Dermot turned on his side, stirring the soil that held him; only his foot remained trapped now. Somebody – he tried to see Arthur but could not – somebody had dug him out. He dragged himself entirely free, his ears ringing painfully as he did so. He felt an ache in his neck that he tested with invisible fingers.

"Are you okay?" Arthur was near him.

Dermot drew his hand away; the back of his skull was sensitive, his fingertips sticky. There was a tight pain he couldn't lose in his knee, but nothing anywhere felt broken. Dermot felt sick; he bent over and had to hold onto his legs for balance. Recovered, he braced a hand against the roof and took a blind step forward.

"What about the others, Arthur?" He walked towards the voice.

"I don't know, Irish. It's just us here. Bertrand is dead; I think it's Bertrand. His body is behind me."

"Jesus Christ."

"The cave-in starts about five feet back, and I found you at the other side."

"Is it shut?"

"Completely blocked. I've no idea how far it goes."

"Bloody hell."

Arthur's voice seemed only feet away. Dermot stopped moving. Who could believe that such a large man as the Lieutenant could disappear so completely?

"How many do you think were up front?" asked Arthur.

Dermot racked his brain. His head was sore. He was trying to account for his men. "Three? Maybe four. I think I passed Dardenne on the way up here. Have you heard anything from any of them?"

"I haven't heard a sound at all. No noise at all, Irish, till you came back. I thought I'd been buried alive."

They were near the end of a sapper tunnel, one hundred yards from the mouth of their trenches. They'd been digging under the German lines to mine the enemy defenses. Dermot's hand fell on a shoring post that had likely saved their lives. He leaned against it to take the weight off his knee and reached forward towards Arthur's voice. He found Arthur sitting down.

"You've got me."

"Well, this is certainly cozy."

"Do you want the good news or the bad, Sergeant?"

"Right now, I'm just happy to be here."

"Glass half full, Dermot. Glass half full. Could you do with a drink?" asked the Lieutenant.

"I've got my own... no, what?" He touched his pockets in vain. "Where the hell has it gone?" Dermot looked around out of habit.

"I took the liberty earlier, and helped myself to your pockets. Sorry, Sergeant, but I wasn't sure you'd be needing it. Here, have a sip yourself."

Dermot reached out slowly, fingers grasping, then met the big hand coming towards him. He received his half-empty hip-flask back and gratefully worked its top.

Dermot took a sharp swig. He felt much better for the instant glow. "Thank you kindly. You're a fine man for looking after it, Lieutenant." He raised the flask to toast him. "You mentioned there was good news?"

"You just drank it."

Dermot paused to consider this. "And the bad news, Arthur?"

"Well, my Celtic chum, it occurs to me there's a distinct possibility we'll both end up dying down here."

Dermot unwound the bottle cap he'd just screwed back on and took another liberty. He tried to look around, one hand on the post, his boots stuck in the mud beneath him. He was dizzy from the pain of his sore bent knee, and the ringing in his head persisted. He was fighting to know which way was up, still disoriented by the darkness. His stomach rolled and he heaved and gagged, but he kept his liquor inside him.

"Let me have a feel about, and let me have a think on it. It happened an hour ago, you said?"

"I think so." Arthur was the officer, but Dermot was the expert.

"No tapping, no voices, no scraping?"

"Only from me."

"Jesus Christ. You've got no matches, I take it?"

"I even searched your pockets."

Dermot went through them again anyway. He didn't have his jacket with him; the work was too warm to wear it. Dermot shook himself alert. Their predicament needed consideration. He tried to arrange the facts.

Oxygen in fresh air is 20.9% by volume: dangerous below 19.5%; mental and physical impairment at 17%; unconsciousness followed by death comes very quickly at anything lower than that. Assumption that the present air is fresh? Flawed logic. No gauge. Move on.

"Have you felt any air move? Is there any ventilation?"

"Nothing at all that I have felt, Dermot."

Dermot got down on his knees and fumbled through the mud until his hands found the hose he was seeking. The airline, their pipe to the outside world, was pinched somewhere and flat.

An adult at rest inhales one-fourth of a cubic foot of air per minute. 5% of the air's volume is converted from oxygen to carbon dioxide, which you can't breathe unless you're a tree. Am I a tree? No such luck. Two large adults, both of them active? – 1 cubic foot per minute? More? We lose 5% oxygen and we're goners.

"How much space do we have in here?"

"I counted about twenty feet in the tunnel."

Dermot moved back towards the mine face, reaching out with a blind man's hand. His path was soon blocked, the tunnel full of rubble, with not a sound from the other side.

"Twenty-two feet from you," he said, having measured it.

"And my ass is on the other wall."

Dermot paused and considered, his mind racing.

Volume of a cylinder: π x the radius squared times the length at 25 feet? Only this isn't exactly a cylinder. He did the math.

"Not a lot of room," he said.

"I was right? It's not good, then?" Arthur asked, his voice low.

"No, Français, it isn't." He was reluctant to speak further.

"What are we looking at, Irlandais? I'd rather have it clear."

Dermot shifted. He sat down on his heels and rested his back against the tunnel wall. A strange calm descended on him. "We have air problems and water problems, as you might have guessed already. If it's raining, it will start to seep in, and it might not drain away fast enough, though we're above the water table. But we haven't drowned yet, Français, so that makes air our biggest concern. Any water will displace our air even further."

"Not good, no?" Arthur sounded solemn.

"And the walls are shot. Completely unstable. They might collapse on us further, though I think not unless we try to dig out. And don't make too much noise."

"Noise will bring down the ceiling?"

"No, but my ears are bloody killing me."

Back in the void, Arthur may have cracked a smile. Dermot liked to think so. "But you don't want to dig? The stability? Or do you?" Arthur was uncertain.

"I don't know," Dermot answered truthfully.

Dig or wait? Both options were fraught with risk, but he preferred to be the master of his own fate. To sit and do nothing and suffocate before rescue came... the idea put his teeth on edge. He made up his mind.

"We should dig. Up. We're a fair bit down, but it's either that or try to go back, and that's not happening without shoring. Only thing is, we're behind enemy lines."

"Then we'll sneak back to our side come nightfall."

"Well, that will be the plan, if we get out. But if we're caught – well, they don't treat sappers too kindly. And we still need to get out first."

"Why don't we wait, then? They're bound to send help for us soon."

"You'd hope so. Eventually. Only we're back to the air problem, Arthur, and I've no idea how far back our tunnel is down."

"How deep did you say we were?"

"Deep enough."

"I don't think we have another choice, my friend. I think you are right. Up we should go."

"Maybe. But it isn't good, all the same."

"You think it'll collapse?"

"Yes, I do."

"That's not so good, Irlandais, as you say."

"We should try and find something to dig with. I hope you don't bite your nails, you big French bastard, because it looks like you might just need them."

"Excellent, Dermot, I'd wondered what had happened to your cheery disposition. Let's go see what the Germans are up to."

"This is a bit of bad luck for us all the same," Dermot said, gesturing fruitlessly to a mythical sky while he felt with one hand for a shovel. "Wasn't the rule no shelling?"

"Maybe it was one of theirs?"

"Maybe. But behind their lines? I'm guessing it was one of our boys."

"Then General Nivelle is generous with his gifts. Poor Bertrand here, his mother will thank him."

"He was only seventeen, Arthur."

"I know. What a place to be buried in."

"Well, next time you drop by the officer's mess, you be sure to thank the General."

There was silence, then: "I don't want to die here with Bertrand, Dermot. One hundred feet below no-man's-land. I want to die with the fresh air around me, in the heat of the sun, and the love of my children. I want to die a happy old man."

The burn of the whisky glowed warm in Dermot's gut but even now was beginning to fade.

"Here, have the last drop." He offered the flask back to Arthur.

"Thank you, my friend. You've always been a good sort. I'm sorry to get maudlin this way." Arthur finished the dregs. "I'll keep this so

I can refill it some day."

"You do that."

"I want you to be the first to know, Dermot, I'm putting in for a transfer to the flying corps. Turns out I'm not overly fond of small tight spaces, and I don't think much of the dark."

Dermot laughed heartily. "Then perhaps, Lieutenant, it's time we both got out."

Chapter 4
The Ladies

MICHEL MALENFER WAS DEAD. THE BOY WAS LAID OUT IN A CASKET and kept in a cool room. Black crêpe was hung from the mirrors and windows, and armbands were worn by the staff. The Malenfer women traded their dresses for those of darker hue; all except Madame, that is, for whom mourning garb was already de rigueur.

Mademoiselle Simonne found it oppressive: The house lingered under a veil. She was expected to be patient, to sit and mourn her poor departed uncle. Uncle. She had never thought of Michel that way. He was her mother's baby brother, and Simonne, eighteen and two years his senior, treated him the same. As a child he had only been an annoyance, a little pain that would come into her room. Now he was lying on a cold shelf downstairs, waiting to be buried.

Look at her chewing! Rolling that beef around in there. How long is she going to take to finish it? Just swallow it already!

Simonne was very sad for Michel and had cried that whole first day. When she had seen the girl, she'd known Michel would go; she had believed it and it had come true. Simonne had liked Michel well enough – when she'd thought of him much at all – so long as he kept out of her way and didn't ask stupid questions. They were family, yes, but their formative years had been spent apart. The soil of company in which kinship could flower had been denied them too long.

Simonne was hungry. She wanted dessert now, but had to wait for Madame to finish.

Why must we always endure this? It's like watching a plodding cow!

Her collar scratched her. She looked from her mother, sitting patiently behind her finished plate, to the servants on guard, to the clock that ticked off the seconds. Simonne sat still and endured.

Simonne thought of herself as not unkind. She bore the resilience of youth, an energy that could not long be depressed by dreary thoughts of death. She was very aware of her body. She had her own friends and counted her fiancé among them. She had her own thoughts and opinions and dreams, and Michel had scarcely intruded on any of them.

Simonne liked to read; Michel had not. Simonne liked music; Michel had liked to shoot – his ear was dull to anything other than the sound of a hunting gun. Simonne liked to paint and go for long walks. Michel had complained bitterly about having nothing to do. Dying, Simonne reflected, was the most interesting thing that her uncle had done in years.

Thoughts of death put Simonne in mind of her own departed father, and as it ever did when this happened, her mood slid into melancholy. She didn't like to think of him for this reason. He had been conscripted and had gone away to fight when she was thirteen. Four years ago her mother had brought Simonne with her to the Manor, after she'd gotten the telegram – such a long time ago. Her mother had been born and raised at the Manor, so for her it was returning home, but for a young girl, quickly becoming a woman, the house was nothing but a jail: remote, isolated, and no one around to be your friend. She had always heard the voices before, but here they were so clear.

Simonne scratched at her neck again. The black lace itched something sore. She stared over the vast polished table, down to where her grandmother sat.

Grand-mère.

Another night waiting, waiting...

And for what?

Ennui could make her bitter.

"What are you staring at, girl? Sitting there like a stunned duck!" Her grandmother spoke to her sharply, stretching out her words. She would be sixty soon, if it could be believed. How did anyone live so long?

Ancient wizened creature. Just hurry up and finish!

"Staring, Grand-mère?"

Michel was always your little baby, and now your baby is gone.

Madame had allowed Michel a latitude of behavior she hadn't tolerated in anyone else. It wasn't just that he was a boy, although that certainly made a difference, but he had been treated with the sickly fondness of a lonely child. Michel had been her pet and was her last. Madame had doted on him with a mother's right that Simonne's own mother never got.

Michel makes five. You've outlived five of your own children. How does that make you feel? There you sit, preaching and controlling, telling others what is right and wrong. You don't even look at her, do you, your own daughter? Too full of misery for losing your beloved family name, and never enough care for those of us still living. No, keep pretending, keep pretending every-thing is normal; pretend you're not detestable to those who have to endure you.

Madame looked hard at Simonne. *Objectionable girl.* No, the girl had become a woman. *She's a beauty, though, just like her mother, and like I was back in my day.*

Madame Malenfer had married her Colonel forty years ago. The Malenfers, in 1879, were already the establishment. Her husband had distinguished himself for Napoléon III at the Battle of Sedan, and though the Prussians won the field that day, taking her husband, the Emperor, and 100,000 troops prisoner, that wrong had recently been righted. It gave Madame no little satisfaction, though she thought it a terrible shame her husband had not lived to see it.

The family was conservative and valued its traditions; it long had sided with the church and good-thinking rural people. The nonsense coming out of Paris these days was a blasphemy to hear. Madame had done her duty – there had been six children from their union. Arthur had been her eldest; she had been scarcely nineteen when she bore him. *Only one year older than Simonne is now,* Madame found herself re-flecting. Arthur, her boy, who had served in the Great War and hadn't come home again.

Sophie came one year after Arthur. Was it fair to judge her only daughter by her match to that useless husband? Madame had dwelt more often of late on that very question. It still rankled her. *Careless frippery!* It annoyed her to even think about it. Sophie was weak! Madame was wont to blame herself for her daughter's selfish indul-gence, and there was not even a male issue as compensation, only Simonne with her dark scowling.

Madame had lost three children in infancy after that, her preg-nancies coming quick in succession. It was a dark time, one on which she didn't like to dwell, and then... nothing. After a while she had thought herself barren. But twenty-one years after Sophie's birth, she had found herself once more pregnant. Pregnant at forty-three. Michel had been a gift, a present. Her last son had been a blessing, and now he was taken away.

To lose five children? She had tried to understand, tried to reason, but there was no political or biological logic. The answer she already knew: The Curse of the Malenfers had taken them all – the Beauvais Witch had spoken truly.

Your name will be wiped from the earth.

And so it had come, she had run out of sons, and this table was all of the family. Three generations of women, and all of them in mourning – that was all that was left. *She*, Madame, was the last to hold the name, and it was *her* job to care for their safety. The Malenfer line had come to an end; but who, after her, should inherit? Who could take care of the estate? Who amongst them all was worthy? Sophie showed no will for it, and was a widow, after all. Then what about pretty Simonne? *Stupid, headstrong girl.* Madame looked hard at her granddaughter, who stared back with her glazed, smart eyes. *If only she weren't quite so strange. We could have gotten her a better marriage.*

"I'm just wondering when dessert might be coming, Mémé?"

Simonne was the only person who called her anything other than Madame, occasionally using the familiar affection, its irony not lost on her either.

"You keep an appetite like that and you'll get fat, and then your fiancé won't take you."

Simonne looked furious, which pleased Madame, who went on slowly chewing.

"You stare like a sphinx, Simonne," said Madame. The only noise in the room beside her own voice was the clatter of cutlery against the china. Madame smelled rebellion and didn't like it.

"Keep your daughter better mannered, Sophie, or we'll have to raise her dowry." Madame passed a forkful of boiled white meat past her thinly pressed lips. She ground it like chewing tobacco.

"Simonne, please don't stare at Madame that way." Sophie's voice was tepid. "It's rude to stare, you know."

Simonne turned her eyes on her mother, who wouldn't meet them. "I was only wondering, mother, whether we'd have a chance for dessert before bedtime. Grand-mère, like so many of these old people, thinks the world waits for them..."

"Please, Simonne." Sophie sounded embarrassed, as if fearful of an argument. But Simonne had no mercy for her mother – a pawn in her grandmother's games.

"And perhaps it's me that will send Robert packing," she threatened. "Perhaps I'm not so keen on him."

"Robert is a charm. You are fortunate to have him."

"I dare say he even loves you." Madame said it as if the commodity were scarce, like sugar. "Are you trying to annoy me, Simonne? I don't know if we'd find a better match anywhere, even accounting for all of your money."

"Is that why you like him, Grand-mère? Because you think that he loves me? You just want me to be happy, no other reason?"

"Insolent girl. He treats you well enough; think yourself lucky. What more do you expect? He presented himself properly, and we were happy enough for you. His family is common, true enough, but Robert has education with the prospect of an income, and his father has envious connections.

"Face facts, Simonne. You are a lonely child, and your mother is a pensioned widow. Both of you are dependent on my good will for all of your allowance." Simonne did not need to be reminded of that. "The match is suitable. He gains the prestige of our family, for which he clearly hankers, and you get a comfortable future. Yet who would take you even for a dowry if they suspected... instability?"

Sophie looked away. Simonne's face darkened.

"You should try harder to fit in." Madame pursued her grand-daughter mercilessly, the point clearly a sensitive one. "I heard some talk concerning you recently, from just before Michel's death." Madame kept a keen eye on her, scanning for reaction. "I heard you stirred up everyone downstairs with nonsense talk again."

There was no denial forthcoming.

Madame clattered her cutlery down onto her half-full plate. "It's exactly this sort of thing you must stop immediately! Whatever was your meaning? Why must you disturb them?" she asked, exasperated. "This is what I'm talking about. Who would marry a woman like that? Who would want one? Tell me."

"I can't help it if they're upset, Grand-mère."

"Can't you learn to hold your tongue, girl?"

"But I saw her, I did." Simonne was defiant.

"Sheer nonsense." But Madame was shaken. She hadn't expected a confession and didn't want to hear one. Her object was to quash these differences, not to parade them around the room.

"I saw her." Simonne was unrepentant.

"Saw who, dear?" Her mother tried to help.

"The lady, the Witch." Out it came. "You know it's true, you know it, Grand-mère, and I knew that Michel would die."

"Enough, girl!" Madame thundered. "We will not hear such child-ish talk here. Keep in mind you are a grown woman and one that is soon to be wed. No one likes your infantile games. You had best learn to keep your mouth shut."

Cowed by this dressing down, Simonne did not move or reply.

"Really, Sophie," Madame turned her ire on her daughter. "What kind of a husband will take something like that?" She jabbed a fork at Simonne. "We'll be lucky if anyone takes her off us. Anyone at all.

Talk to her. I insist. You must talk to her and straighten her out, and the sooner you do it the better."

Sophie had covered her mouth with her napkin through the whole exchange. She didn't answer now.

Madame kept on: "You are an heiress to the estate, Simonne, or has that fact escaped your notice? It is your duty to ensure this marriage proceeds without any possible trouble. Remember, girl, it is not just your reputation you must think of, but the children you will bear for your husband. They should not have to go through life hiding their mother's shame. Think of them. Think of them. Think of your family for once in your life, and stop being so utterly selfish."

Simonne cracked. "There are no real men left at all!" she burst out. "The beastly war took them all, and those it spared..." She faltered for a second. "Those it spared are broken men and old men and false men... and little else besides. You can't make me do anything. You can't."

Madame was soft-spoken, her voice as sweet as candied almonds coating bitter arsenic. "Simonne, my dearest. Whatever it is that you're talking about, please mind your tongue and show some respect, and know that your elders know better. Young Robert is hardly detestable, and I have your best interests at heart. Just try to be a little more normal. That's all I'm saying. I'm sure you'll be happy together."

"He'll take me as I am, or maybe I don't want him."

Madame stared, disapproving. "I'm tired enough of your hysterical theatrics, Simonne. Your outbursts and inventions. You'd be far more eligible if you could finish a meal in silence. Could you try doing that for a change?"

"What is it you think I am? It's true what I tell you, and you know it."

"Simonne!" Madame brought her fist down on the tablecloth, and the plate service jumped an inch. "You are a silly young girl, and you must take good counsel." The last three words were pronounced distinctly as if read from chiseled stone.

"What do you know about anything?" Simonne rose up, a head of steam upon her. "You've watched over nothing but dead children and decline! What sort of example did you set?"

"Intolerable girl!" Madame hissed her reprove.

The fight was affecting Sophie. She clenched her napkin to her mouth, her habitual tick when anxiety took hold. "Please, Simonne," her mother implored, though neither faction took note.

"Now don't get too excited, my dear." Madame was patronizing again, and seemingly enjoying it. "Fancies such as yours can sometimes seem real when emotions are all in turmoil. You will come to see that we are right, and your imagination will calm down." With Simonne, Madame was a master of platitudes, and she scattered them now like confetti. Simonne regularly took her meals with a supplement of these conferred wisdoms. Tonight, however, she had no appetite.

"Always duty. Always responsibility. But really it's all about you. I mean look at this table... just look at it!" Simonne seethed as she gesticulated down and around the long dining room.

Her mother and grandmother looked about as bid, the same view that they beheld every evening; twelve could sit without touching elbows, but only three lonely women sat eating. Simonne had made her point, if that was it: The room was hollow and nearly empty.

"This is your pride? Our great Malenfer family? I don't see anyone here. Look where your damned duty has got you. You have no right to preach to me."

Madame's hand moved fast. It caught Simonne sharply across the face, turning her cheek and stopping her outburst cold.

"You will mind your tongue, young lady."

A tear collected in the young woman's eye during the silence that followed. A tear; but only one. Simonne's head slowly turned and met the cold dark stare of the matriarch.

"It's a new world, Grandmother," Simonne stood up from the table. She marched out of the dining room, leaving her family behind her.

Madame trembled in fury once she had gone, the door closing behind her granddaughter. "Insolent, selfish girl!" she hissed, to no one in particular. *She'll come around.* Madame forced down her temper. *She is, after all, blood of mine. She'll do just what is expected.*

Dessert that night was a pear charlotte. It was a special treat from cook that used half a week of rations. It was Simonne's favorite, but she went without. Madame ordered that none be saved.

Simonne was furious at herself, but only for showing a tear. She picked up her heels and ran. Each step lightened the burden of expectation that she'd felt on her back at the table. She moved deftly, soft-slippered feet quietly covering the distance. Through the twisting, turning hall she went, skipping across the balcony steps, wending her way beneath the paintings of glowering dusty ancestors. The portraits, in fading oils, watched their progeny's flight down the hallway.

Simonne moved forward with a purpose. The paths down which she fled were as part of her as the veins and arteries that laced a web beneath her own pale skin. Simonne knew she was at the staircase without remembering how she arrived there. Up she spiraled and then crossed the landing past the hollow suits of armor – beaten steel that had fought in wars long before this last one. The armor guarded the last run of steps that led up to the topmost landings; Simonne now took them two at a time to the summit of the Manor. Here she stopped, and only now, for the third floor was her refuge.

Her breathing as she arrived was loud and hard of pace, but she soon enough recovered. Simonne then stood dead still and quiet as stone as she listened for anyone coming. The sound of the wind was a comfort to her; the storm outside was brewing. She heard the roof creak, refusing to yield, and a clatter from somewhere near. She thought at first that it came from the north hall, down around Madame's rooms, but the distant bang was only the unrestrained hinge of a swinging shutter. Nobody was following her. She was certain of her escape.

Her grandmother was the only living soul who occupied this level. Madame's residency was a good thing, a ward against intrusion. If you managed to avoid her you had the floor to yourself, for no one else came up here unless summoned by the bell. The servants skirted it from habit. As a rule they preferred to roam as close to the ground floor as possible. Simonne knew well that the staff drew straws to tend the third floor call.

With her breath back and no hint of pursuit, Simonne collected herself to move forward. She reached over to a short table and fetched the stump of a candle. There was always one here to be had in a box she kept for this purpose. She lit it from a half-torn book of matches. Holding them high, the candle and matchbook both, she turned southward into the dark hallway. In this wing of the house, going away from Madame's bedchamber, there was no lamp to light the darkness. She passed the head of a glass-eyed stag whose rack butted into the shadows. She continued on towards the noisy shutter that grew louder with the wind's howl. She wound her way with a confident step through the twisting and staggered passage, back towards the end of the house where the last of the rooms were found. Back to the hall at the end of which the attic stairs came down.

Beyond the walls, the wind bit hard and made the eaves sing shrilly, while the rains tapped their persistent appeal on the glass outside each window. Little stairs stumbled in ones and twos before rising again in gaggles; the hallway fingered a torturous path around the stone bones of the manor.

Simonne knew the route well and could have walked it blind-fold. Her feet skipped as she ribboned along until she stood at the last door. A closed door. The old nursery door. It was flaked in a paint of cracked indigo hue that wrinkled under the candlelight.

She heard the voices more clearly now, little whispers almost dis-tinguishable. They were growing excited because they'd heard her approach, because they knew that she drew near. And this was why Simonne had come, for it was company she wanted.

She put a pale hand on the brass doorknob, polished bright from wear. She blew once, hard, to extinguish her light, for none of them liked the candle, and with the acrid smell of a smoking wick the last dim light was swallowed.

Simonne turned the handle and entered.

Later that same evening, hours after Simonne had run off, Sophie found herself standing sentinel outside her daughter's room. She held her breath for a moment. Hastening feet approached from the direc-tion of the main stair, but the tread was lumbering. Sophie was disap-pointed even before the fulsome Berthe appeared.

The Malenfer housekeeper drew near. "Begging your pardon, ma'am, but Mademoiselle is not to be found anywhere. No one's seen her since dinner. Perhaps she went outside, do you think?"

"No, I think not, Berthe, but thank you for trying all the same. I think I'll wait for her a while longer."

"Shall I let you into her room, ma'am?"

"Thank you, Berthe, but I'll wait for an invitation." She had her own key anyway. "I suppose I'm being a little silly here," she confided to the trusted servant. "I'm trying to mend fences, you see. A chair would be welcome, though, I'm feeling a little low." Her own voice was little more than a whisper.

The housekeeper went off, happy to provide a service.

Time then moved more slowly, and no one else passed by. Sophie sank into a despondent mood, alone in her own thoughts. She would do anything for her daughter, she told herself, Simonne was not to blame.

An hour later Simonne had yet to return. Sophie gave up waiting and went at last to bed.

Chapter 5
A Request

DERMOT DID NOT WAIT FOR AN ANSWER; HE PICKED UP HIS HAT AND he went. The door of the Swan closed behind him and left him on the step. He found the courtyard ominous and cold, where earlier it had been welcoming; the noise and warmth were all at his back, and the dark and the quiet before him.

Surely it had been Arthur – his old Lieutenant – standing by the tree? What trick was his mind playing? Whatever was going on, he had to leave. *Got to get away.* Go somewhere with fewer people around until the feeling left him. Because it wasn't the crazy notion of what he saw, but the certainty he felt that scared him. Dermot pulled his collar up against the chill and put a foot on the wet smooth cobbles.

"Dermot? Is it *really* you?"

Ivy smothered one of the walls at the side of the brasserie. The words came at him from somewhere in there. It was a voice that Dermot had never forgotten – he knew it from down in his sleep.

"Arthur?" he heard himself say.

The figure stepped out under the gas streetlight where Dermot could see him clearly. "You're a hard man to find, Dermot Ward."

"Josephing Mary. For the love of God."

Arthur still looked young from a distance. "I've been chasing you up for days."

He'd always been meticulous about his dress and grooming, down to his walrus mustache. The men had called it Arthur's "Kitchener," after the British lord. Arthur had cultivated his whiskers when he'd won his commission in the army of France. They'd been a foil to overcome his boyish good looks, but they weren't a prop anymore. Arthur had grown into them long before now; he was a man who had seen things he shouldn't.

"What the bloody hell are you on about? 'Hard man to find?' You're meant to be dead!"

"I know," Arthur agreed, disturbingly. "Isn't that a strange thing?"

"In that hospital…"

"Yes…"

"I left you in that hospital. They told me you were dead."

"Well. There's an explanation there, Irlandais."

Dermot took a step back, his head reeling. As the first shock of recognition passed over him, it was replaced with something else. "In the ambulance. I went in that bloody ambulance… to that hospital with you…" His voice, accusing.

"Ah, yes…"

"You bastard! They said you were gone. I was there all along. In that ambulance."

"It's difficult to understand…"

"Why, Arthur, why?" Dermot sucked for air as if he'd just been punched. He doubled over, feeling winded. "Why didn't you say anything?"

Arthur took a step towards him.

"No, you bastard! Don't you move a bloody inch. Don't come any nearer." He shoo'd him back. Reason had turned on its head. He rose up, and scrubbed his knuckles at his head. "Think, think." He spoke to himself. *What is going on?* "I helped them carry you. I was there. They told me you were done." All the guilt. The sleepless nights. The haunted dreams of failure. "Why did they tell me that?" he pleaded with Arthur. "Why didn't you let me know?" Tears welled up of frustration and anguish mixed with relief and joy. "Bastarding French bastard." He cleared his eyes on the back of his rumpled coat sleeve.

"Well, you know…" started Arthur, his palms turned upward. "It's good to see you too."

Dermot ran forward. He covered the distance in three, four, powerful strides. He grabbed Arthur around the arms and shook him in a bear hug. He tried to hide his tears. "Why didn't you let me know?"

"Ah, old friend, it is good to see you, and I'm so glad you can see me too."

Something was wrong. He had felt it as soon as he'd grappled the Lieutenant. The man was as light as a rake. Dermot wasn't listening.

"Arthur?" He released him.

Arthur reached over to him and put his hand on Dermot's face. It wasn't what Dermot had expected.

"What the hell is this?" Dermot backed away. There was something not right here. He pawed at his cheek as if to clean a dirty mark where Arthur's fingers had touched him. Dermot had an image of the laughing woman knocking the plate of food. Arthur's touch felt like a smear of oiled fish that ran down to his chin.

Right then, the door of Le Jardin des Cygnes banged open and a group of revelers spilled forth.

"What's going on, Arthur?" He heard his own voice too loud in the night. He heard it starting to quake.

"We should go somewhere quiet." Arthur tried to calm him. "I'll explain."

"What do you mean?" Dermot wiped again at this face, the sensation slightly wet. "You're all cold," he challenged.

"Dermot, don't talk anymore," Arthur soothed. "You're attracting some attention."

He was right. The well-sauced group had noticed Dermot and heads were nodding their way.

"Look." Arthur became anxious. "Come away with me for a minute. Maybe stay quiet till then."

"What are you on about, Arthur?"

"Please, Dermot. Stay quiet."

"Hey. Look at that." It was the group.

"Poor fellow."

"Crazy as a barrel of monkeys." A laugh followed by another.

"Better leave him be. Give him room."

"Onward! Single file."

The bar mountaineers passed amused eyes over Dermot's tarantella. As if roped together they ascended the alley, the last of them waving goodbye.

Arthur sighed. "Just come away with me for a minute, so we can talk. I'll explain, Dermot, I will."

"What's going on Arthur? Why were they looking at me that way?" The side of his face still felt slick. He kept wiping without relief.

Arthur seemed to sag. He capitulated. "OK, I'll tell you, but take it easy. And only if you'll promise to come."

Dermot noticed a note of despair. The friend he hadn't seen for nearly three years looked desperate and scared.

"I promise, Arthur. I'll hear you out. Don't worry. Just tell me what's going on."

"You were right the first time, Dermot. You were right."

"I was right?"

"You were. I am here, but I'm not. Not really."

"What the hell are you talking about?"

"Please. Calm down. Take it easy. Try and understand, Dermot, about the hospital. It did happen. It did."

"What happened?"

"I died."

There was a pause.

"I'm dead," he clarified.

"Jesus, Joseph, and Mary. What have you been drinking?"

"Please. Listen," begged the Lieutenant.

"Bugger. The hell. Off."

"I *am* here, but I'm not. I did die, Dermot. I'm dead."

"That would be funny if I didn't feel sick."

"I died in the hospital. But I didn't go away. It's true enough. It happened."

"Away to hell! Aw, come on Arthur, let's go get a drink. I'm sorry I got all weird on you."

"It's true, though."

"Now don't rub it in. I've been on the sauce myself. I thought I was seeing things. I was thinking to myself I'd gone mad."

"Please keep it down, will you? You'll draw attention. People will look at you odd."

"Arthur. Come on. You win, I'm sorry. I should have been happier to see you. What kind of joke is that, anyway? Never mind. You're a sick bugger, you are. Let's go get a drink and make up. You can tell me where you've been."

"I knew this wouldn't be easy."

And Dermot laughed. What had he been thinking? He'd had his reservations – it had seemed so strange – but he'd seen crazier things through the war. A squad of men torn apart by shelling leaving one guy in the middle untouched. You took what was. You had to. It was Arthur here, however it happened, and there was nothing else about it. Dermot grabbed him in a headlock and rubbed his knuckles across his scalp.

"You big French bastard! What a story. You totally had me wound up. Where the hell have you been hiding? When did you get out?"

"You can let me go, Irlandais... thank you." He picked up his fallen bag. "Okay, a drink. Do you have a house we can go to? Somewhere we can talk?"

"You sure you don't want to go in there?" Dermot thumbed at the Swan. "No? Well, I've got a room. It's none too pretty, though."

"That's OK, it will do. Give me an hour and I'll tell you every-thing, and then I must beg a favor."

Dermot didn't give it a thought. "Whatever you want, Lieutenant. You don't even have to ask."

Dermot led Arthur as quietly as he could past the shuttered door of his landlady. *Miserable old trout.* He raised his hat. "Bonsoir, Madame," he whispered. His rooms lay at the top of the stairs. They cautiously ascended, but did not get too far.

"Monsieur Ward." It was the propriétaire's voice from below.

"Ears like a bat."

"Monsieur Ward!" Loud enough for the neighbors.

Dermot leaned gingerly over the banister and looked down on the gray-bunned head.

"Can I assume from the late hour that your wallet still works? Your credit is good in the tap rooms? Rent day is tomorrow, and you are already two weeks behind." She shut her door with a slam.

"Beastly woman. Face like a bayonet."

Dermot and Arthur wound up the stairs like an hour hand chasing the minutes. "The door's unlocked, please go on in."

"You'll have to open it for me, Irlande."

"Open it?"

"I'm afraid that I'm not able."

Dermot played along. He showed Arthur into the living room. It was his bedroom too, and his study, and his dining room besides; a bachelor of simple means is the consummate utilitarian. Dermot cleared clothes off a chair that served him as a wardrobe.

"Please, take a seat."

"Thank you, but I'm OK here. I think I'd rather stand."

"May I get you something to drink, then?" he asked with polite formality. "I can do tea if you won't touch the hard stuff, but I'm out of coffee and wine. I suppose you could drink water? The pressure is good at this time of day if you're needing any."

"I'm good, thank you. I'll pass." Arthur took off his hat and laid his small suitcase on the floor.

"I'll fetch one for myself, then," Dermot wasn't going to pass up the occasion. A bottle was kept in his tiny kitchen for just such an emergency. He cleared two nights of dishes from the table on his way to collect it. "Make yourself at home."

Arthur took a look around the room while Dermot rattled down the hall. The ceiling rose fourteen feet high. A lifeless fan in its center waited patiently for summer. The walls of the room were papered heavily in a peeling burgundy pattern – a hint of faded richness that had long ago departed. The signs of frayed empire were everywhere, from the chip of the cornicing to the scratched pillars that supported a preposterous fireplace. The place would have been something in its day, but that day was now long over. It looked unlikely to soon return.

"There you are." Dermot was back, offering the glass that hadn't been asked for.

"Is that the cathedral?" Arthur looked from the window. "No, thank you." He refused the drink.

"Yes, they know how to ring those bloody bells. You'd think they do it for sport. I can't say I've set foot in the place. Don't feel the need anymore."

It should have been awkward, but somehow it wasn't, and Dermot felt pleasantly fine. "Sorry for the state of things," he apologized. "Cleaning lady comes first day of the year, only she took this decade off."

"No, it's fine." Arthur looked again at the piled bed sheets, books, and newspapers, the tools and the cups on the bench. A rucksack. "I heard that this season, squalor is 'in.'" His lips widened in a teasing grin.

Dermot radiated happiness. "It was precisely what I was shooting for. So hard to get it just right, you know? Place keeps slipping into 'tidy' or more often just 'mess.' It's a balancing act. I'm glad you noticed. Not all my guests appreciate the work I put into the place." He raised his glass in mock thanks, and took a little sip.

"So you left the army after all?" Arthur asked.

"Yeah, yeah. Sometimes though I have a bit of trouble believing the whole thing's actually over."

"You didn't want to stay on?"

"Christ, no, Arthur. I've had enough of that for ten lifetimes. But I'm still figuring out what to do. It had changed, too... the Legion, I mean. It was filling up with Russians. Not that I mind Russians, you understand – cheery bunch of miserable buggers – but nearly all of them were Tsarists. Divine right of kings. Arse kissers, all of them, and that I couldn't take. La République's got lots wrong with her, but she sorted out *that* issue."

"So you took your discharge."

"Yeah. I've been out of uniform since Christmas, and I can't say that I miss it."

"Why did you stay in Paris? Why aren't you back in Irlande? Why are you hanging about here?" Arthur had at last settled himself on the corner of the bed.

Dermot had a distant look, as if it wasn't an easy question. He swirled the contents of his chipped glass.

"Do you remember where I'm from, Frenchy?"

"A distant bog, as I recall."

"Exactly. I left Ballingarry in 1914 and I haven't been back since.

Nowhere outside of something small near the little village green."

"But it's home, isn't it?"

"Well, that's quite the question." Dermot sighed. "My father died last year."

"I'm sorry to hear that."

What was the point in sharing? What would Arthur remember anyhow? It was years ago. His little brother. He took another sip.

"How do you go back, Arthur? How do you go home to *that* after all that we both saw?"

"Many men have done so. And yet I find you here."

"Exactly. You're right. You get on a bloody boat, that's how you do it. You just get onto the train. Back home. If that's what's important to you." He pulled another long drink from his glass, not quite finished it yet.

"You had a brother. A younger brother. He was, what? Ten years younger than you? Did he eventually sign up?"

Dermot finished his drink. "He was fifteen. Fifteen, Arthur. All stirred up by the Easter Rising three years back, he went and got himself killed."

"Oh, Dermot. I didn't know."

"Nothing to know. I was here. He was trying to do the best that he could and ended up in a ditch. Well, maybe the rest are doing all right. I hope they are. I'm just trying to look after me – I'm no good for anyone."

Dermot saw Arthur's face, looking at him.

"Christ, don't you start too. I can't go there, it's not home anymore – or it is, but I'm not me." Dermot pumped his arm as if priming a dart, chasing the elusive target of what he was trying to say. "I mean, look at ourselves, man – things are different now. I've probably gone insane and you supposedly died years ago..." He laughed between another mouthful, tasting the irony as much as the whisky. "So both of us are having a rough time. How do you go home and say it's all good, with this crap in your head?"

"You get on a boat," Arthur replied.

"Exactly. And maybe I will. Maybe time *will* change things. Maybe that's all that will."

"Maybe."

"I'd like to go home, Arthur; one day I really would. She won't be doing great, my mum, not right now, but she'll be doing all right. When I can help her, I'll go, when I'll be good for her – but not right now. Not right now for me."

"Or when you run out of money?"

"Or when I run out of money. I might go then, that's a point. Cheeky bastard." He was smiling again, however. "So why were you looking for me, Arthur? What did *you* come here for?"

It hadn't escaped Dermot's attention that Arthur had not brought it up. Whatever it was that was important and pressing, he needed to work up to saying. Dermot thought the time had come; it was time to get some answers. He turned the tables on Arthur. "Why aren't you at that farm of yours, that big house you talked about? You used to make us all jealous. See? You're not the only one of us that hasn't forgotten a thing. Why aren't you back home, Arthur? Are you in a spot of trouble?"

"Yes, my friend. I suppose that's it. I suppose that's why I'm here." He sounded like he wanted to talk, so Dermot stayed quiet and let him. "Do you remember the tunnel, Dermot? Do you remember what happened that day?"

And how could Dermot ever forget? He relived it himself every night. "I remember," was all he said.

"I tried to ask you for something. I was going to ask for a favor."

And Dermot was back there, transported by the memory; the walls of his room turned to dirt.

Dermot, if I don't make it... if I don't get out... I need you to....

"Yes, I remember, Français. Only we were a bit busy at the time."

"Please listen, Dermot." Arthur was sincere. "I need your help now, I desperately need your help. I'll beg for your assistance or do anything it takes."

"Jesus, Arthur. Calm down, man. Take a seat." The thought of Arthur having to beg, after all he'd done to him.

Arthur sat down again. "We didn't have many secrets, Dermot, but I kept from you one. I had children, Dermot. I *have* children. Two boys. Twins. I was young... an indiscretion, and their mother... she died giving birth."

Dermot paid attention now; he'd never heard any of this. But why Arthur was bringing this to him tonight he could not yet understand.

"My own father took care of things," Arthur continued. "He made sure they'd be all right. But I did her wrong, I see that now, and also my two sons."

"Christ, you're a sly bugger keeping that under your hat. What do you mean, *took care of things*? What happened to them, then?"

"None of this was told to anyone. My father covered it up."

"But what happened to your kids?"

"They were nursed away somewhere, and then later brought back to the farm. My father saw that they were cared for, but I couldn't speak of their existence and did not acknowledge them as my own."

"But he died, didn't he? Your father died years ago. Didn't you tell me that?"

"He did. And I let things carry on. I got to watch them both grow up and work around the estate."

"Well..." Dermot wasn't sure what to say; he didn't want to judge. "That's great, isn't it? So now you've got two kids!"

"Just recently, my brother Michel passed away. The question of the estate's inheritance remains to be decided."

"But you'll get it, won't you?" He racked his memory. "I thought you were the eldest?"

Arthur just looked at him and puffed out his mustache. "When you see things as they really are, you'll better understand; but they, by rights, should get their share and be very well looked after."

"You said they work on the estate?"

Arthur shied from the question. "I've not been a good father, Dermot, but I need to do this much for them."

"And your family doesn't know?" Dermot repeated Arthur's own words to try to keep things straight. In his head the absinthe bath was slowly unraveling everything.

"Growing up, I thought the twins might suspect, or my mother would know the truth. But now I know I was wrong. I have to tell them, Dermot, don't you see? It will mean so much for them all."

"I don't really know, Arthur."

"The Malenfer line isn't over! The family name lives on!"

"And this is a big thing in your neighborhood?"

"You should come and see for yourself."

"And why do you need me again? What am I supposed to do?"

"You are the one who must tell them."

"That's still the bit I don't really get. Why don't you tell them yourself?"

"Because I told you, Dermot! I am dead, I really am, and no one else can see me. So you'd be really helping me out."

"Oh, I remember. It's coming back now. You *did* tell me that bit, yes. Good, good. Nice to get that straight. So I'm sort of being haunted then, is that what we're saying? You're either messing with my head or you're driving me mad from the grave?"

"Old friend!" Arthur objected. "Please don't think it so. I'm in need of a little assistance, and I thought that you might oblige."

Dermot ruminated a moment while he drew again heavily from his glass that was getting dangerously low.

"OK," he proposed. "So a few things might be happening here."

His mind had been at work. "Scenarios one and two are what I think are likely, but there is a scenario three."

"Go on."

"You don't think I'm serious?"

"I'm intrigued."

"Well.... Well, that's all right then, I suppose. So. Here it is. Ready?"

"Ready."

"Good. One: I've gone mad, like I long suspected, and should really lay off the drink. Until I do I can now expect successions of dead friends and family to parade through my life as they please."

"It's likely just me. There aren't a lot of us." Arthur tried to help.

"But that's OK." Dermot talked to himself, ignoring Arthur for the moment. "I'll lay off the absinthe for a week. See what happens when I finally dry out. Except I *can't* do that. It's the green fairy in the bottle that keeps all the bad thoughts away..." He pondered the conundrum. "So how am I going to sleep if I can't be touching the absinthe? This is a pickle I'm in."

"I don't follow you, Irlandais."

"You don't?" Dermot readmitted Arthur to the dialogue. "See, if I'm mad, then there's no need to help you because it's all going on in my head. In fact I should really not be doing anything, even talking to you. I should lock up the door and stay safe!"

"What is your option two?" Arthur interrupted. Dermot blinked.

"Option two? Yes. Very strange. Talking friends that shouldn't be here... Well, option two is what I'm counting on, as it's definitely the best of the bunch."

"For me or for you?"

Dermot gave the question consideration. "Definitely for both. Option two is that *you've* lost your marbles, but that you're alive and you're really here."

"Oh, I'm here."

"Then there you go!"

"...but please, continue all the same."

"Well. How I see it is I've had a rough night... obviously... but I'm lucky enough to have met an old friend." He looked here hard at Arthur, the shifting colors that made up his body, the ravine of scarred flesh down his face. "And *you've* had a rough night too, by the looks of you. And you're a nutter now, obviously, which means you've been locked up somewhere and just got out, or you've gone wandering about on your own. Maybe you're an absinthe jockey like myself, eh, Arthur? Do you like the green and sugar? And somehow you've come to think that you're dead..." A thought just occurred to him. "You're not playing with my head here, are you? It's not a funny joke if you are."

"No. Sorry, Irlandais. No joke, I'm afraid."

"Well. That's too bad, though looking at it objectively, I suppose it could be amusing. Now, seeing as how option two says you are mad, it behooves me to help an old friend. Get you safely back to the loony bin from which you've obviously fled. That sort of thing. Kids or no kids. Do the best I can for you."

"And option three?" Dermot stalled; that had sounded OK to him. "Option three?"

"Now I don't really like that one."

"Let's hear it anyway."

"Option three is things are just exactly as you've said."

"Aha!"

"That you're a ghost and I'm not mad and that you've actually got two kids."

"Just so!"

"But even if that were the case, I think that still makes me insane."

"Not so much insane. Difficult to accept, perhaps; courageous even; but not so much insane."

"I need another drink." Dermot drained the remains of his glass and poured Arthur's into his.

"Come to Chaumont with me, Dermot. Help me make these things right for my children."

"Now, how could I do that?"

"Tell my family about my boys for me, that's all that I'm asking from you."

"They're going to believe me? A story about hidden children. Now you really are nuts."

"I have proof: their birth certificates! I hid them in the house."

"Judas's arse."

"It's easy."

"What a story. I've clearly gone off the deep end."

"Then think of it as I'm really here, and you're just escorting me home."

That struck Dermot as better somehow, though none of this was going too well. Practicality occasionally smites a man who is well into his glasses, and Dermot sensed the time had come for him to lay his head down. *Things,* he thought, *might seem a little clearer in the cold light of the morning.*

"How about we talk this over one more time at breakfast?" He was practically horizontal already.

"An excellent idea. Can I take the floor?"

But Dermot was already asleep. If Arthur had known, he'd have pitied Dermot, for it wasn't a peaceful place. Sprawled out in the chair he was far away, back down in the tunnel again.

Chapter 6
The Tunnel

DERMOT SALVAGED BROKEN TIMBER FROM THE FLOOR. ARTHUR HAD found a pry bar. They picked a spot in the roof that had collapsed on them a little, and there they clawed, struck, leveraged, and pulled, clearing what fell down on them back towards the mine face, and then returned to the roof once more.

The plan was to keep their own end open as long as possible, in case rescue, by some unimaginable hope, did come for them. Dermot's forearms and shoulders burned with the strain. He had long ago become numb to the unending fatigue from muscles held elevated above his head. They shielded themselves from whatever fell and then scraped and dug for more. They had nothing else, no other hope, and soon that was all that fueled them.

Time slipped by. Arthur's pocket watch, a tick tick tick without reference. Dermot found its persistence slowly picked away at his mind. The darkness was unending.

"Above!" Dermot called the warning. He'd worked a rock free, and it dropped on them unexpectedly. It spilled off Dermot's shoulder and must have hit Arthur. He heard him groan and fall to the ground. The watch fell silent.

"Are you all right?" Dermot called down.

"I'm fine." There was the sound of broken glass being shaken. "That was a present," he said.

"I'll get you another for your birthday."

The watch gone, time now passed unquantified, left to the imagination. Dermot found this disturbed him more, but there was nothing to be done about it.

Sometime later, he called for a rest.

"It'll be a long go. Let's pace ourselves." He didn't say anything more, their progress difficult to measure. He tried to visualize the dimensions of the room that encapsulated their existence. He fought down his growing despair. There was, by now, six inches of water in the tunnel and a thick viscous mud underneath it. Resting was uncomfortable, and the thought of sleep terrifying – to be swallowed whole, unexpectedly, and wake up with your choking lungs full of muddy water.

The air about them grew heavy and foul, and Dermot was breathing hard to get it. Soon they were fighting for the depleted oxygen even when they rested. Dermot knew their time was fleeting.

"Back at it, Lieutenant?"

Dermot heard Arthur rise up, felt the stale thick air move around him. His friend's large hand found his shoulder.

"Dermot, I may die here," Arthur said slowly. "And if that happens I've got something to tell you."

"You don't love me, do you, Frenchy? It's been worrying me something terrible."

"You're a good sort, Dermot Ward, but not my type. But I do have a favor to ask of you."

Dermot heard the change in Arthur's tone, the resignation. It saddened him. "Go on," he encouraged.

"If we don't get out... if *I* don't get out, I need you to..."

There was a second in which the whistle was audible, very faint and behind them.

"Down!" Dermot yelled, and they dropped into the muddy pool just as the whole earth shook around them. The explosion bucked Dermot like a mule. The roof ripped from the ceiling. Dazed and stunned, Dermot turned onto his back, shaken and uncomprehending. Blurred shapes swirled in front of his face that were now becoming clearer.

"I can see. Arthur. I can see!" Dermot looked up at the hole, his fingers moving and stretching before him. A ray of light silhouetted his hand. He felt a splash of runoff or rain. "Arthur? Arthur!"

Dermot pulled at him, dragged him up out the water, and lifted his head clear. He was rewarded with a heaving splutter as the big man caught his breath. Arthur coughed and choked, clearing his mouth of the dirty water that had collected in his throat. He gasped to regain his breath. "Dermot." He spoke too loudly then cradled his head in pain. "My ear!"

"You're OK, you're OK." Dermot soothed him down, although he saw the trickling blood and knew immediately that Arthur had ruptured an eardrum. *He could see!* "Don't worry, your hearing will clear. If you can hear me at all, it'll clear. Well, probably... It doesn't matter, Arthur," he continued quickly. "We're out, Frenchy! You lucky bastard. Did you hear me? I said we're out!"

"Out?" Arthur cast about, as if aware all of a sudden that he was able to use his eyes again. "What was that? What happened? Another shell?"

"I don't think so. Maybe, but I think it came from back there." He thumbed at the direction of the cave-in. "I think they're trying to get us out or kill us in the attempt." Dermot was all cheer.

"And the hole?"

"We must have gotten pretty close to the surface, and then that last blast loosened it up. There's light, Arthur, which means there is air. We're safe. We're going to get out! Jesusing Mary, I never thought. I'm going up for a look."

"Wait a second," Arthur gripped his arm. "Why don't we just stay here instead? Wait for them to get through to us?"

"Are you nuts?" Dermot shook him off. "Who knows how long they'll take? Another hour? A day? And this place isn't safe by a long shot." He looked up at the ceiling as if to prove his point. The danger he'd envisioned in the dark was now confirmed by the penetrating light. "No, I tell you, we're both getting out of here right away. Pack your bags, big man, it's been a lovely time and all, but I think we've overstayed our welcome."

Dermot shimmied back up the tight chimney they'd painstakingly carved out together. The light went out for Arthur beneath as Dermot filled the chimney.

"Shouldn't we wait for night and cover?"

"Maybe." Dermot's voice was muffled as he squirmed forward, widening the opening with his arms. "I'll only take a peek."

He had to writhe and wriggle but at last he was out, reborn from inside the earth's hot womb into a brand new world. Only it wasn't. It was a familiar world of wire and bodies, of mud and freezing rain. He was on the side of a large crater – thankfully not the bottom. It was a lake down there, and had they come up under it they would certainly have been drowned. Dermot sank to his hands and knees. He drank deeply from the clean well of air like a straggler who'd reached an oasis, a man who thought he'd reached his end and couldn't quite believe it was real. He felt the unnerving sensation of falling, falling back into an ocean of space with the open air around him. He fought against the tears that ran from his eyes, and took a second to collect himself.

He'd been gone, he knew it. He'd given himself up for dead. It was only for Arthur that he'd kept it together, too ashamed to show him his fear. Soiled from the mud and the dirt of the hole, Dermot sank to his knees and he prayed.

"What's it like?" It was Arthur's voice from below, the only answer he heard.

"Lovely. You should see what they've done with the place. Come on up, it's all clear."

Dermot, keeping low, lifted a German rifle from a boy who wouldn't be needing it and crept up to the crater's edge. He inched forward, writhing on his belly, until at last he peered over the rim.

At first he didn't quite understand what he was looking at; it took a few seconds to comprehend. "Bastarding Jesus, this can't be happening." He watched for a short time more, judging the wind and direction. But it was. "Jesus, Mary. No."

A noise behind him distracted him and Dermot reluctantly turned. He turned in time to see Arthur emerge from out of their tiny hole. Turned in time to watch Arthur stretch to ease his knotted cramp. Turned to see Arthur stand tall, his long bony arms held high. Dermot turned too late to stop him.

"Arthur, get down, you fool!"

The bullets came from behind Arthur where the German trenches lay. Arthur whirled, sent tumbling to the ground, as Dermot shot wildly in reply. He saw no-one, firing blindly only to keep heads down. He scrambled over, frantic now, until he reached Arthur's side.

"Christ, you stupid bastard! Look what the hell you've done!"

Arthur lay gasping, stunned by the shock. His mouth was open as if trying for sound that seemed unable to form.

"Christ, you've taken one." Dermot could see the mess. "Jesus. Maybe more."

"Go! You go," Arthur managed, forcing the words, as he clutched his own arm tightly.

More shots, but overhead. Dermot let off a couple in reply to give them something to think about, and then he dropped the rifle down the hole.

"What did you do that for?" Arthur still had the sense to wonder.

"Things aren't good. We're going back down."

"They'll find us. There's no point. You've got to run."

"They'll not be looking for us pretty soon, they'll have other things to worry about." Dermot grabbed Arthur by the shoulders and lifted, pulling him a few feet, his boots dragging in the mud. The Lieutenant let out an ungodly scream when Dermot touched his shattered arm. "Sorry about that, Français, can't be helped." Arthur had almost blacked out. "Christ, you're bastarding heavy." He heaved. He'd got Arthur's feet into the hole.

"Why?" Arthur stammered. "Why go back down?" Anyone would

know their cave was a deathtrap – one grenade would finish them off. But Arthur had seen Dermot's face and was clearly scared by what he saw: Dermot was crying. "What is it, Irlande? What's going on?"

"Christ, Frenchy." Dermot sniveled and wiped his eyes on his shoulder. "You really don't want to know."

Dermot let go. Arthur dropped like a stone, sliding down the wet walls, screaming as the fall jarred his bones. Then there was silence below. Had Arthur blacked out? Had he killed him? But Dermot's thoughts moved on. He was thinking again about what he had seen over the crater lip. He wasn't worried about the Germans at all.

Beyond the crater rim was flat gray ground and the boiling yellow cloud. *They* were attacking. His side! And they were sending over the gas. The weapon they feared more than any other, more than bullets or knives or bombs. The weapon that killed in silence; the air that melted the skin.

Dermot ran to the scattered soldiers' bodies he'd taken the gun from, going through their kits, searching, searching frantically, casting a look back over his shoulder but remembering to keep crouched down.

One! There was one. He tore at the box for the mask. But that was it, no others. There weren't any more. Dermot looked to the edge where the trenches were, then back once again to his own, and he saw the first tendrils spin in the air as they mounted the crater's wide brim.

"Merciful God. Please no." The yellow curls looped like incense trails, bidding his prayers up.

Dermot ran, sprinting now to the hole, the yellow air only yards away. He slid on his belly and wriggled inside, sliding face down into the tunnel. It was a short wild descent. He landed on top of Arthur. Arthur must have been unconscious, but the shock of being fallen on brought him around.

"Sorry, Français." Dermot apologized, rolling off him into the slurry of water, "but please shut the hell up. I'm trying to think here!"

Dermot stared up into the chimney, into the dribbling rain. He had seconds only, he knew, and his arms were starting to shake.

"Christ God!" He clenched his hands, trying to stop it, his whole body shaking in fear. He sat and squeezed his arms tight round his legs. *Think, think, think, man, think!* It would be coming any second; it would come and spill right in. The gas, he knew, was heavier than air, and it would seep into any low space.

Dermot pulled out their only mask and pulled it over his own head. It was different from the kind he was used to, which tied around the face. "Arthur, I'm sorry." His own voice was suddenly louder. It was this, or both of them dead.

Dermot had a plan. He took his shirt off and then pulled off Arthur's too.

"Dermot, if I don't make it..."

"Shut the hell up, Français."

"Dermot, promise me please..."

He found their one lone jacket next, long abandoned on the floor. The Irishman climbed back into the chimney, and it was then he felt the sting.

He saw nothing, no obvious change. The hood made everything cloudy, but nothing was obviously yellow. He forced himself up. The flesh of his wet dirty chest now sizzled, like cold batter dropped into a pan. He wailed as if scalded yet pressed ahead, and worse the pain became. His hands seared now, his finger tips most of all, as if a too-long-lit match had run down to his nails, but he bore it and still labored on.

He was at the top now, sucking hard breath, and then he put his head clear out. From rim to rim he could see nothing more, for the cloud had consumed all the earth. Quickly Dermot spread out the wet shirts and jacket he had brought. He erected a tent to cover their hole and keep the foul air out. A good half he got done – the jacket was good, but the shirts were proving too small.

"Bastarding Jesus!" he cursed out loud, and sobbed at the pain in his hands. He made his best efforts to cover it up and could finally bear it no more. With the shirts in place he lowered himself, and once more their prison was dark.

"Arthur! Don't you dare die!" He pulled the Frenchman up, getting a wheezing breath from the unconscious man – and then hope. There was a gap now, a tiny thing in the wall. A hole through the caved-in tunnel behind him that hadn't been there before.

Dermot fell to his knees and shoveled with his hands. He could feel the air start to sting around him. He dug with his blistered pin-pricked hands as Arthur coughed sharply behind him.

"Please!" He shouted though the widening gap to the rescuers on the far side. "Quickly now!" There *was* someone there, and they were coming for them! A shaft appeared that became a small channel, perhaps only two feet around.

Dermot could not open his hands. His bare skin felt basted, as if they'd been plunged into hot oil; seizures started, a helpless trembling that ran up both his arms. *No, please!* he pleaded to no one. *Some more time is all!*

"Gas!" said a voice from in front of him, and then two hands gripped his own. Dermot was pulled hard forward, sucked headfirst into a straw.

"Out you come!" said the voice close by.

He was through to the other side.

"There's a man alive back there," he choked. "I've left my friend on the other side." He lay on the floor, shaking hard, his body now losing control.

"Gas! Gas!" The cry went out, and there were legs around him everywhere.

"Go back if you want," the voice told him, "but I have to seal up that hole."

Dermot managed to lift himself and slide the hood back off his head. He rolled over and looked through the tiny gap that was smoother from his passing. Through the tube there was a clear view to his friend at the other end.

He saw Arthur slumped on the tunnel wall, coughing and broken and torn. His shoulders, perhaps, were too wide for the pipe, and the poisonous mist settled lower.

Dermot's tears now ran freely, unhindered down his face. "I'm sorry, my friend, I'm sorry," he sobbed. The miners closed Arthur in.

Chapter 7
A Malenfer Funeral

By tradition, the Malenfers buried their dead on a Wednesday. No one was quite certain why. The unkind would observe that a Malenfer funeral was as far from the Sabbath as possible; they let the implications hang in the air. But whatever the reason behind it all, the practice brought complications.

For this reason it was much easier for all concerned (the departed perhaps excluded) if a Malenfer died on a weekend. This afforded appropriate time to make ready the preparations. Over the generations, such a consideration solidified into ambition; indeed it was not unusual for the eulogy to be colored by the deceased's regard to time-keeping. Rightly or wrongly, Malenfers everywhere conspired to expire on a weekend.

The tradition was superstitious, unorthodox, and possibly heretical. It was nonetheless true for all of that. A Malenfer understood that dying prematurely led to storage in the root cellar, molding slowly like a fine blue cheese, hidden out of sight.

Any priest who values his daily crust knows well the habits of his benefactors. A priest of Darmannes (in which the noble estate lay) is careful of his appointments. When infirmity lingers over that tribe, he curtails his Wednesday diary. It would be rash of a cleric to book out that day with baptisms or weddings.

Rationality must take a parlor seat when visiting such traditions. In one form or another, these are rife in older families, a curiosity to those outside and a burden to those who serve them. Reason might present its card at the door, but admittance will never be granted.

So it was that on Wednesday, the twelfth day of February in the nineteenth year of the new century, Master Michel Malenfer was to be brought by carriage to the St. Jérôme Chapel. Horses dark as Alsace coal mines towed the hearse in which he rode, each mare plumed in ostrich feathers dyed to match her coloring. The browbands of the blackened bridles shone with burnished silver. The quarantine on the house had been lifted and the family was free to attend.

The coffin itself was walnut, a sarcophagus lying flat in the bed. The pale, gaunt boy that rolled inside was out of proportion to its scale. And yet Michel barely fit in that large polished box, for to be buried with him was his name.

Eight men it took to hoist the casket into the wagon bed. The chapel was only a short ride away in the village of Chevecheix. The hearse moved off with a rumble of wheels, and two coaches followed behind it.

The family sat in the first of these, which they shared with their local priest. Madame and Sophie sat together across from Simonne and Father Meslier. He, like they, wore flowing black robes, but alone eschewed a veil. Father Meslier, a jowly man, clasped the Good Book between sweaty hands and gripped it tightly to his lap. They said not a word through the whole trip; Michel's coffin made more noise.

Behind the hearse and both the carriages walked the servants of Malenfer Manor. Following them came a larger host, who were the tenants of the estate. In this parade arranged for the dead they paid their collective respects, or failing that, at least ensured their attendance was duly recorded. They walked at the pace of a slow-beating drum, and many would wait outside when they got there, for the Chapelle St. Jérôme was tiny and could hold but half their number. Already it was nearly full, and the coffin had only moved off. It was swollen with the ranks who came up from town and dignitaries from wider: bankers and creditors, men from the guilds, and a flavor of elected officials. The Army was present out of respect to Madame and the family's history of service – for Madame's husband, the Colonel, and her son Arthur and the others who had served before them. Newspapermen hovered nearby, drawn by the whiff of celebrity.

In the middle of this procession, alone in the second carriage, sat the fine, polished figure of Monsieur Crevel, a neatly groomed gentleman of fifty. Crevel held the distinguished title of Mayor of Darmannes – an impressive badge susceptible to tarnish if the influence of the municipality was appreciated. Crevel seldom let that bother him, and certainly not on this occasion.

Today he sported a long wool overcoat that he had chosen to leave unbuttoned, a concession to his peacock pride in his chest of medals. A gleaming array of trinkets and trophies were on view upon his doublet, worthy baubles of civic service and serving the rank of his title. They hung from his neck and were pinned to his breast and dangled from his lapels. His suit had been pressed till its edges cut, and then starched for extra crispness.

Crevel at this moment sat in thought. His manicured fingers twisted and rolled his carefully waxed mustaches. He was thinking about the small speech he was to give at the service for Michel and how well it would go. He mused pleasantly on the accolades he would receive from it, and the tone he should take in reply.

His carriage, his private carriage (the other one being at home), Crevel shared with his only offspring, Robert. They were alone together, father and son; Crevel's wife had gone some years before and so missed out on this occasion. It was a shame, he mused, for in her time she had always loved a good funeral.

Crevel had raised the boy the best he could, which is to say, not quite so well at all. He was a man committed to his professional life and to "getting on in the world," and in grieving the loss of his passing wife, he'd redoubled his ambitions.

Crevel was not indifferent to the boy – he had not, for instance, delivered him wholesale to the care and affection of a wicked housekeeper – but the chore of raising a child exasperated him, and he thought himself ill-suited to it. Understanding his own deficiencies in the matter (which he did not underestimate), he ameliorated them by the traditional remedy and packed Robert off to boarding school. Crevel now had ample time to advance his aspirations, and he pursued his political goals without further distraction.

As Crevel's fortunes improved, so did Robert's schools, and the familial bond was renewed at holidays when he came home between the terms. He consoled himself with the certain knowledge (when the need infrequently required) that many a father had done worse for a boy, and damned few had done much better.

For Robert's part, he adapted to the change as children of an age do – he accepted it as normal. One day he had a mother, the next not. One day he had a home, the next a dormitory. If he was sad and lonely and cried every night for the first week or month, he scarce remembered it ten years on.

When he was seventeen and his days at school were almost up, the War had already started, and all the boys of his acquaintance were giddy to join in. His entire final year was spent enrolled in the Officer Training Corps, and he and his friends enjoyed tremendously the shouting, marching, and dressing up that went along with the performance. Robert had expected to take a commission when he came of age, but then found himself excused from service. The University had beat the Army's letter and offered him a place. He duly reported to the Sorbonne in Paris, but dropped out after only one year.

This event did not entirely disappoint his father. Like many parents, he extolled the value of an arts education as long as his child took up medicine or the law. In the summer of 1918, Robert gave up city life and returned to his home in Darmannes. Crevel greeted his son's return (and the money it saved him) with tears of fatherly joy.

Robert's time away had blessed him with the makings of a fine education and given him connections aplenty. It was a sound enough base upon which, to his father's eye, a career could be built. It was Crevel Senior who arranged for a position inside the municipal administration, a job with prospects, yet not too demanding, that would serve well his son and heir. Most importantly, the job Robert fell into was designated as Protégé – protected. In the Byzantine world of the French civil service, the position carried an unspecified strategic worth: a stamp of gold, richly prized, for its occupant could not be spared. Robert was kept from the army's grasp; Crevel had showed his affection.

Robert was like his father in many ways and yet in others not. At college, in the company of friends, he had pursued a feckless lifestyle. Rumors persisted of bacchanalian nights and smoky parlors of poor reputation, all of which contrasted sharply with his father's rural conservatism. Crevel Senior cultivated a public persona that was puritanically straight-laced – his public expecting nothing less – and what he did behind closed doors was no one else's business.

Physically they were more closely matched. Robert was a fit young man with a mane of curly dark hair, hair that he let wild. He didn't wear it neat, like his father did, or cut it short, and this alone was distinctive for it obviously wasn't army. Beneath this ruffle was a strong chin, and when he smiled, which was often, his teeth showed straight and even. His father liked the look of him; he called his Robert "honest." If consensus is a truth of sorts, then Robert was handsome without a lie. His features might have come from his father, but to their arrangement he was indebted to his mother.

News of Robert's return soon spread fast about the town. Many a girl looked on his lips – on a woman such lips would be termed "full" – and thought wistfully of them romantically employed, pressed hard against her own. Many a mother of a girl of Darmannes had exactly the same sordid thought. Maidens all, devoid of adventure; all the men gone off to fight.

It wasn't just that he was pretty to look at (though he was), but he carried a scent of the exotic. His wardrobe from the capital was a little more fashionable than that of the local men, and there were unfounded rumors that flitted about of a dangerous passionate past. Robert wore this aura well, charmingly unconcerned by how he stirred the hearts of ladies in these rural parts.

Back in their carriage, Robert stretched out wide across the bench. He tapped a foot against the door and wrung his hands out like a towel. He couldn't settle down. He glanced out the window before staring back down at his palms. At twenty years of age, other men might have outgrown their youthful impatience or mastered its physical displays, but Robert was different in this respect and wore his temperament on his sleeve. He laughed out loud at that which amused him and scowled deeply at every frustration. Robert, then, was an open book — a frustration to his father, for Crevel could be unreadable when he wished and considered it a quality worth having. Right now something obviously bothered Robert, and it was interrupting his father's reverie.

"What's the matter with you, then?" There was little point in asking him to sit still.

Robert paused. He had wanted to talk for quite a while, but he knew his father would fill his ear. He wasn't sure where to begin and didn't know if he should start. He found the courage, and in the long tradition of bad news bearers, did his best to soften the blow.

"I've been thinking about something," Robert said, "and when you calm down I'm sure you'll see it's for the best."

But by the look on Crevel's face he wasn't so sure anymore.

"And what," Crevel spoke slowly, annoyed already despite his best efforts, "have you been thinking about?"

"Simonne," said Robert. Mademoiselle Simonne, his fiancée.

"Simonne?" Crevel was caught unawares; he'd expected another entreaty on moving back to Paris or joining the bloody Army.

The war's over now, son, you'll have to wait for the next one. You can thank me properly then.

"What about Simonne?" he asked, suspicious.

Robert had met Simonne one month after his return to Darmannes.

It was expected that Robert stay in his father's house in the center of town, and so he did. There, after only two weeks back from the city, he was already bored to tears. To salvage the little he could from this life, Robert did what he could to have fun. He made it his conscious duty to attend every concert, every dance, every play. He shamelessly courted invitations to parties when they didn't come his way. Being the exotic son of the Mayor, his calendar was naturally soon filled. If there was a paucity of society in Darmannes, it was only in quality and taste.

Of all the unlikely places, it was at a church lunch that he met Simonne. Robert was enduring the dreadful event, one he'd been pressed into attending for some war cause or another. "I hate these things," she'd said to him. "They think they're actually helping."

"Scrap iron for the war?" She was apart from the other young ladies, long black hair and deep green eyes; he'd been watching her since he got there.

"No, silly. Religion."

"That's a bit strong for a church lunch, wouldn't you say? The old girls here are liable to eat you alive if you keep saying things like that."

"I'm Simonne," she extended her hand, "and next week is my birthday."

Mademoiselle was turning eighteen and had the presumption to invite him along, the dashing young man from Paris. His father had been very pleased to hear of it. He'd gone, of course, and the courtship had progressed by bounds. The war had ended on November 11th, and to celebrate he'd asked for her hand.

"Yes. I suppose that's what comes next."

He remembered that when she'd said it, the world had seemed so bright.

"What are you saying about Simonne?" His father repeated himself.

"I don't think I want to marry her after all."

Robert watched as his father digested the news; he didn't think it had gone down very well. His father made his distant smiling face, the one he wore when he wanted to kill.

Crevel finally continued in a soft, slow staccato. "And what would make you think to break off your engagement with the eminently suitable Mademoiselle?"

"I don't know." That wasn't the right thing to say. "I don't know, it just doesn't seem right," he tried to elaborate. Robert was surprised at himself. He'd managed to say it. "She's different, father, and not in the normal way. She's nice and all, but the things she talks about sometimes... the way she looks at things... I'm not entirely sure she's all there."

"And what" – Crevel often started his sentences this way when he was annoyed (his voice was in the habit of pitching high over the 't') – "does *that* have to do with anything?"

"Well, she is, she's great... but she's going to be my wife, father. I mean, I'd like one that's right in the head." He stumbled a bit for his words. "It's just, well, it's forever, you know, dad? There's so much out there to do and none of this has to be now, and maybe Simonne isn't right?"

Crevel restrained the urge to lift his cane up and rap Robert's thick curly head. *Tact*, he thought, taking deep breaths, *use tact.*

"I thought you loved her?" Crevel went for the reasoned approach. "I thought she was *everything* and a *delight*?" He mimicked his son quite well.

"Oh I do, I do," Robert defended. "Well, I thought I did."

"You've met another girl?" Crevel interrogated.

"No, no! It's not that. It's just Simonne. She's just... I just think that keeping her happy is going to be a bit of a chore." Robert sighed.

"Dear God." Now it was Crevel's turn to sigh. He thought for a moment. "Have you told her this?"

"No.Not yet."

"What about anyone else?"

"No, just you."

"Then look here, Robert, there are a few things you should take into consideration, a few things it's important to know."

Robert was listening. He was happy to listen to advice; it was taking it that he sometimes had difficulty with.

"You're going to marry her," Crevel said.

"But I don't think I want to, father..."

"I hear you, Robert," Crevel cut him off, "but in this instance you are going to do what you're damn well told."

Robert looked sulky. Crevel ignored this and relayed his advice.

"You'll continue to pay her attentions, but don't fawn over her – women hate fawners." He paused then went on, as if reading now from a list. "Pay her a compliment, do so regularly, but don't ooze it, it can't seem contrived. Sparingly, but it should seem sincere; spontaneous is better yet.

"The next bits are important," he went on, as if consulting a manual. "Don't ever forget her birthday or your wedding anniversary, and if you can manage it, surprise her with something on the day that you first met, that anniversary too, she'll love that. The first two are absolutes; treat the latter as a bonus. Importantly, if she says she wants nothing or needs nothing or you should pay such things no heed, do not for a single moment believe her! Are you listening?"

Robert nodded, though unsure of where his father was going here.

"Now, this funeral is a great opportunity for you," Crevel resumed. "They're all a little fragile about poor Michel." Crevel wrung theatrical tears from his eyes. "What you need to show here is that you are a pillar of strength! You!" He jabbed a finger at Robert. "They like that. It shows dependability, a strong arm to lean on. Good husband material." He painted the air with his hands.

"But I'm already engaged to her. I don't want to marry her now..."

His father ignored him. "You must play her like a fish, Robert! And what a fish she is!"

"No, father. I've got her, I just don't think I want her..."

"Nonsense!" Crevel boomed, and then quieted down. He feared the coachman would hear him over the trundle of the rolling spokes. "Do you know what it is you have here?" His voice turned thick like cold treacle as he asked the question of his son. There was no answer forthcoming, so Crevel provided the answers himself.

"Is she alluring, beautiful even? Yes she is, she is ravishing, and still only half the woman she might become. Just look at her mother... no, you're still far too young. Consider yourself lucky and just take my word. Then consider, Robert, whether she is intelligent. A match for you and more... don't look sour, boy, you don't want a boring one." Crevel was being unkind but not insincere. "Is she of a suitable age? Eighteen and a peach, ripe for the plucking; no dowager for you, my boy! And is she of good family?" Here and only now did Crevel pause as if his train of thought had hit a washed out bridge or was going so fast as to leave him breathless and incapable of speech.

Crevel had hunched forward over his knees as he spoke, leaning into Robert, forcing his son to retreat. But now he sat back, sprawling in the coach as Robert had done, lolling like a libertine. He glanced out of the window at the fields and gray sky as a carefree man of leisure might, knowing the day before him was his, and whatever he chose to make of it.

"Simonne's an heiress, my boy. Michel is dead. This isn't a farm we're rolling through, son, it's an Empire in the making!" He capitalized the word for Robert's benefit. "This sweet little girl all of eighteen years old has fallen for you, and the Fates have gifted her a picnic basket with everything you see stuffed inside it. All you view here will one day be hers!

"Let me tell you, Robert." Now Crevel was steaming, his boiler lit and stoked well. "Let me tell you!" he repeated. "If she were half as rich with one third the brain and plain as stone to look at, you would still damn well marry her for what she brings. Do you understand me? Pennies from heaven, Robert, these are pennies from heaven!"

Crevel fought to control himself; he saw Robert was sulking and changed tack to accommodate.

"Some things we do from the heart, Robert, and some things we do from the head. In the matter of your engagement, I wish you could satisfy both."

Robert was quiet. He didn't argue – he already knew where this was going.

"But if that's not to be," Crevel continued, "then don't be a fool. Do the right thing, Robert, marry the girl, and find your happiness elsewhere."

The procession eventually arrived. It was a regal affair inside the chapel. The Crevels shared the front pew with the Malenfers, Robert and Simonne sitting together, the crowd filling the place and beyond. When it came time, Crevel rose, as arranged, to say a few words. He chose a route up the center aisle to reach the dais, his purple sash of office crisp and unmistakable across his medaled breast. All eyes that day were his.

He did not rush or hurry or fluster, nor did he tarry, but in his bearing and pace he conveyed both the weight of his elected office and the occasion that had brought them all together.

He spoke of the Michel that he might have known – memories of a youth with a tanned smiling face, a boy he saw running through high grass, pumping legs chasing after a ball. He spoke of a lad full of life and promise, a boy that cared about others (Robert raised an eyebrow only here), a joy to his family, so full of potential, and taken all too soon to the grave.

The war had touched so many, and the flu was everywhere. There was not a family present that couldn't relate to the speech. Crevel himself even managed a tear.

Sixteen years old, dear God. Crevel reflected on the Fates. *In pace requiescat, young man. Rest in the peace denied the rest of us.*

Chapter 8
The Life Hereafter

DERMOT WAS UP EARLY DESPITE HIS LIBATIONS OF THE PREVIOUS EVE-ning. His excesses were only externally evident around the shadows of his eyes. Arthur was already awake.

"Still here, I see?" Dermot said. "No change of heart?"

Evidently not. Arthur was dressed and sitting in the solitary chair. The Lieutenant smoked contentedly on his Meerschaum pipe.

"Darmannes."

"What is that?"

"Darmannes," repeated Arthur. "It's the closest station to where I live."

"Do you know the time of the trains?"

Arthur did. Unless they fancied overnighting it there wasn't much time to spare.

Dermot washed at the only basin and changed his shirt for an-other. He kept on the suit he'd worn the previous night; indeed he had no other. The rest of his things fit easily into a duffle kit bag.

"I thought *I* traveled light," Arthur said to him, noting Dermot's Spartan bundle.

Dermot finished shaving. He dried himself with a towel, and then used it to wrap his few toiletries in. These were the last to go into the top of his bag before he pulled the laces shut.

"The hand luggage is easy," he said. "It's my trunk that weighs a ton."

It weighed a ton.

"Give us a hand." Dermot dragged the large lock box from out of the corner where it had been covered by a blanket.

"I can't, *mon ami*. I'm no help at all." Arthur was regretful. "It's a problem with the life hereafter."

"Oh, you're still on about that, are you?" Dermot had hoped it would pass.

"You're not trying to steal out past your landlady?" Arthur chastised, seeing the room now quite deserted. "Are you planning on coming back here?"

"Well, that depends a bit on you, don't you think?" The Irishman strained at the load.

The gray bun guarded the street door, disapproving of the noise and the early morning disturbance. No one was sneaking past lines while she was on picket duty.

"You look better than you should, Monsieur Ward."

Dermot settled his accounts with her and went out to hail a motor taxi.

The trunk was loaded and secured, though not without bad language, and they made the Gare de l'Est with an hour to spare before their train's departure. Dermot, giving Arthur a look, surrendered to the porters. At ten past eight the stationmaster blew on his whistle shrilly; the guard signaled with his flag, and their carriage gave a shudder. It lurched again, bucked, and creaked while both men looked out the window. They set out first class to Malenfer Manor with Dermot refreshed from the joy of travel. They floated east on clacking track, each saying their own farewells to Paris.

"Tickets, please." Their carriage was at the rear of the train, the furthest from the boiler.

"Two for Darmannes, one way, please." Dermot asked.

"Two, monsieur?" The conductor checked.

"Yes, two, and he'll be paying."

"He?" said the conductor.

"I told you," Arthur said helpfully.

Dermot looked like a man hit by a snowball in July. Arthur, sitting across from him, shifted in his chair, and raised his broad wide shoulders in a "What can I do?" appeal. Dermot turned to the conductor. "Are you telling me, honestly, that you don't see that man right there?" He pointed to make it clear, lest there be confusion with all the other empty seats.

"Monsieur." The conductor was a sensitive man; he had fought in the war himself. He had known men that returned home troubled, and he had a measure of respect. All the same, this was a first class carriage, and he had a job to do.

"If Monsieur needs assistance, perhaps he best take some air at the next station? Otherwise, a one one-way ticket to Darmannes will be two francs, ten centimes."

"Two francs!"

"And ten centimes."

"Do you have two francs on you, Arthur?"

"I regret, Dermot. Money means nothing to me now."

Dermot dug out two francs. It left a hole in his wallet big enough to crawl inside.

"Merci, monsieur." The conductor left him alone.

"You know what that means?" Dermot continued after a minute for reflection.

"Prices have gone up?" Arthur suggested.

"It means I really have lost it. I'm on a train to goodness knows where, I've quit my rooms, and the friend I'm helping is only in my head." Dermot seemed resigned.

"Not one bit of it, my friend," Arthur continued sucking on his pipe. "Choosing first class! I do like your style. But you see what I mean about behaving around others? Mind how you act – you'll get funny looks otherwise."

"That's great advice. The talking thing in my head is now giving me advice. This keeps getting better."

"I am not a 'thing.' You're doing well. Honestly, sit back, it will be fine, don't worry. You'll like the place when we get there."

Dermot raised his eyes to Arthur at last. "You're really not in my head. Are you?"

"Well, no and yes. I know what you mean. I'm not your imagination."

"Jesus wept." Dermot examined his hands. He thought he should find them shaking. "How did this happen, Arthur?"

"I told you last night," he replied.

"Well, last night I wasn't really asking."

"I don't know," Arthur told him again. "It just did. I'm not sure why or what or anything. But I died. I died, and then I was still here."

"It's a long haul to Darmannes, Arthur. I'm in a listening mood."

And so Arthur told his tale.

Lieutenant Arthur Malenfer sat alone on the empty terrace, tightly wrapped in his plaid blanket of red dyed wool. He was sunk low in the wicker seat into which he'd squeezed himself. The spot Arthur took, *his* spot, as the Lieutenant liked to think of it, commanded a clear view over wide lawns and bedded gardens that only now were emerging, hours since his vigil began, from the mist of a winter's dawn.

A towering maple tree with branches bare stood in the center of the garden. Bearded moss dripped from it. The tree caught the first morning sun in its dewy coat and glittered good cheer. The ground beneath it opened gradually to the human eye's caress. It was a pleasant view over which Arthur gazed, and it was familiar to him. He knew, though could not yet see, that in the distance behind the grand tree, beyond these manicured lawns, there was a high brick wall behind a hedge that marked the end of the hospital grounds. And in this wall was a tall wooden gate that the staff would lock at sundown.

His fellow convalescents, those who were physically able, were encouraged by their doctors to take the air and seek out the gate in the wall. They would stroll out to the wood, under the canopy of ancient trees that pressed up tight against their garden. The wood stretched its limbs invitingly and beckoned you to join them. Arthur liked that route and took it often. If you opened the door in the tall brick wall and followed the path behind it, it would bring you to a bridge of sorts, rough planks and windfall branches. Someone (he'd often wondered who) had gone to a lot of trouble. The bridge itself spanned a small fast creek, the last obstacle before the fields.

At this moment, Arthur could hear the distant churning of those waters, the stream in spate from the heavy rains that had fallen the preceding evening. They'd gone on, uninterrupted until two hours ago. Arthur had noted the hour. To this faint burble of worldly song a trilling tune was added, the morning chorus in the country air that lofted through the branches. Arthur felt a beauty in that moment, one that perhaps existed for him alone in all the broken world. Not a stir had he heard from the army hospital whose rooms sat close behind him.

The mist on the garden shifted. Arthur drew up and peered over the balcony, alert to the emerging scene. Tiny things still, small green fingers, pushed up from below through the grasses – crocuses had sprouted in a tight druid's circle from the roots of the giant maple.

It was a faerie vision, life sprung from the frozen ground, and it was filled with such bright promise! Here he was in February, the month not yet half over, and here was the gift of flowers. Crisp flint blues and spotless whites, the whole flecked with gold. Soon, he knew, their blooms would shine, and spring would surely follow. They were inconsequential in their own way, but for Arthur they held a hope. They were proof of a sort, evidence even, that the earth held not only the dead things.

Lieutenant Arthur Malenfer smiled at the picture and wrestled with his blanket once more. It was a pleasure he knew, and he'd take what he could, but it brought no peace to his soul.

Before the Great War, the hospital in Épernay had been a country residence for one hundred and seventy years. It was owned by a grasping family, a tribe of palming pompadours who leased it only grudgingly to the Ministry of the Interior. They got an unfavorable rent for it, draconian terms imposed by the Prefecture of the District and presented to them by a Commissar. In June of 1914, the Ministry took what it wanted.

The oily patriot in the Commissar's hat had made himself quite clear to the family – history itself expected acquiescence and their full and total agreement. The plan for the property was simple: The house and grounds would serve splendidly as an infirmary for any casualties in any conflict in the unquestionably short time it might be needed, and refusal on their part to cooperate (though surely unthinkable) might necessitate a *compulsory* purchase. It was hinted that appropriate recompense, in the event of such an outcome, would be determined by a notoriously Jacobean branch of the Estates Office in which the Commissar himself, he told them sweetly, had a first cousin of no little influence. The Commissar gave them a smile that could press olives. He conveyed the news most delicately.

The family in Épernay was a mercenary brood, but not without some sense in it. Angry clouds were mustering to the east where empires rattled their sabers. Russia and Austria-Hungary traded words, and Germany, always Germany, was not so very far away from them. To take umbrage with their grasping government might mean months before the courts; to take umbrage with the Kaiser would mean a great deal more besides. In the early summer of 1914 the winds of change were blowing, and the family in Épernay signed over. They sold their furniture and thumbed their noses and took sail for Martinique directly. The Commissar got his hospital and considered them most foolish. He had thought the grounds most admirable, and especially the maple.

The Épernay Infirmary for the Rehabilitation of Veterans (it had seen three name changes in the last five years) had become more democratic in its guest list since that time. During the torrential fighting at Aisne in 1917 the casualties overran the bedrooms. Soon the drawing room and library were full, and then the stretchers spilled out into the gardens. The lawns had disappeared under tents, and still the men kept coming. The terraced balcony, through the war years, had catered to patients in the hundreds. The dining room had been transformed and was used for operations, its kitchens turned to boiling bandages and sterilizing instruments. Gangrenous limbs were amputated at the same table where game had been carved. The stains it held would never wash clean – the blood of a generation.

Unless Paris fell, the hospital was far enough away that it would not be overrun, but it was close enough to the Western Front that its trade and business remained steady. By the end of 1917 the front had stabilized, and the battles moved further on.

In March of 1918, the hospital's role changed again to one of convalescence and rehabilitation. The spirit of liberté remained, but égalité and fraternité were discharged. Democracy was put aside, and the hospital was reserved for officers. Reconstitution of *their* flesh and spirit, it was judged, could be better served in the absence of the common soldier.

Arthur had seen much of this change.

"Do you remember that ambulance, Dermot?"

Arthur had arrived in the second week of May, 1916, in an ambulance choked with rotting flesh and delirious opiate ramblings. He'd come with the crushed and torn and rendered whose cries drowned out the engine. It had been a four-hour ride from the last hospital, the field hospital, a journey he wouldn't wish on anyone.

At the field station before Épernay, the triage doctors had been busy. They had waded through the piles of mangled men strewn on the ground before them. It was their job to decide who should go under the knife and who would lie out in the rain.

"They called your wounds 'hopeless'," Dermot said mistily.

Men with a better chance were going to get help before Arthur. The Lieutenant was lucky to find an ambulance that had room enough to take him, which carried him to the gardens of Épernay, though it might have been Elysium. The men in the ambulance were the rejects. When the orderly at the field hospital shut the ambulance door, he did so on the damned. No one expected them to make it, and he looked relieved to see them gone.

They fit eight men into the tiny ambulance, stacked like sardines and laid out flat. Dermot rode with the driver. Only six survived to hear the crunching pebbles under the tires on the Épernay driveway. Arthur was operated on that day, and twice again on Sunday. It was May 14th, 1916. He remembered it like it was yesterday.

"I waited," said Dermot. "They wouldn't tell me anything at first. I sat in that lobby for hours."

The Lieutenant knew the details from his own medical records. The files gave the facts but lacked the brushstrokes, and they did nothing to show the pain. It read, he'd thought, like a menu: Arthur Malenfer – a dish upon a plate.

For starters, please consider the burns to the side of the face: juicy and disfiguring (though not life threatening) and posing a risk of infection. A suspected fracture of the right forearm is next, likely the ulna, and though mortally insignificant it looks a dreadful mess. The house specialty now follows: two bullet wounds, serious but controllable, very tasty indeed. Both bullets had exited the patient, one through the broken arm, the other through his waist; the chef is proud to say, however, that the organs remain untouched! The dish is very lucky and the wounds have been sown shut; garnish with infection risk (you can't really have too much!).

But it was the dessert that was disappointing, the dessert that let him down: lung was on the menu, and it all boiled down to air. The chef seemed out of recipes for that poor ingredient he found.

Of the eight broken men who shared the ambulance journey from Aisne to Épernay, only one survived the week. Arthur wasn't he.

Lieutenant Arthur Malenfer died in the Hôpital des Armées at Épernay on Sunday evening, May 14th, 1916. His burnt poisoned lungs finally gave out, the last of his strength no longer capable of shoring up his chest.

It was to his not inconsiderable surprise, therefore, that his spirit lingered on, and almost three years later, as he told it to Dermot, he was still no clearer as to why.

Arthur's pleasant seclusion on the frigid patio was interrupted by the intrusion of two fellow patients sneaking outside for a smoke. Arthur still thought of himself as a patient – he couldn't place himself anywhere else. He couldn't reasonably think of himself as staff, though by now he'd been at the hospital longer than almost everyone. Most of the staff were medical, of course, and he wasn't helping anyone, least of all himself. There were janitors and gardeners and orderlies, true, but he wasn't doing work either. Not having a purpose somehow annoyed him. *Am I now the resident ghost?* he'd ponder. *What the hell am I meant to do?* Should he haunt the place? Make a nuisance of himself? Arthur found that his education and experience had prepared him very poorly for a life in the afterlife. He knew little about being a ghost.

His first memory of life, of this *new* life (this was how he liked to term it), came when he was standing over a bed in the recovery room alone with his own body. There was no one else in the room; the nurses had left them momentarily. He was looking down upon himself and it wasn't a pleasant sight. In truth, he looked a state.

"I remember thinking: *This isn't good*; and that, as they say, was that."

"You could see yourself? You could see what was going on?"

"Oh, yes. I was apart from it, but it was me. There was no mistake about that."

Arthur found himself fully aware, not drugged or dazed as his mind had been only seconds before. There was a feeling of cold, as if a breeze was blowing up his backside – as he soon discovered there was. Arthur, the new Arthur, *this* Arthur (he felt an identity crisis in the making) was dressed in the gown he'd died in, and the damned thing was open at the back. The gap up his backside embarrassed him and was more than a little chilly. Modesty, then, had claimed him first, an admission he later felt shamed by.

I'm dead! I'm really dead!

His cadaver lay prostrate before him. After sorting out his drafty gown, the import of this dawned.

Arthur the spirit gave his prone body a push, a shove on the foot. It felt unusual; that is, it didn't feel of anything. Well, it did, but not in the usual way. *He*, his dead he, didn't feel anything at all. Not that he was aware of. He, his *ghost* he... (that's when Arthur first thought of the word) felt only smooth wall. No sensation of skin or hair, or heat or curve or toe. Whatever he tried to touch at all was empty but some-how solid, like magnets of the same polarity pressed against each other. No matter how hard he leaned into it, nothing seemed to give way, but pushed back all the stronger. The science experiment now quickly over, panic settled in.

"Help!" he shrieked, in a most unmanly tone – he was able at least to speak. "I'm dying in here!" He cursed himself for waiting; he should have brought assistance right away. Where had the nurses gone?

There was no reply.

Arthur went to the door to fetch the doctor, only he couldn't grab the handle! He swiped at it and swiped at it but felt the smooth wall only.

"Bloody hell!" he cried now in frustration. The door blocked his path. There was no other obvious exit.

"Help me!" he cried again, but still there came no reply.

The door and room looked very solid, but he himself was sheer. Not invisible, but he could see through himself – not bones and veins and muscle, but clothes and hair and skin. He existed only in water-colors, tinting the world with his presence.

I'm not white, he thought as his body lay lifeless and uncared for. *I thought ghosts were meant to be white. Or is it dark?* The uncertainty bothered him.

He refocused. He had to get help. It was only a door. He took a few steps back and charged it. Shoulder down he ran full force, closing his eyes at the last second.

"I can't run through doors, Dermot. I learned that lesson the hard way."

Arthur's head hurt quite a lot now, though not as much as it might have. This detail he only understood later from experimentation and reflection.

Arthur the corpse lay still and quiet on the bed, the chemicals in his body already preparing for the first steps of decomposition. His dead self, at least, was aware of what was expected of *it*.

Five minutes passed before a nurse checked up on him. Arthur had calmed down by then. "I've died," he told her, though she didn't hear; by now he'd sort of expected that. "I think I sort of stopped breathing," he informed her regardless.

There were a lot of them in the room then: the doctors, four nurses, and a couple of others. He was pushed out of the way, knocked into the corner, tumbled as one might cast aside an empty hat box. Arthur hadn't expected *that*. He was bigger than all of them and dwarfed the tiny nurses. He took it with good grace, though; he was already start-ing to accept things. He stood on a chair out of the way to watch, and ducked his head to miss the ceiling.

His body was shaken and slapped. His dead eyes were held open and a light shone into them. The doctor said his name loudly, over and over, shouting into a deaf ear. Arthur found it unsettling to stare back at himself, but he could not look away. They felt for a pulse at his wrist and then at his neck, they pulled his mouth open and showed his strong teeth, they pushed down on his chest. They put a mirror in front of his face; not a breath, perfectly clear.

Arthur felt himself a little hungry as he watched them shake their heads. A glance at a watch, a scribbled note on a clipboard, then the sheet drawn over his head. *I really have died.* Somehow it all felt official; he thought of his family for the fist time.

"I had to be quick. I jumped down and snuck out the door before the nurse. She closed it behind her. I didn't want to stay with myself any longer – my old dead self just lying there. No one could see me and no one could hear me and I didn't know what to do next."

"That's... that's terrible, Arthur."

"Yes. It's what the Americans term a 'raw deal'."

Chapter 9
The Young Couple

WHILE A DESPONDENT ARTHUR MALENFER WAS TURNING INTO A urine-splashed alleyway off the rue des Trois Frères in pursuit of an elusive Irishman, his niece Simonne was on a quest of her own, the coincidence of which was known to neither of them. She slipped from her room without disturbing the dust and slunk down the stairs like a black cat. She left the house by an inconspicuous side door, the secret of its key one she guarded closely. It was bitter outside, miserable compared to her warm vacated bed, but she was resolute and unbowed by the sudden change. A Ural wind redoubled its torment and Simonne lifted her hood by reply. She paused only to let her eyesight adjust, for she carried no lantern nor candle. Certain that the coast was clear, Simonne set out down the road. Her rendezvous was a ten-minute walk around the bend. Engines off, headlights dead, the car would not be seen from the house.

Robert's cigarette gave him away long before Simonne made him out. He was standing on the road beside his father's pride – a Peugeot Type 153. (Robert had told her its name a great number of times – he seemed to think it important.) It had polished brass trim and a gleaming maroon body, which looked smoky under a dry moon. It was barely distinguishable now.

Robert heard her step disturb the gravel before he made her out. "Darling!" he said, and he dropped his cigarette, ran to her, and held her tight in his arms. He pressed her cold lips in a strong embrace. Simonne was a little taken aback. She wasn't used to spontaneous displays of ardor. Robert hadn't been like this in a while.

This was the spot where they had been meeting privately for months. At the beginning, Robert would come as often as he could, which was as often as Simonne would let him. He had been quite forward with his hands at first, until she had set him right. She was stirred by his passion, but more than that was the appeal of what

Robert represented: escape – freedom from her small boring life. Robert had an agitation for living life that Simonne found irresistible.

Back then they would go for short rides in the car or walk hand in hand through the woods. They would sit and talk and trade sips from his pocket flask. Simonne had no doubt that Robert filled it from his father's bottle and that they smoked Monsieur Crevel Père's cigarettes. She didn't care – it felt so daring and exciting and, importantly, such fun. They would interrupt their stolen time with kisses.

It was here in the misty twilight of a November evening that he'd surprised her with a question. Simonne remembered sitting on his knee inside the car, snuggled against him to keep them both warm.

"Simonne... darling. I've been thinking a bit," he started. "I've been thinking that for something to change, you've just got to make it happen. Do you know what I'm trying to say?"

She didn't, but was too polite to say so. They had been talking about the war, as everybody was – soon it was coming to an end. The papers were full of an imminent armistice, and Simonne was forced to believe them for once. She could hardly remember a time of peace. Everyone was talking about what came next.

Robert tried his best to clarify. "I mean that *we* decide. Us, you, me, *our* generation. No one else is going to change things for us." He was flustered when he spoke, his ears glowing red, and Simonne read this tic as conviction.

Such sentiments never failed to strike a chord with Simonne; she was vulnerable to pulpit plauditry. She didn't need clarity or facts and figures but had a strong sense of right and wrong. *We decide.* Her gut told her 'yes.' It was then that he asked her the question. She was sitting on his knee, so he couldn't go down on it, and Simonne hadn't seen it coming.

"Simonne... darling. I think it best that... I think it best that we get married." It just popped out. He ran the words out at the end. He seemed relieved to say it, as if he had been bottling it up and now it was just spilt ink. "How would you like it if we did?" He grew enthusiastic. "Can you see how wonderful it would be?"

Simonne did not know. She was a little taken aback. She felt rather silly sitting there on his lap, but there was no polite way to climb free.

She liked him fine, Robert, her man – he was a way out for a lot of things. She considered herself rather sweet on him, but she hadn't expected this. She'd been thinking of letting him leave a hand on her thigh, maybe allowing him to touch her garter strap. *Madame Simonne Crevel!* She had played the sound in her mind once or twice, even practiced writing her signature (that fancy had gone on the fire). It wasn't that marriage had never entered her mind. But marriage? Really? Right now, and to him? Robert? Where had she thought this was leading? What had she been doing? Her complicity filled her with shame.

But then, she thought, why not? The war was over, and things *would* change. Robert was right to say so. Was not she already eighteen? It was time to take charge of her life. Was she, Simonne, going to kowtow to Grand-mère and live under her thumb all her life? Did she want to be parceled off – or elope into nothing like her mother? Wasn't she, Simonne, her own person, and couldn't she do as she wished?

Robert seemed anxious beneath her skirts. Time was passing by.

"Oh, Robert, I'd love to!" It arrived on the spur of the moment, like many of Simonne's decisions. "We'll get married, yes. Yes, we will. I suppose that's what comes next. And we'll both be terribly happy."

Right then in the car at the side of the road, the future had seemed so bright.

"I've missed you, Simonne." Robert's lips tasted bitter, of tobacco. He had one arm around her back, gripping her close, and the other one down on her stocking.

Robert's work had become demanding, and he was now only able to see her on weekends or when he came up to the house by invitation. Robert's kisses were not as urgent as they'd been during their first weeks of courting, but Simonne had heard the other girls talk and knew that sometimes happened.

That was what made tonight so unexpected; he hadn't held her like this for months! He seemed so... urgent and needy. Simonne responded with a heat of her own.

"Oh, Robert!" She leaned into him, her hands high around his neck. "I missed you too!"

Robert released her and she unwound herself reluctantly. He held the door open on the passenger side and offered his hand out to help her. Simonne took it for balance, and then, mindful of her dress, she stepped up on the running board and climbed into the car. Robert closed the door, walked around front, and joined her on the other side. They sat close together on the sprung leather seats in their intimate little box. The roof was up and fastened snug. He didn't start the car.

"I've brought cocoa." He produced a flask from behind the seat after passing her a cigarette. To Simonne it seemed symbolic of the change; she'd have preferred a stiff drink.

There was a lot about Robert she did like, and his kisses were right up there on that list. He could be funny, and he was handsome and honest (though it could run to cruelty behind people's backs). He had a secure job and his father's car and he was almost twenty-one... a real man from Paris, something special amidst a farm.

It was just that Robert, now that she knew him better, wasn't really the "doing" type. All talk and no trouser. Little things and large. His résumé was a casserole of baked ambition that never seemed to play quite out. Simonne recalled that when they first met, Robert had been full of zeal about enlisting in the army. "A black eye to my interfering father." The sentiment resonated with Simonne. She had begged him not to go – selfish reasons of her own – but Simonne was not immune to the patriots' drum and she knew how young men were perceived. But Robert? Obstacles seemed to materialize to obstruct his fiery pronouncements. Robert only did things that were easy, and Simonne wondered if that meant marrying her.

Shouldn't there be something more? A passion? A spark? Or was marriage like Grand-mère had said to her – the best match you could get? Simonne just needed to talk to him more, to see how things would work out.

She took the offered cigarette and the chocolate cocoa both. The vacuum flask steamed when he opened the lid, and she balanced the cup upon her leg.

"Robert. My mother and Grand-mère have been talking about us. They're a pair of old busybodies, it's really none of their business."

She had hoped by this path to lure him into the conversation, but was surprised by his response.

"Your family is against me now." It wasn't a question. "I was fine for you when Michel was alive, but now they want something more. That's it, isn't it?"

"No, no, it isn't," she objected automatically, not seeing where this could come from. "No, it isn't. They like you a lot."

"You're a token for them, Simonne, a prize to barter with." He wasn't mad or annoyed, he was the pleasant and cheerful and attentive Robert – Simonne was unbalanced by that. "You're an heiress now, the papers have it. Did you see what they said about you? Madame's just looking out for you. I'm sure she thinks you could do better than me, and probably she's right."

"No. No, really. That's not it at all." She found it hard to speak. The appeal in his words brought on shame, but he'd got it the wrong way around. How now could she put it into words, the truth of what she was feeling? *No, Robert, listen. Grand-mère thinks you're the best I can get. It's me that's having second thoughts!* "My grandmother likes you a lot."

"It's all right, I understand." He seemed hurt. "I just want you to know that when I asked you to marry me, it was because I loved you, Simonne. And I still do. And I know I always will."

Tears ran freely down her cheeks. She felt so cruel inside.

"I understand, though, and I know that you have to do what you feel is right." He put a caring hand on her shoulder. "What's right for you and your family." He took a heavy breath. "I release you from your promise, Simonne. I want you to follow your heart."

She sobbed; great racking sobs of jumbled "sorrys" spilled unchecked from her mouth. Her hands shook so, it was difficult to put her chocolate down. She threw her arms around Robert and hugged him and cried into his shoulder. Embarrassed and ashamed by what she felt, she clung to him like the first time.

"Oh, Robert!" she managed at last. "Whatever was I thinking? I'm so sorry, my darling. I will marry you, Robert, I want to. Just set a date. We'll run away if we have to. We can steal your father's car!"

"I rather hope not! He's terribly fond of the thing!" He tried to embrace her but was fearful of the cocoa. He laughed again and squeezed her hand and affixed a happy face. "You're such a funny thing! Don't worry, my darling, everything will be wonderful." And then he did kiss her again; he kissed her tears away.

With a tremor still in her gut, Simonne opened up a little. "I've just been feeling a little troubled of late. You know, things going around in my head. Thinking about us, and what's to come, and then of course Michel's death."

"I'd been meaning to ask you."

"It's okay now. It's still sad and all, but everyone has lost someone."

"Is it true darling? What they say, I mean."

"What *do* they say?"

"They say you talked." She felt his hesitancy, even a sense of fear. "They say you talked to a spirit or something and that you knew how it would end."

He couldn't look at her. Simonne felt alone once more.

"Would it matter to you Robert, if I did?" She tried to be funny with him, reaching out for his trust.

"Of course it's all nonsense, I know it is, darling. Witches and things. But it gives people ideas."

The rain came on heavier all of the moment, and thunder rolled low overhead. She leaned in tight against his shoulder and hoped to feel his arms embrace her. She longed to share, to be herself, but how could he understand?

"No, I didn't talk to a spirit at all, if that's what they're saying."

"Good girl." He seemed relieved, and he put his arm around her then. "Just making things up to scare the servants?"

"That's right. That's what it was. Keeps them on their toes."

"Good girl!" Another compliment. "You've got a curious sense of humor."

"I think I should go now, Robert." She didn't want to spoil things. She knew she had to leave.

"No! Why? Look at the rain out there!"

"It's OK." She slid out from under his touch. "I rather like it." Simonne opened the door herself. "Thank you Robert, for understanding. I'm glad we're getting married." Then she stepped out of the car and closed the door shut and retraced her steps up the roadway.

It was true enough, Simonne thought – she really did love the weather, and the rain obliged by piling on hard while lightning broke the heavens. And it was also true enough, Simonne thought, all that she'd said to Robert. She had not *talked* to the witch, very true; that wasn't at all how it happened. She'd felt the girl near – a presence, was all. She remembered her deep disturbance. And the witch girl visited only now and again. She wasn't like most of the others. The girl came only when one of the family was soon to be injured… or die.

The Curse. She'd grown up with the talk and all the yabber and the secrets and whispered wisdoms. But fear and sadness, that's all the spirit really was, loss and a terrible sorrow. She'd felt it in the witch – it's what gave her form – but there was also something darker: a sense of satisfaction and a leering toxic pleasure that Simonne was troubled by.

The leafless branches creaked and swayed, and a limb tore off quite near her.

"Just calm down," she scolded the trees. "There's nothing to get excited about."

Then she turned down the path back to the Manor, and the house lit up with the sky.

"I'm going to be married very soon, and I'm going to be very happy." But the rain and the wind and the sky and trees didn't take her announcement so well.

Once safe back inside her room, she curled up into bed. Tucked under a blanket of romance, she now dreamed of chiming bells. But she slept less soundly that she might have, fearful that Robert should learn her secret.

Robert was late home that evening. After leaving his fiancée, he had driven through half the night, keeping company with his thoughts, which the headlamps could not pierce. He closed the door quietly after rolling into the garage, but on entering the house he noticed the low burning light in the study. His father had waited up for him, as all good parents would.

"Well?" old Crevel asked, the hour and intrusion not seeming to incommode him.

"You should thank me," replied young Crevel, "You'd have been proud of what I did."

"Good lad," said Crevel, genuinely pleased, triumph stamped large on his smooth scheming face. "Off to bed then, son, sleep well. You've earned your rest this night."

Robert took the stairs slowly, his conscience weighing him down. He felt slightly embarrassed and partially soiled but mostly ashamed of himself. Simonne was very pretty, and she could be very nice. If only she wasn't so strange sometimes and full of so many ideas. It might work out, they might be happy; it could work out just fine. But now he had to plan for a wedding after all, and the work *that* was going to entail. The thought of the effort in running an estate made him miserable to think.

How did it happen? So much to worry about. Things were much easier when I was back in college.

Sleep did not soon find Robert, dispelled by his troubled mind. He wallowed in a soup of reheated self-pity and tossed and turned till dawn.

Downstairs in the Mayor's house, Crevel Senior stayed up till dawn. That brain was a whirl, a Swiss clock of reasoning, an assemblage of permutation. Possibilities and probabilities meshed and ground and whirled, and however Crevel looked at things, the outcomes were all good. To Crevel, alone in his drawing room, the future seemed bright indeed; he allowed himself an indulgent cigar, and smiled a conqueror's grin.

Chapter 10
The Train to Darmannes

FROST-FRAMED FIELDS PASSED BY THE TRAIN'S WINDOWS. PARIS WAS long behind. The conductor had checked on him only once, but Dermot was wise to his coming – the rhythmic opening and banging of doors heralded his arrival. Dermot waited till the fellow moved on before conversing again with Arthur.

"And what happened after that?"

For the next few days, Arthur behaved like a dog following an old master around. He trailed along when they buried his body, and slouched behind when they returned. The cemetery was vast. White crosses grew like a tropical crop in an antipodean plantation, his but one monotonous stalk in an overly fertile field. With the first shovel of earth on the lid, Arthur decided to break away. His flesh didn't need him now, and no one else had claimed him.

"I had to get back to the regiment. I couldn't go to your funeral."

"I don't blame you, Dermot. What could you do? I only tell you how it was."

On the third day following his death, Arthur made a decision: The theological implications he would set aside while he focused on practical challenges. *A history of sensation* was how he came to describe it. It was the way he kept his reason.

Arthur found that he got hot and he found that he got cold. The change took a while, like it was sinking in, his nerves dulled but not forgotten. Since he was stuck in his hospital gown (he could not pick anything up to wear, though not for want of trying), he was often uncomfortably chilly. Unsuitably dressed for the seasonal weather and unfashionable around town.

Arthur lingered in the common rooms, the canteen and kitchen, but he didn't think of it as haunting. He hadn't found a label for it – he was happier in the company of the living. In the public rooms he would usually find a fire lit. This was important until the weather changed for the better, and besides, the public rooms did not make him feel intrusive; he was still uncomfortable in another's private space. "I would make my bed on the couch most nights, but sleep came slowly to me."

Arthur found himself hungry at meal times, but he did not need to eat. He conjectured that these were phantom feelings, a hangover of his corporeal life. The sensation passed an hour or so later, and he wondered if it would dull over time – if, unlike him, it would learn to fade away forever.

The kitchens prepared roasted capon one week after his death. Arthur's stomach growled audibly when the gravy boat appeared. He went out from the dining room and hid away from the scent.

If hunger was a torment, it remained a blessing in comparison to his toilet needs. Arthur had no idea why, he couldn't fathom the possible reason, but three times a day he was compelled to search for privacy. The next twenty minutes were sheer toil as he tried, futilely, to clear himself of whatever demonic infestation seemed determined to come... almost, almost, but never did. He hadn't been dead one month before the inevitable happened. Ambushed by an ulcerated patient, a sweaty man who barreled in on him, Arthur was evicted.

"I only got out by climbing the wall, the fellow had barely seconds to spare. What would have happened if he'd sat down on me? The thought just fills me with dread."

After that, Arthur threw modesty to the wind. He picked a good spot in the garden's rose beds where there was little risk of disturbance. On public display, he could only hope this torment would someday end.

Arthur had been thirty-three when he'd enlisted. He'd had sweethearts, of course, but none suitable for marrying, and he had never gotten engaged. In the long lonely hours when the patients had retired, he now mused on these circumstances, how those things might have changed. There was no young girl back home in Darmannes, no one to whom he would write. No long letters now interrupted, no lover who'd be crying all night. His children didn't know of their father; their mother was long in the grave.

During the years of his army service he'd had two city leaves, and both had found him up in Paris in his uniform and stripes. He remembered the dancing halls of Montmartre fondly, the girls who liked soldiers there. He thought of them a lot now, and more so with every day.

At the hospital at Épernay there were a number of nurses, and every one a pretty sight. After two years of service in the trenches, there's no such thing as a plain-looking nurse. Arthur found their presence almost torturous. When he was good he hid himself away from them, and when he was bad he hovered. Arthur lasted almost one whole month before he succumbed to the growing torment. By now his situation had given him the habit of talking to himself. No one seemed to object.

"And why not?" he asked his conscience.

"It's not polite," he pointed out to himself.

"Who says it's not polite? Who makes up these rules? Maybe this sort of thing is perfectly fine when you're dead like we are."

"And that's why you're asking yourself? Hmmm? You think this is what a gentleman would do?"

"Prude."

"Beast. Get a grip on yourself, man. And what exactly are you hoping to get out of this, tell me? How is this going to help?"

He thought himself blush, and his conscience pressed its unfair advantage of knowing exactly what he meant.

"What? You think you're just going for a look, do you? Don't kid yourself. You're a dirty pervert and well out of order – you should learn to control yourself."

"I'm just looking. They'll never know..."

"It's useless anyway," he interrupted himself, "it doesn't even work. So why bother with it? You're just making it worse. Go stand out in the rain."

Arthur paused for a minute, and his conscience thought he'd won.

"The urge lives on, my friend, that's why. What's a man to do?"

That evening, as the night shift arrived, he followed the nurses in. He felt ridiculous in his dressing gown, but what was there to be done? He crossed the door into the ladies' changing room under a pall of shame, and there he watched, jaw to the floor, as they laughed and talked and changed. Not all of them showered, but the soap was used by some. Arthur stood spellbound and groaned with despair as they unpinned their long hair. He wrung his hands in torment as they hung their towels on pegs. Arthur watched the water steam as they lathered up a storm.

The brassiere of one with a ponderous bust lay upturned on a pile of loose clothes. Arthur caved in and lowered his face, feeling its nuzzling warmth. Then he turned his back on that angelic host and fled without a word.

"I never went back."

"I feel dirtied, Arthur. You're a disgraceful letch." Dermot made a face.

"Please don't start. It's terrible. You can't possibly understand."

"Did she really have big ones?"

"Dermot. Please. Be kind."

Arthur had shamed himself. He felt sorry for himself. And after that night, he fell into a despair worse than any he had as yet known. It wasn't just the flesh he craved (though he did crave the flesh), it was the company and the contact that was gone. No one there to chase him out with a laugh or a harsh word. No one to share a meal with him and harangue him for what he'd done. *What was the point of it all?* he wondered. *Nothing matters anymore.*

"I could not conceive why I was still here, or what 'here' really was, or what to do with myself. All meaning had simply gone. I was haunted – haunted by the life I could no longer have. It is not the dead that plague the living, Dermot, but the living that torment the dead."

The next three months were difficult for Arthur. He'd fallen into a sort of sulk, the malaise of the disowned. He'd exhausted all thoughts of what he should *do*, culled by the crushing knowledge that he could only observe. Never to interact; never anymore. For a man that was used to action, this was very hard to take. An eternity of it stretched out before him, and he impotent to change.

He thought of his family back home and how they were taking it. How were they getting on? But what was the use in such thoughts as those? The War right now was everything; there was only that. The ambulances came with their regular haul, and broken men kept dying. Arthur attended the funerals always, and quietly hoped for a friend. He always walked back alone.

Then came the day when he couldn't take it anymore, when he came to the edge and stepped off. *Can the dead themselves actually die?* There was only one way to find out.

"The janitor was fixing shingles. I got up on the roof."

His guts felt tight and his heart beat faster, and then he took the step right off... There was a second, then another, and then: "God, man, how it hurt!" He lay for an hour on the pebbles and then crawled back up the front steps. Arthur lay on the couch feeling splintered inside, but the pain left him after a day.

He thought perhaps the distance hadn't been enough to do the job. It took more courage to put his head down under the ambulance wheel. But he did. He needed two days on the couch after that.

The last go proved decisive; Arthur knew he should have thought of it first. Épernay was pleasantly rural, and the doctors would often go hunt. The land was well provided for in terms of rabbits and birds.

In a canteen that had to scavenge supplies, game was never turned down

Arthur followed a shooting party out one early evening. He put his forehead to a barrel trained on an unsuspecting pheasant. He looked into the shooter's eyes that looked straight back through his own, but seeing nothing but eternity he had to shut them tight.

"The noise was immense. I awoke in the field. It was dark, wet, and cold. I felt very badly hung over. My sore ear hurt even worse. Everyone was gone, it was the middle of the night, and I didn't even know which day. But I was still here, there was no denying it. I knew then that I could never leave that way. The whole thing was rather depressing."

Arthur's pipe had gone out, and he lit it again from a box of matches he retrieved from his jacket pocket. A thought came to Dermot.

"How is it you're not wearing your hospital gown now?"

Arthur puffed up a storm. "Turns out I can lay ahold of anything in the possession of a newly dead man."

Dermot looked again at the suit, the pipe, the watch chain, the suitcase, and the fine polished brogues of his friend. A ghoulish collection they made.

"I'm not going to ask you how you found that out."

"I don't think I'm going to tell." He puffed for a while before resuming. "All of this went on much as I said until the last few weeks."

"And what changed then?"

Lieutenant Arthur Malenfer sat on the empty terrace, alone once again. The staff and patients were inside the hospital enjoying a heated lunch. The dawn that had emerged from the gardens that morning had lent him a sense of calm. The crocus sunrise felt like an omen for change, and all day long could not shake the feeling that he would not be immune.

He could hear the wireless: Paris was in the news again, the treaty negotiations continuing at Versailles. Arthur liked to hear the news. He read the papers too. The hospital received the local, which carried notices of death, and it was from these that he got most of his information about the newly departed. Arthur read the obituaries in the national press as well; the hospital got Le Temps from Paris, which was particularly morbid and good. All sorts of people were dying in Le Temps every day, and Arthur followed their fortunes like a racetrack gambler studies the forms. Arthur had an unknowing accomplice that enabled his macabre habit – one of the Épernay doctors read the papers front to back with religious observation. He snuck them off to his private office after lunch each afternoon.

The wireless in the day room had moved on to grain prices – Arthur didn't call grain prices "news." This, however, was his cue. Arthur rose, and made his way up the hospital stairs to the open door by the landing. This room had once been a child's bedroom and was still painted in faded yellow, the color of baby chicks, or baby chicks that had been smoking. This was the doctor's office. Arthur walked in without invitation and the man in the white coat shut the door. The doctor retreated to his desk, where he made a poor show of inspecting the thick files in front of him. He ignored the Lieutenant, who paced the room patiently, but Arthur took no offense; as usual, he was looking at the photographs that hung around the walls. They were familiar to him: sepia posed family groups, other people's frozen lives that made him think back on his own.

Whoever was in the medical files was never as important as the headlines, and before long the pair of them were peering over the broadsheets.

On page twenty-three he saw it. It was there, and he saw it. He read it three times through until every word had sunk in.

Michel Malenfer, son of the late Colonel and Madame Henri Joseph Malenfer, in Chevecheix, Haute-Marne, on Sunday, February 9th, 1919, of influenza, age 16. Service to take place this Wednesday, February 12th.

"My little brother."

It was Monday's paper he was reading, published yesterday, so the funeral was tomorrow. And there was a commentary, one of the rare editorial compliments that accompanied social worthies. Underneath the announcement, *Le Temps* explained that the Estate had suffered greatly in service to country and that the diminished, though not inconsiderable, fortune of the Malenfers would now likely fall on a lone grandchild, a certain Mademoiselle Simonne. A photograph went with the piece, but not of the dead Michel. Rather it showed an attractive young lady who had possibly come into a fortune. The editorial leered; there was not a journalist or reader in existence that didn't approve of a beautiful heiress.

There was a sharp knock at the door and Arthur looked up, recognizing the junior doctor.

"We'll soon be ready outside, sir."

"Thank you. Take at look at this, will you?" The senior doctor showed the junior man the picture.

"Nice looking girl," said the younger.

"And loaded along with it!"

The senior doctor removed his reading glasses before rising and leaving. Arthur didn't follow him out, for the man had left his newspaper. It lay on the desk, still folded at the obituaries.

Michel is dead? Simonne's to inherit?

They'd never been close, the age gap a moat, but still, Michel was his brother. Arthur was shaken – not for that, but rather for what the obituary omitted.

"I have two sons, as I told you Dermot, and neither of them was mentioned."

That crocus dawn had prophesied a change and the budding of new purpose.

The following morning, the hospital warden drove into town at such an hour that he went without breakfast. The route took him past the railway station. The warden was not aware of his passenger, but Arthur traveled with him. It was a cool dry Wednesday in Épernay, the morning of Michel's funeral.

Arthur had with him a leather suitcase into which he'd put a few books and small pieces, arranged the night before – the sum of his new existence. He had said his few farewells before he left, to the sofa, and the maple tree, and the nurses. There was no one there to wave him goodbye or shake his cold hand warmly, and in the end Arthur's last few years were reduced to the car door closing. There was a sound of the tires spinning on gravel, and then the hospital was behind him. Arthur didn't once look back; he only now looked forward.

At the wicket in the railway station, a family was buying second-class tickets to Paris from an envelope heavy with inflation-touched banknotes. The father counted them out in a hurry, as if they lost value with every second. Arthur watched them go – the line moving up, the short man in the uniform who skillfully punched the tickets. He timed the gap and followed on and went through unobstructed.

Arthur stood apart from the few dozen who waited on the platform. Épernay was not the first station on the line, but he didn't have to wait long. Scores of pigeons rose aloft from their nests in steely branches; they flocked and turned beneath the sky of dirty glass-paned arches. Billowing white from its colic boilers, the train hove into sight.

Arthur boarded where he could and settled in an empty carriage. He removed his raincoat and stored his case and waited for the whistle. At the last minute, he gave up his seat for a woman and her daughter. The train surged forward and pulled away with Épernay behind them.

The girl was excitable, as children of an age will be. She roamed the seats in the face of censure from her overbearing mother, and stopped in front of Arthur.

"What are you staring at?" her mother admonished. "Stop staring like that!" she contradicted. The poor child couldn't win.

The little girl – she couldn't have been more than five – looked him in the face.

"It's all right," Arthur said, surprised and pleased, but not sure if she could hear him. The girl turned her ear as one might do when catching a distant sound.

"It doesn't hurt, not anymore," he touched his cheek. "You don't have to be frightened, you know."

"Come back here!" ordered her mother, and the child slowly complied. The woman took a sandwich from her basket and passed her daughter an apple. The girl did not offer to share, and Arthur returned to his reading.

It was a little after one when the Épernay train arrived at the terminus, an hour later than expected and without thought of explanation. Arthur stepped down: a mistake. He scrambled for shelter behind a pillar as the swarm of humanity moved past him, a rock in the stream observing the current that churned as it parted around him.

Being tall has its benefits, and Arthur took advantage. He looked over the cresting water of hats, beyond to the mouth of the river. There stood an amphitheater, the grand hall of the Gare d'Orsay, and filling it were carts and bags and flecks of colored dresses, and earthy suits and uniforms and barrows heaped with packages. It was a wall of sound. Here was the coming and going of the masses of the transient living, those moving with a purpose and those forced to linger a while at this terminus. Beneath a pendulous four-sided clock, spectators crooked their necks at departure boards. A chorus of bedlam echoed from the girders to the beat of marching legions, while a locomotive at a nearby platform erupted in a screech of wheel. Arthur watched, horrified, picturing himself beneath it. It jarred and shuddered then stuttered forward, coaxing its cars a few feet. Arthur fled it, spilling with passengers onto the concourse proper.

He was drawn to a café with an open façade from which he could better view humanity. Here were people smoking, passengers filling time drinking coffee from tiny glasses. *They have coffee!* He was cheered, sharing in the small pleasures of the living. There was a free stool at the counter and Arthur took it.

A scruffy looking boy was peddling Gitanes from a tray around his neck. He was doing the rounds of the outside customers, busking the café's few tables. "One centime, monsieur. Ten for a pack. Do you need matches?" The boy moved on and Arthur's attention turned instead to the women.

Women everywhere. Épernay had been but a dripping tap, while this was an open faucet. Hats and gloves were obviously in fashion, coats and skirts falling more than often just below the knee line. When they walked, the ladies clicked along cheerily, their heels tapping on the marble floor. An occasional ankle caught his eye when the crowd contrived to spread. The army had been a man's world, and despite the nurses, his hospital had been one too. Arthur looked at these women because he liked to, but also to avoid the men. These past five years had not been kind: amputations, scars, and burns. A clean shirt could disguise only so much – disfigurement was common.

A shoddy fellow beside a ticket line caught Arthur's attention. For a fleeting moment Arthur took him for another apparition. Then Arthur saw the truth of it. He stood apart, twitching, seemingly invisible to the queue. The tramp pawed his face repeatedly like a cat trying to clear a stain, and he talked and mumbled and pushed the sky and jerked around to look. No one in the ticket line paid him any attention; they all conspired to let him be, to leave him with his demons as they went about their day. Arthur studied him for another minute and then had to look away.

There were old men in the station and there were boys, but where, he thought, were all the rest? There didn't seem enough of them, a hole that wasn't filled. Young men walked stiffly, leaning on canes that their fathers had no need of. There were uniforms, uniforms moving about, but not marching anywhere. No shouting orders. No swinging arms. No purpose to their bearing. Arthur lifted a hand to the scars that decaled his own face. His fingertips found the hard ridges that defiled his symmetry.

From his stool at the café counter, Arthur could see clear to the north. Beyond the station gate he glimpsed horse drawn-carriages, and crowds, and passing cars. There was a scrolling metal sign – he knew it spanned the Métro hole that led the people down. Those steps, if he wanted, would carry him through Paris till he got to the Gare de l'Est, and from there a train could take him to Darmannes and the Malenfer estate.

Arthur had made his mind up when he read the doctor's paper:

He was going to return to Malenfer Manor and set the record straight. But he had a problem too. *How* was he going to tell anybody? *Who* was there to help?

The stories and the séance rooms agreed on a few things. If there was someone he could reach out to, that person might have a connection. It would be someone that carried a link with him that stretched beyond the grave. Arthur had had a lot of time in Épernay to think about whom that might be.

His family? He thought of them affectionately, but none of them were close. Such moments of reflection made him feel a hollow man – an honest recounting of a life reveals the counterfeit within.

He had one idea, however.

Arthur picked up his case and, glancing at the Métro station, turned away from it. He exited the Gare d'Orsay and emerged into a Paris under sun. It was a sight to lift the heart of even the most miserable of the dead.

A metropolis in which to find one man. It was not going to be easy. *Suffering Jesus, you big French bastard, the answer's out there somewhere.* He knew the Irishman was here. Arthur remembered the first bullet and choking in despair. He remembered digging the hole. He remembered the stinging air. He knew that somebody had pulled him out and got him into that ambulance. If there was anyone in this world that Arthur owed, it was his old friend, the sergeant. And if Dermot Ward had survived his war, then he would surely be here in Paris. He hoisted his case and looked both ways. *But where on earth to start?*

Chapter 11
Malenfer Manor

It was the long side of three o'clock before they reached Darmannes. There were few people on the platform; a single track and solitary office were the station's sum and total. Dermot looked up and down. A porter was not to be found. Dermot dragged his trunk, furrowing with an edge, until reaching the safety of the waiting room.

"You told them we were coming?" Arthur inquired. There was no one there to greet them.

"Just as you said."

Madame. I knew your son Arthur in the war. I bring news. Arrive from Paris today.

Dermot had attached his name to the telegram before boarding the train.

"How far from here?"

"Not much more than five kilometers. There's a nice route over the hill." Arthur was stretching his shoulders, rolling his arms behind his back one way and then the other. It was dry but cool, and the air was very still. At this time of year it would be dark after five, still plenty of time to get there.

"So I follow my imagination off into the wilds?"

"Not with that trunk, you don't. We'll have to sort that out."

Dermot rooted out the Station Master and asked for his luggage to be delivered. He repeated an address that Arthur provided and was surprised to find it accepted. The man was most helpful, effusively accommodating for a specimen of government employee. The trunk, he said, would be brought up that night or the following morning.

"This is the nearest town of any size within distance of our estate." It would be bright and cheerful come the summer, the window boxes full of flowers, but at this time of year the chapel's double steeple looked across huddled masonry. Red tile roofs sloped sharply down over shuttered bone-gray buildings. They set off following Arthur's instructions, and Dermot nodded greetings to curious residents as they wound their way from town. "There's only one place closer – Chevecheix is its name. Place is barely a village. Hasn't changed in two hundred years. But you need to come here for all but the basics. After Paris it seems too small."

"Does this village of yours have a pub?" Dermot asked him.

"Is France not the most refined of countries in all the civilized world?"

"What's its name, then?"

"Another test? You doubt me still? It's the Café du Viaduc! Its proprietress has inspired the cause of more than a couple of fights."

Dermot knew he had never been anywhere near this place, he *knew* it absolutely, and yet here he was. No one else could see Arthur – he was sure of that – and he was following him to God knows where.

With Darmannes behind them, the land opened out to the broad fields of the Haute-Marne. The cart path they followed was straight and long, and he was happy to stretch his legs. Even after the rain came on, Dermot stayed warm from exertion.

"We used to have cakes, with cream." Arthur emphasized the latter, in answer to Dermot's latest questioning. "And we bake our own bread down in the kitchen in an enormous cave of an oven." Dermot's mind was on his stomach. "And we eat it with soft cheeses that are churned and set from the milk of the cows on our farm."

"God, you're killing me."

"And we grow our own grapes, too. My great-grandfather set down the vines. The best of the vintage we keep in the cellar for family and our guests. You won't regret coming, I'm sure."

"Well, if it's so nice, why didn't you go back there straight away?"

Arthur didn't answer immediately. "I have happy memories of the place, and some I might wish to forget. But you will be well looked after, my friend. You can be sure of that."

"Come on, Arthur, your kids being here and all – even if I swallow everything else, that bit I just don't get. Why didn't you go see them earlier? What was there to stop you?"

Arthur laughed dryly, but it didn't seem in fun. "I said it was nice for visitors, but not the same for family."

"But why wait till now? Why not 'fess up and claim your children years ago?"

"It was the best for them," he answered cryptically.

"Because your father told you not to? That isn't right. You're a bigger boy than that."

"You don't understand." They approached a fork in the road. Arthur drew up. "My father... he was protecting them. As was I by staying silent."

"Oh, yeah?"

"Yes."

"From what?" If he was going to make an arse of himself, Dermot wanted to know the facts. Besides, the Arthur he'd known back in the war wouldn't have run out on anyone.

Arthur seemed to be weighing his options. He shifted his feet. "I didn't plan on telling you this. I thought I'd spare you the fuss. But it's not as if things are simple right now, so you can have it for all it's worth."

"You're going to tell me why you left your children alone?"

"Not alone, my friend – looked after. They were never alone. And everything was for their own good."

"Excuse me for saying so, but that sounds like an excuse unworthy of you."

Arthur sighed, resigned: "Hear me out before you judge." Then he took a few moments as if ordering his thoughts, as if not sure of where to begin. "Ours is an old, old family, Dermot, and we've lived in these parts for an age. Something happened a long time ago, and since then... well, since then we've had nothing but trouble."

Trouble? "What kind of trouble?"

"The dying sort. The sort of trouble you wouldn't wish on anyone you care about."

"I don't get it."

"I knew you wouldn't. Our family. The Malenfers. Well... we're cursed."

Dermot laughed; but Arthur looked, if anything, more troubled. "You can't be serious?"

"I wish I weren't."

"Ah, come off it."

"Our curse – the Malenfer Curse – it leads you to a bad end. That's what I was protecting them from. That's why my father hid them."

"You're pulling my leg, surely."

"The man who talks to ghosts on trains now doubts the existence of curses?"

"Aw, don't start that again." Though it seemed a difficult point to shake. "I'm just saying..."

"You don't have to believe it, Dermot, but it is exists all the same. Those who carry the Malenfer name end up in a very bad way. Hiding my boys might have saved them from it. That was the reasoning, anyway."

"Plenty of people live under a curse, Arthur – my family too. Most just call it poverty, and get by the best they can."

"I understand what you mean, and you are right, of course. I was dismissive myself at the beginning. My father, however, took it very seriously. When I found out I was going to be a father, I took the news to him. I thought he was going to be furious!"

"And was he?"

"No, he was deeply concerned. A boy may pretend otherwise, but he hears every word that his father tells him. If you lived at that house you would know. He saw it as an opportunity to escape our fate and made me swear that I would not tell. By hiding my children from their legacy, we hoped to keep them safe."

"And you believe this still?"

"Listen, Dermot, what can I say? I died years ago and yet I find myself here. Excuse me if I'm willing to consider anything within the realm of the possible."

"But then why change? Why change your plan now? Is it for the money? You want the money for them? But won't you be exposing your children, risking them by giving them their title? Won't you be bringing the curse down upon them?"

"This is what I can't explain. Of course I hope not, but perhaps. Perhaps I am risking them, and God help me if that is so. But perhaps the curse knew of them all along, and I was only fooling myself. Perhaps the curse is a fantasy cooked up in our heads and I was a fool to listen to these tales. I can't explain any of it to you – you aren't family, so how can you hope to understand? But you must trust me. Trust me that it feels right. Trust me that I know what's best. My boys must be looked after, Dermot. It's something I must do."

"It feels right?"

"It does. They are Malenfers, and they need to know, for the good or the bad it will bring."

"It just sounds crazy."

"I know. I don't ask you to judge, my friend, I'm just trying to explain. And I want you to know that I am grateful to you, for the help that you've been."

"I haven't done anything yet."

"But you're here aren't you? And you've agreed to help, and so I know you will."

Dermot felt no better.

Arthur started meddling with his pipe and then seemed to notice where they were. He beckoned Dermot up the path.

"Come up here to where the road forks, there's something you should see."

As Dermot approached the land fell away and afforded a view through the valley.

"Have a look over there. Isn't it fine?"

"What is it? Is it ancient?"

"It's our 'Viaduct.' The river is the Suize. It's actually a railway bridge, but it looks a great deal older. Six hundred meters of tiered stone arches like a Roman-built waterway. Pretty, isn't it?"

It spanned the meandering pedantry of a mature and swollen river. The Suize sluiced beneath the viaduct on its way to a distant sea.

"Let's go." Arthur turned away. "Let's find out what they're having for dinner. Chevecheix is just below us, but this other path runs by the Manor."

"The village is down there?" asked Dermot.

Arthur nodded. The veiled shapes of low clustered buildings could be made out through the sheen of rain; insect light from tiny windows and the hint of solid stone.

"I'll just be a second. You stay here, Arthur." Dermot advanced alone.

Chevecheix huddled by a stream above the banks of the much bigger river. A small inviting hostelry commanded this end of the village. A painted sign of the namesake bridge hung above its entrance: *Café du Viaduc* was written large, illuminated from the interior.

Café du Viaduc – just as Arthur had told him. It was real! And so was the ghost of Arthur with it – Dermot had no other explanation. He hadn't read it in any book. He had never set foot in this place. No other soul could see Arthur; it was entirely in his head. *Am I being called to account for leaving him? Is this a judgment of me?* But in that moment he gave up his excuses and accepted the madness it meant. Arthur had returned, and Dermot knew that he must do his best to make amends; but Dermot knew not whether this meant his salvation or whether it damned him to hell.

He turned his back on the Café du Viaduc and made his way back up the hill. Soon, ahead, lay the fork in the road and he could just make Arthur out – a dark looming figure, massive and marked, consumed by the fading light. Arthur raised one long arm, beckoned him to follow, and Dermot fell in beside him.

The big house had been hidden by trees, but it now rose up around the courtyard. A curtain twitched on a second floor window and a pale face looked out for a moment. They had been spotted.

A bristling young man with a glaring face approached from a nearby barn. "This is private land. We have no work or alms." He shoo'd them off.

"Pierre!" said Arthur. "It's Pierre, Dermot. This is one of my boys."

Once you accept the talking dead, there is not much left to faze you. "Are you Pierre, by chance?" he called out. The fellow pulled up, wary.

"I don't know you," he answered, suspicious of the stranger. "Who are you? What's your business here at the farm?"

"My name is Ward. Dermot Ward. I was a friend of Arthur Malenfer." There wasn't much of a reaction. "I served with him during the war. I sent a telegram to his mother this morning, telling her I would come." The young man seemed to give this some thought. Dermot felt the cold of the rain. "She's expecting me. Will you see me in?"

He was scruffy and bore a discontented look on his otherwise handsome face.

"My boy! You've grown into a man! Don't you see me here before you?" Arthur appealed with outstretched arms. In their frame and bulk there was a resemblance between father and son, though Arthur's jaw had slackened to jowly where Pierre's remained firm and tight.

"So you knew Arthur, did you?" the young man said finally, as if the benefit of the doubt had ebbed in Dermot's favor. He never once so much as glanced at Arthur, who was on top of him by now. Arthur was invisible to him; to his father's pleas his ears were deaf. "I'm not Pierre, though, he's my brother. I'm his twin, Émile."

"Some father you are," Dermot breathed aside.

"Émile!" choked Arthur, and was he crying? "My boy, it's been far too long."

Dermot extended his hand to shake. The young man seemed unsure of the offer but reciprocated after a beat.

"A pleasure to meet you, Émile."

"I am Madame's groom. It is a pleasure to meet you, monsieur, if you are who you say you are. You haven't brought anything?" Émile's eyebrows grew tight again.

"My trunk is being sent along from the station," Dermot explained to him. "They said later this evening or perhaps tomorrow."

"Well... this way then, I suppose."

Arthur's son escorted them across the cobbled yard. "Mindful of that puddle," he called back, swerving before the bottom step of the short run to the door. "That crater swallows people whole."

They did not ring – Dermot saw no bell – and their guide didn't wait for admission. Émile gave a heavy push to the panel, and it opened with a long grinding creak. They stepped inside. Émile pulled the large slab shut; they felt the shudder through their soles. Arthur Malenfer had returned back home. For Dermot, there was no turning back.

Chapter 12
Daughters

"Please wait here, Mr. Ward. Don't wander." Émile disappeared up a staircase.

"Trusting lot," Dermot remarked, when he thought they were alone. Glad to be out of the drizzle, he stood staring around at the place. Arthur hadn't exaggerated; it was a marvel to behold.

A grand house may achieve its distinction by honest means or foul. It might impose itself on you through a sweeping staircase or a vast height to its walls. It may hoodwink you and deceive your eye through a careful line in the wallpaper, or flatter falsely and pretend by a crafty use of lighting. A house can lay a claim to grandeur through its taste in art or furniture, and risk its reputation on the moods and temperament of fashion. But a visitor to the Malenfer Manor felt grandeur in a curious way, one difficult at first to apprehend yet immediately unsettling.

The house was grand because it *shrank you*. Inside its walls you were pressed and squeezed and made a little smaller. The place was somehow diminishing, and in so doing it became that much larger. Perhaps it was that the doors inside were a little too wide for their height? And this was true, for a cart could be driven through many of its halls. Perhaps it was the exaggerated masonry, much larger than engineering called for? The ground floor was stacked on such coarse pieces, their facing left mostly exposed; panel and plaster were reserved for the galleries that Dermot found later upstairs. Whatever it was, there was an expansive feel – you were a child in the room of your parents, and the spell was strongest lower down where the rooms seemed for bigger creatures; ogres and giants might dwell within and feel themselves quite comfortable. The furniture was of a size to match, and the entry hall no exception. Dermot was unaware of the spell, but he found the sensation comforting. The place exuded a density, a permanence of matter that he immediately took to. There was nothing airy about the old house; in every sense it was solid.

He noticed the deep fireplace with fuel stacked on its cold hearth. It was wide enough to roast an entire deer without nearly touching the edges. A penetrating draft whistled down in the absence of a welcoming flame.

Arthur had moved into the room, running his hand over a table. Arthur seemed to share the Manor's scale, its ratios and dimensions. The mortar to him might be cartilage, his bones taken from the same quarry. Dermot didn't disturb his friend, but left him with his memories.

There were three paintings in the room. Two were of large rural scenes, and dominated the room. The first of these, the nearest to Dermot, placed the manor in ripe summer fields, only the profile of the house was at a different angle from the view he'd glimpsed on arrival. The second painting hung opposite the first and was its twin in perspective alone; it was a bright winter's day of frost and breath, and icicles from the roof – sharp crisp lines and bare fallow fields against a cloudless sky.

"My great-aunt did those." Arthur saw him looking. "I think someone's switched them around." He looked unsure.

Neither picture bore any resemblance to the palette he'd just walked through. Outside was a sky the color of gun smoke and blasted twisted metal, and Malenfer Manor blended into its farm on a drab and washed-out canvas.

"That wasn't here before." Arthur pointed out the third picture.

The final painting, smaller than the others, was on the biggest piece of wall. It was the furthest from the doorway and Dermot guessed why it had been hung there. It asked you to walk towards it and resolve its tiny figures. One glance was enough to draw you in; it beckoned you to step forward. Dermot felt its lure physically and surrendered to its direction.

The figures were plants and animals and men, but each of them twisted reality. Children's fancies tormented and warred, they violated the senses. Sticks and scythes, beak and claw, and unnatural little horns; swords and daggers prodded and tore and laid each other open. The artist had given life to the scene in a brew of primary colors. It stirred with a violence all of its own, though mere flecks on the canvas before them.

"I like it," Dermot smiled, cocking his head back to Arthur. "Who painted that, then?"

"It must be new. I haven't seen it before."

"It is Mademoiselle Simonne's garbage." Émile gave his brusque opinion with a tone of the long suffering. He had appeared behind them suddenly without any sort of notice. "Madame's granddaughter," he clarified.

A clock chimed a quarter of six, a grandfather clock with leaded-glass doors through which Dermot could see the guts moving. Cogs and wheels and chains and weights with a pendulum like an axe head. It was draped in crêpe of funereal black that hung from its tall wide shoulders.

"You'll have to wait for Madame," said Émile. "I don't know what room she'll have you in."

There was a rustle at the top of the stairs.

"He'll be in the Blue Room, Émile. Go at once and fetch Berthe." The voice was clear and sharp, one familiar with being obeyed.

"Of course, Madame," Émile replied and hastily made off.

Madame Malenfer was regal in mourning; she wore her darkness well. She drifted down the wide staircase like smoke from a blocked-up chimney.

"Mother!" Arthur appealed, but she looked right through her son. Death in a family casts textured shadows, and Madame had woven them all.

"I understand you knew my son."

"I did, Madame, I knew him well. We were very close, in fact."

"Is that so? And yet you are not French, I don't think."

"You have an ear, Madame, you're quite correct there." He didn't feel the need to explain himself any further. "Might I say, I regret my intrusion at this difficult time on your family – I understand you're all just after losing Arthur's brother. I am very sorry for your loss." He bowed his head towards her.

Something in Madame commanded respect. She wore sacrifice like a medal. But some medals are well-earned, Dermot knew, and he was not one to judge her. He felt uncomfortable besides, an intruder despite Arthur's invitation.

Madame, who had been prickly at first, now seemed to thaw just slightly. Dermot didn't know if it was a habit of hers or as a result of his attempt at manners.

"Well, that is so, we will miss Michel, just as we have missed Arthur." She was composed. Her tears were spent, or had dried up, or had never been there to begin with. "Your telegram came as a surprise. I take it you plan on staying?"

"For a day or two, if possible."

"Well, it's very short notice."

Madame liked her silences; Dermot guessed she used them to make other people uncomfortable.

"You mentioned news, Mr. Ward. I wonder what that might mean?"

"Not here, Dermot!" Arthur interrupted, "Not now! You need the birth certificates."

"Eh..." He was trying to appear undistracted. "I do, yes Madame. News about Arthur. News just like I mentioned. But it's something that might be better for waiting until there's time for a private audience."

Madame clearly did not like the sound of that. "I see," she said, tellingly. He saw himself through her eyes. An unknown from out of nowhere who appears at the end of their gate. A friend from the war, likely sniffing for a handout, playing on old times' sake. And Dermot did recognize himself in that picture too; she wasn't so far off. He judged it not a time to blabber about favors for men from the grave.

She was a striking woman for her years. Petite. Diminutive. It seemed implausible that she could have borne a child, let alone one of Arthur's dimensions. Chalk lines in her hair, more gray than white, and tiny wrinkles betrayed her aging, yet she was cold and hard – there was more warmth from a statue. Her size belied her presence. Dermot held his ground before her, but he knew who ruled that family. Émile had gone scurrying off, and Dermot could hardly blame him. Madame shared one physical resemblance with Arthur, and they were looking at him now. Her eyes were his, or his were hers – he found the match uncanny.

"I am very pleased that you've come, Monsieur." She showed all the emotion of wax. "We are all of us here far too miserable. You will cheer us up, I hope."

"I'd be glad to try, Madame."

"You were with Arthur's regiment?"

"No. Seconded. I was with the Legion."

"Your rank, Mr. Ward?"

"I was a sergeant."

"Indeed. Not an officer, then."

"I was an engineer, ma'am, but I'm now discharged from the service."

"My family has a long honorable tradition, Mr. Ward. My husband was a Colonel. He fought in the last war with Prussia and was recognized for it."

"So I understand. My condolences again, ma'am."

"*This* war has almost done for us, Mr. Ward. My family is very close to me, and there isn't much left of it now."

It seemed rehearsed. She held her hand out, palm down to him, and Dermot didn't know whether to shake the thing or kiss it. He floundered and did neither. Madame withdrew her small hand with a murmured "Hmmmmm" and a look he couldn't fathom.

Noisy footsteps preceded the return of Émile. Accompanying him was a bulwark of a woman on the downside of middling years.

"Berthe here will show you to your room" – Madame took notice of his damp condition – "that you may change. Where did you put the bags, Émile?"

"The luggage is to follow, Madame."

"Well, you're wet," Madame observed, "but we'll take care of you." She looked Dermot over. "Berthe, see to it that everything is provided for."

"Yes, Madame," said the housekeeper.

"We dine at eight sharp, Mr. Ward," Madame announced. "As luck would have it, we are on a farm, so we can offer you a dinner. Starvation is about the only thing we haven't died of lately."

"Thank you Madame," Dermot bowed; addressing her this way seemed natural. "That would be just grand."

Madame did not return his smile nor give another word. She turned back to the staircase and returned the way she'd come, but a quarter of the way back up the steps a sharp cough broke from her lungs. It racked her chest and paralyzed her; she leaned against the banister. Dermot thought to move and help her but was stalled by the reaction of the others. The servants ignored the episode completely; they behaved as if it had never happened. It passed in seconds, and Madame took her leave without further explanation. Dermot and Arthur shared a look. Both of them were left to wonder.

"If you'll follow me, sir, I'll get you settled. And welcome to Malenfer Manor."

The doughty housekeeper brought him to a door, down a wainscoted hall, up one flight of stairs. "Please make yourself comfortable in the study, sir, while I arrange for your rooms to be made ready. It shouldn't take too long." Not waiting for an answer, the efficient woman turned and made off, the tightly pinned bun of her hair not the only reminder of his landlady. Dermot watched her retreat. He was going to say a word to Arthur when he caught sight of another figure, a sober-looking woman, observing him from a distance, the open stairwell between them. Dermot lifted an arm in greeting.

At first Dermot thought it was Madame. Like her, the lady wore mourning dress and was of similar frame and coloring. His confusion was only fleeting, however, as this woman was clearly younger.

"And now you have seen my sister, Sophie," said Arthur, a tone in his voice betraying him. Arthur waved, hopefully. He got no sign of reply.

"Are all the Malenfer women good-looking?" Dermot wondered aloud.

"You're a disgraceful man, Irlandais." Arthur didn't sound annoyed. "Her husband was a nice enough fellow; he died the first year of the war. It's her daughter that painted that picture you saw, downstairs in the hall."

It all fit for Dermot. He saw the family now. The Malenfer boys all gone. Madame left with her sole remaining daughter, the pair of them both widows. And then there was the still elusive heiress. The three women all rattling around in this grand old house of memories.

"Can she see you?" Dermot asked. "Perhaps she sees you and doesn't recognize you?"

"Hello, Sophie!" Arthur bellowed. "Your brother returns and walks the earth, doomed to life eternal!" He slapped the wall for added effect, but Sophie didn't so much as blink.

"I guess that's a *no*, then."

Arthur seemed sad. "She was born one year after me. We both grew up here together. She left home as soon as she was married, and she married very young. My mother hated him, her husband." He didn't elaborate. "I missed her sometimes, back then." Arthur gazed after her. "It can't have been easy on either of them."

Dermot, conscious of his audience, raised a hand in greeting again. There might have been the briefest of nods, and then the woman walked away.

"Friendly lot, your family," Dermot said, tongue-in-cheek. "I think she likes me."

"Let's go into the study, or Berthe will be annoyed with you." Arthur took his eyes from his sister, a mournful look on his face. "You look like you could do with a drink."

The study was warm and cozy. Unlike downstairs, there was a fire going, with four leather smoking-chairs camped around it. There was a round end table bearing two decanters and a collection of glasses. A single kilim rug took up the center, pinned in place by the furniture. There were two bay windows that Dermot found as he opened the drawn curtains; any view they had to show would have to wait till morning. Dermot's shoes brought a creak from the wide-planked varnished floor. With the door closed the place was snug; it kept the heat in well.

"Brandy?" Arthur suggested.

Dermot didn't refuse, and poured himself a glass. He slaked his thirst with the relish of a temperate man gone bad. Standing with his back to the fire, the steam rose from his pants.

There was another door leading from the room.

"What's through there?" Dermot asked.

"The library," Arthur told him. "But don't get lost – Berthe will be back and dinner can't be far off. And there's the matter of the certificates."

Dermot, for whom books were a weakness bordering on vice, tried the handle out of curiosity.

"It's open. Fancy that."

"Enjoy yourself," Arthur motioned him away. "I'm staying here for a while." The ghost of Arthur dug out his pipe and slid his hip flask from his jacket.

Some libraries are made for show. Such shelves are half-filled and harbor dusty curios. They play host to ornaments or the bric-a-brac of the unenlightened. The Malenfer library was no such thing. It was five times the size of the study. The room was stuffed and its shelves sagged down beneath its substantial inventory. The stacks must have risen twelve feet up until they scraped the ceiling. The shelves were tightly spaced, admitting the minimum of daylight, and were swollen with a multitude of volumes, some of which looked antediluvian. Dermot set out to meet the inhabitants and make a few new friends. Most were locals, the titles in French, but some were foreigners like him – the English and the Germans, he noticed, had muscled their way in here.

As in a crowded barracks where the soldiers outnumber the beds, so the books were crammed on shelves and had set up makeshift posts. Leaning towers waited to be billeted wherever space permitted, and Dermot found the passageways jammed, inhibiting his progress. Great slabs of books were piled on their sides, like slate cairns ready for toppling. Dermot was wary lest he knock a pillar and send the temple down.

It was as he slipped by such a pile that Dermot heard a curious sound – the noise of little whispers and the scuffle of shuffling feet. "Hello?" he asked, and was answered with a child's retreating giggle. Dermot peeked around the shelf, but the children must have moved on. They couldn't be far, whoever was there, past the next shelf over but one. As he made his way around to follow the noise he heard them move further off. They were talking again in excited murmurs, but he couldn't make out their words – the young voices of little people, full of excitement and fun. Dermot crouched low and stared through the shelves, but couldn't catch a peek of the children. He decided to beat them at their game and fixed on a plan to ambush them. He tried to keep as quiet as he could and crept up very slowly.

It was dark at the back of the tall heavy shelves, where the light from a sconce barely penetrated. As he wove between the books, his back to the light, he filled the space up with shadow. They no longer retreated and he was gaining on them; he could hear their whispers getting louder. Only one more row to go. "One, two..." he counted in his head.

"Got ya!" he shouted, as he pounced.

There were no children at all. No scurrying feet; no small hands; no hushed secret voices. To his great surprise there was only a charming young lady, who looked up from her page.

"You're new," she said in greeting. She wasn't flustered at all.

He didn't know what to say. Where had the children gone? Where had the whispers and giggles come from? Who was this lovely girl?

"My name's Simonne," said the girl, lowering her book. "I suppose that I'm pleased to meet you."

Dermot stood gobsmacked. It dawned on him that he must look an idiot. Madame had been regal, Sophie aloof; but this girl, this *woman*, was stunning. Her raven tresses ran loose and wild, spilling past her shoulders to her waistline. Her hair framed a bosom that was high and tight, which Dermot tried hard not to notice.

"Dermot Ward," he managed, only starting to recover.

She was unblemished, like a cameo piece. Her lips were thick, pulled wide in a genuine smile, and dark next to her pale skin. She had a small fluted nose and tiny ears that defiantly held the hair from her face. Her eyes were green but flecked with hazel, and Dermot was lost in their gaze.

"Mother said you might be here."

Dermot noticed she inclined her forehead every time she spoke. She was slender and short, and her eyes met his through wisps of lovely dark locks.

Dermot awoke. With great embarrassment he saw that she'd extended her hand in greeting; a doll's hand it was, a porcelain hand, with shaped clean healthy nails. He tried to free a hand, juggling the books he'd lifted, but was incommoded by the brandy glass that he'd brought along for company.

"Dermot..." he shuffled the books back. *Idiot!* he thought to himself.

"Ward," she answered. "You've said that bit already."

What am I doing? Sharpen up, man. Pay attention, won't you!

He managed to liberate one of his hands with which he took her own, and at her touch a joy consumed him, far warmer than the alcohol. He held her fingers perhaps a moment longer than propriety allowed, and once having released the Mademoiselle he found he missed her touch.

"Mademoiselle," he managed with what he hoped was confidence. He smiled as he cringed on the inside. *What is the matter with me?*

"You like books, Mr. Ward?" She smiled at him again and he loved it when she did so. He nodded like a fool. "Good," she said, "I like them too. That's a coincidence."

"Simonne?" A woman's voice came from the far corner of the room. Dermot hadn't been paying attention.

"Simonne?" Someone was walking towards them. "Ah, there you are. Why didn't you answer me when I called?"

Sophie drew up when she saw the tall Irishman leering over her daughter. Dermot recognized her from the hall.

Dermot bowed from the neck. "Madame, we have not been introduced."

"His name is Dermot Ward, mother." She smiled mischievously. "He's stealing the books and drinking all the brandy, but he seems all right besides that."

"Really, Simonne. Please ignore my daughter, Mr. Ward. I saw you, of course, and I heard your name mentioned earlier. I must say we're curious to know what brings you."

Simonne piped in. "There is never anyone new here, Mr. Ward, so strangers bring us running. And we rarely get news, and your telegram spoke of news, so you're a very popular fellow." She tilted her head to one shoulder. Dermot smiled back like a marionette happy to have his strings pulled. "Mr. Ward is a reader, mother. Aren't you, Mr. Ward?"

"I didn't mean to disturb," he said. "They're making my room upstairs..." Why did he have to explain? "Wonderful place you have here," he went on, needing to talk. "And this is very special." He waved his leather bound book for their view, and raised his glass to salute to the pair of them. "An illustrated Dumas and a Calvados... and the pleasure of two charming ladies!"

Simonne laughed heartily while Sophie only stared, perhaps shocked by the liberty of her houseguest. Arthur at that moment appeared behind her shoulder, and Dermot felt somewhat relieved. He felt he was making an ass of himself and needed the moral support.

"I see," said Sophie, not enamored, any suspicions about her new guest seemingly confirmed. "I'm glad to see you laughing, Simonne. We haven't had much occasion to be happy of late, Mr. Ward."

Dermot's jaw hung loose for a moment while his brains searched around for his manners.

"I wished to say also," he began, "to you both, I mean, how sorry I am for your recent loss... your brother Michel, Madame; your uncle, Mademoiselle."

Simonne calmed down, the ladies both nodding their heads in polite acknowledgement of the ritual.

"But you must call me Sophie, Mr. Ward, Madame is only my mother."

"Trying times for the family," Dermot continued. "I didn't mean to intrude."

"Why *are* you here?" It was Simonne that asked, sincerely and pointedly. "What *news* can there be about Arthur?"

"Simonne. Manners," her mother censured.

Dermot felt he could refuse her nothing. *I have brought secrets to share?* What could he say? He glanced up at Arthur for answers.

A curious thing happened. Simonne turned her head to follow his gaze, and then flexed as if struck by something. She trembled.

Arthur didn't notice anything. "Don't look at me, Dermot. Tell them what you want."

Is she listening? Dermot saw the once laughing girl become quiet, pensive and troubled.

"But I wouldn't let the cat out of the bag until Madame hears it first. You'll end up in her bad books. And you still don't have the birth certificates."

Why wouldn't Arthur shut up?

"Are you all right?" Dermot asked her, concerned. Simonne's head snapped around to Dermot as if only just seeing him now.

"Why did you come?" she spoke harshly, urgently.

"I have some news," he stumbled. "I promised an old friend."

"What did he mean, 'cat out of the bag'? What is the secret you're keeping?"

Sophie intervened. "Simonne? Simonne!" She took her daughter's arm, forcing her attention.

Simonne came to as if from a daze, fading in and out of lucidity. "It spoke to you," she accused.

"Pardon?" Dermot was unnerved.

"You know it did. Don't you?" She reached out her hand towards him, as if skeptical he were real. Her face was in awe, as if the world she had known had been usurped and replaced.

"Simonne!" her mother shouted and slapped her daughter's arm away. Simonne stopped, chastised. Then seized by a madness none could determine, she turned and twisted away. Breaking free of her mother's hold, she up and fled the room.

"I'm sorry," Sophie apologized.

"I'm sorry." Dermot was red-faced.

"She's a nice girl," defended her mother. "Sometimes she has these... episodes."

"It's perfectly all right," Dermot answered, embarrassed, but he was talking to Sophie's back. The mother had gone after her child.

Arthur clicked his teeth on the end of his pipe. "She knows I'm here, Dermot. You heard her."

Chapter 13
An Envelope

THE BLUE ROOM TURNED OUT TO BE A SUITE OF SORTS, FAR GRANDER than the garret he'd vacated. Off to the side of a four-poster bed there was a sink and his own private toilet. He tried the flusher and pronounced the receptacle in splendid working order. A sprung settee and mismatched chaise longue dominated the cluttered living room; they commanded the space in front of the fireplace, displacing a school desk to the corner. The Azorean wallpaper was a disappointment – Dermot had visions of sapphires.

"I remember this old fellow. He's been here forever." Arthur was petting a bedraggled badger, a specimen of ingenious taxidermy. The beast was perched above the mantle, posed rampant and imperial. Though steely clawed and fang bared, it instilled a measure of sympathy. Arthur seemed to remember it fondly. Dermot dropped his hat on its head.

"You'll find everything where it should be, sir." The Malenfer housekeeper was all efficiency. She invited Mr. Ward to ring for anything, though the tone of her offer lacked sincerity. She left with a final scan of the place as if tallying the candlesticks and linen. With the doughty Berthe out of the way, the subject returned to the library.

"She knows something, Dermot, it's perfectly clear." Arthur referred to Simonne. He talked to Dermot from the requisitioned couch, his ankles crossed over one end.

"I thought the same thing. But what 'episodes' was your sister referring to? Didn't you find that strange?"

"She was just a young girl when I saw her last. I don't know if Sophie was covering for her, or if she's behaved this way in the past."

"And where did the children get to? That I want to know."

"What children? What are you talking about?"

"I was following... oh, never mind. It's not really important. Regardless, Simonne knows."

"Yes, I heard. She knew I was there, or she knew that something was."

"There can be no doubt – she repeated your words. But I'm certain that she couldn't see you."

"It's exciting. I'm excited, Dermot. It's so good not to be alone. I'm sorry that it distressed her, but I can't deny it gives me hope. We may have discovered an unexpected ally. I was right to come back, I know it."

"I'm worried that we frightened her, Arthur."

"You're going to have to tell her something. An explanation is in order. She certainly thinks that *you* saw something. I think that's what upset her the most."

"I rather picked up on that."

"This makes things *very* interesting." Arthur was looking pleased.

"Look, Arthur..." Dermot was less amused. "No disrespect, but I'm just coming to terms with events myself. I'm here to help you, and then I'm leaving. I don't really need this..." What was he going to say? Distraction? "She seems a very nice girl, and all. I just hope that she's all right with you here."

Truth was, the thought of seeing the young Simonne again was foremost in his mind. Uncomfortably so. Fortunately, Arthur didn't pick up on his discomfort and changed the subject to the practicalities at hand.

"Well, I'm sure that she'll get over it. We'll find out soon enough. Now. To business." He sprung from the couch. "The birth certificates. We have some time before dinner and we had best make use of it. If you're going up against my mother soon, you had better come ready and armed."

Dermot prodded at the teeth of the snarling badger. "She struck me that way too."

"They're not likely to come right out and say it – too damned rude – but they will want you to make a clean breast of your news and get to the point pretty soon."

"I got a taste of that in the library. I don't blame them, I'd be curious myself. Strange man shows up, peddling a story... I'd say 'Out with it or get right out.' They've been generous to let me stay." But here Dermot was hesitant. Wouldn't they be upset by the news? Would they throw him out on his ear? He had rather enjoyed his reception so far and, despite his protestations, was in no mind to leave right away. Malenfer Manor had much to offer that he hadn't considered before. "I think it best if the certificates do the speaking for both of us."

"You are quite right, Dermot. I couldn't agree more."

"Assuming they're here," he quipped. Then Dermot got a picture of himself as the bearer of unlooked-for drama – for suppose these papers were discovered and he was really to hand them over? It strung his pride, more than a little, that his reputation by this charade would be tarnished. "But... I mean, how do I say they came to me? Do I tell them that you entrusted me with them during the war? And if so, then why didn't I bother to forward them earlier? How does that look for me?"

"Don't worry about that." Arthur was dismissive.

"I just kept them tucked away for a few years and then one day decided to call? I'll look thoughtless at best, certainly negligent, and not the most reliable of guardians."

"Why the fuss all of a sudden? Whatever is the matter? You're an outsider, Irlandais, and what's more a foreigner. Please believe me, there is no amount of bad behavior they won't be willing to credit you with. Tell them you were too busy to write, or that you forgot. You only remembered when you saw the newspaper, or you were in the hospital yourself, or tell them that you're a drinker and couldn't be bothered to come. Tell them anything you fancy, they're not going to care very much."

"I'm not going to come across as very dependable if I tell them any such story." Dermot was stung. "What kind of a friend would forget the wish of a dying comrade to his children? I'd come across like an ass."

"What the hell do you care? The birth certificates say it all, you don't have to... oh, wait." Arthur had been waving his arms, growing exasperated, but then settled as if a thought had come to him and the road ahead looked clearer. He nodded his head. "Oh, I get it now. I understand," and he gave Dermot a knowing smile.

Dermot blushed a little redder than he already was.

"Don't worry, Irlandais. She won't think any less of you. They'll be too washed up in the news itself to judge the messenger badly."

"I don't know what you're talking about." Dermot walked to the door, admitting and denying nothing but not convincing either of them for a second. "Well, where are they, then? Where'd you lock away your little secret? I presume I'm not to be lucky enough to find them hidden away in here?" He had a look at the badger again.

"Follow me," said Arthur. "If you'll open the door, monsieur?"

"I hope they're still where you left them. Otherwise I can see your mother throwing me out long before breakfast is served."

"She'd probably enjoy that – don't tempt her."

Arthur made certain the coast was clear, and Dermot followed him into the corridor.

"Down here – it's on the same floor. My old room in the other wing." Having guided him past the staircase without incident, Arthur now ran ahead. "I'll shout if I see anyone coming! It's at the end. You'll be fine. Follow me."

Dermot kept as quiet as he could and walked close to the cover of the wall. He figured if anyone saw him around, he'd just say he was stretching his legs.

There was ample light from the staircase lamps, but the darkness intruded and filled the corridor the further down it he went. This floor, like the library below it, was paneled in whorled wood. Dermot's shadow fell in front of him and stretched longer as he progressed. The grill of a window at the end of the hall seemed to float detached in space. Dermot, wary of where he trod, gradually slowed his pace.

He passed a succession of paintings – the Malenfers enjoyed their art. All in this hall were scenes of Napoleonic wars: cavalry towing artillery and wounded men on stretchers, provision wagons bogged down in mud, comrades supporting friends. Winter in Russia had little to recommend it; he made a note to give it a miss. Moving on a little further, the gilded frames gave way to crossed muskets, muzzle fed, of rod and charge and ball. A rosette of pistols hung around them in a display of bygone power.

Dermot had lost sight of Arthur. There was nowhere to go except deeper down the hallway, and so, one hand upon the wall, he progressed. The paned glass was his target now, its frames like bars to a prison. With painful anticipation he drew near – it gave light to a final portrait. Ensconced within an enormous frame stood a cavalier with sword in hand. He loomed above a slaughtered deer, newly dispatched by his hand. Dermot gave it a casual glance but was taken aback in shock, for it was Arthur he saw staring out at him, the soldier in the canvas. The resemblance was uncanny. But *this* Arthur was centuries old – his equine haircut dated him. The man bore a look of cruelty he had never seen on his friend.

"Long, long time ago." The deep voice was just behind him.

Dermot jumped. "Jesus Christ, man. What are you thinking?"

"One of my predecessors."

"Don't sneak up on me like that. You almost scared me to death." Dermot voiced his objections. They looked at the painting again. "Who's that, then? Your great-great-aunty with the deep gruff voice? That's some moustache she's sporting."

It was a powerful man, richly dressed, but savage and unforgiving. The deer had had its throat cut, and the cavalier was bleeding it.

"I was named after him; he died a long time ago. My grand-daddy's grand-daddy or something. It was that Arthur who established our papers of title and made an estate from one farm."

"The big man."

"And he was the first of the cursed Malenfers. It was him that started it all."

"How do you think they kept all that hair clean? And how would you dry it afterwards?"

"I've always liked the pants myself. You just don't see those anymore."

"The buckles. Check out the buckles on those boots. I'm hoping buckles come back."

"Well, if you're finished denigrating my esteemed ancestor, shall we get back to the task at hand?"

"You'd look good in a pair of those. All I'm saying."

"Strange." Arthur changed the subject. He looked about, concerned.

"Where to now, then?" There was a servants' stairway at the end of the hall, but nothing else that Dermot could see.

"I don't understand why they did this, Dermot."

"What do you mean? What's the matter?"

"It was here." He pointed. "The door was here. My room is right across from the painting." But there was no door now. "They can't have moved the door. They must have blocked it up."

"Maybe on another floor?" Dermot offered helpfully. He had the awful feeling that this was all a fabrication and the joke was about to fall. No birth certificates, no old room, just the ravings of a long dead veteran tearing holes into his mind. He'd take the Malenfers' dinner, dry his clothes, and apologize for the misunderstanding. Clear out after breakfast and book himself into an institution.

"*This*" – Arthur jabbed a finger at the wall opposite – "was my old room."

"Well, there's got to be an explanation." *I've gone mad*, he thought to himself. *That's what's going on here.*

He had a closer look to please Arthur. The light from the landing was just enough to make out the line of something – an edge perhaps? In the light of day the velvet paper would have convinced the eye there was nothing, but the long shadow that was thrown down the hall caught on the tiny ridge under the covering.

"Just a minute." He took out his pocket-knife. The blade slipped into the paper. Soon enough he had cut the shape of a door where before there hadn't been one.

"Why do you think they'd do that, Dermot?"

"It's your family, mate. Let's find out."

The handle to the door had been removed but the mechanism remained, keeping the spring lock shut. Dermot located it with his fingertips and then wedged the blade in tight. "Let's hope they haven't nailed it shut or we'll need a battering ram." The lock turned, clicked, and opened inwards, making a hole in the once solid wall. They entered and Dermot closed it behind him, with the air of the conspirator. Whatever the reason for hiding the room, he knew he wasn't invited.

"Should have brought a candle," he said helpfully; the room was inky opaque. Gradually his eyes adjusted, as he'd known they would in time. He made out the sketch of a bed that seemed drawn in indigo lines. And there was a chair, and there a dresser, and over to the side a desk. It was cold in the room, a stale cold, and it was noisy, noisy too. It was loud like he hadn't heard in the hall; a noise that became intrusive. The rain and wind played like a snare against the pane of a window. Arthur opened the drapes but got little more light as the moon was behind the clouds.

Dermot risked a match, and saw the room in color. He couldn't shake an eerie feeling. Partly it was the suspense of a forbidden room, but it was also in the arrangement of things. Bed sheets crisply folded back, and on the pillow folded pajamas. A trio of what looked to be dolls laid out in parallel, all turned to face away. He lifted an edge of the dustsheet that was draped over top of the dresser. On it he found a man's coiled belt and a handful of change and papers, a packet of half empty cigarettes, and a rosary wound around a crucifix. Personal items, but nothing scattered – everything stacked perfectly. This wasn't a spare room at all – he stood in a museum. The precision with which he saw everything laid out made the hairs on his neck rise straight.

"What am I looking for, Arthur?"

Arthur didn't say a word in answer. He hadn't moved since they'd first entered, as if he were soaking it up. He raised one hand and pointed in answer to Dermot's question.

"You left them in the wardrobe?" He opened the door wide enough to see shirts still on their hangers.

"Behind it."

Dermot put his shoulder down and wrestled the tallboy aside. On the wall behind he found a loose join between two planks of wainscoting.

"Remove it and reach inside."

Dermot teased the board back and felt inside, discovering the edge of an envelope, which he withdrew.

"Open it."

"This is everything?"

"That's it all."

"You want to sleep in here tonight, Français? Seems like they were expecting you."

But Arthur wasn't laughing.

"Shall I bring your dolls back at least? Maybe a comfy blanket?"

"What dolls? What are you talking about?"

Dermot reached to pick one up, but recoiled when he turned it over. The toy on the bed looked back at him with hollowed peeling eyes.

"The love of God." He stumbled back.

Three mummified newborns, side by side – three skeletal swaddled infants. One had rolled, disturbed by Dermot, and it drew his genuflection. Its mouth was set in a frozen suckle; tiny milk teeth fixed in a cry. Its lips were bared, withered and drawn, its gums eaten away by time. Dead these many years it was, frozen in an animate hunger.

"What the hell are these?" Dermot recovered, lifting himself from the floor. He had dropped his match and it had gone out. His hands shook as he lit another. "What are they doing here?" He couldn't escape his initial horror.

Arthur moved up close to the babes and reached out a hand to touch them. "Poor little things. I'm really not sure. They're tiny little children."

"Don't touch them."

"They died long before I went away. I've never seen them before."

Dermot wanted to believe him. "This room is a bloody museum. Is this what you do for all your dead relatives? Is this how she fills this place here?"

"Mother must have had the room sealed up."

"But who are the children, Arthur?"

"I don't know. I really don't. Why would she put them in here?"

The conversation had to wait, owing to a noise from the hallway. Someone or somebodies were coming along, talking as they approached. Dermot snuffed the match and crouched low beside the door, keeping an ear open for danger. Dermot was no lawyer — being discovered wandering the halls, he figured, was little more than an inconvenience, but breaking into a room full of dead babies? How do you explain that away? The voices came closer, and he made out two people.

"... it's a fact, she did," said the one. It was a woman's voice, and though Dermot wasn't sure, it sounded like the housekeeper Berthe.

"Well, she's more fool for it. But she'll set them right. You see if she don't. You know the old bird always will, there's no getting around her."

Dermot didn't recognize the man's slang tongue and he struggled with its French colloquialisms. He tried for a second to peer through the keyhole, forgetting it was papered over.

"And what about that new fella, the one who sent them the telegram? He's all polite and ingratiating but he's common as anything, you can tell. And how come he shows up now, I ask you?"

The pair of them had come to a stop, right outside the hidden door-frame. Dermot held his breath as he listened, but the illusion of the unbroken wall held.

"I tell you why he shows up now." Dermot judged the man older. His voice was more guttural than Émile's. "He's a squeezer is why. Simonne being in the newspapers, you knew they'd start to show up. He's the first of many, mark my words, out trying his luck for an earner." He had a callous vindictive tone and a tongue like a paring knife. "Lift anything he can and feed his face, then get a few francs to push on. You keep an eye on him. You watch him."

"He said he knew Arthur, though."

"*Said* he did. And maybe he did. I'm sure Arthur knew lots of soldiers. What does that prove? Chain him up is what I'd have done. Thrown the bugger out."

"Gustave," Berthe objected.

"Sponging thieves. Bloody foreigners. Send the lot of them back home."

"What about that other thing?" Berthe turned the conversation. "Has Madame said anything more?"

What was discussed after that, Dermot never found out, for the conversation and the servants moved out of earshot. He lifted the wardrobe back, but could not touch the infant – he balked at touching the child.

"Let's get out of here, Arthur. I think I've had enough."

They fled, Dermot knowing he could do nothing about the cut wallpaper. It would only be a matter of time before someone discovered the invasion. But he had the birth certificates. He would tell the Malenfers tonight at dinner. He would eat his fill and discharge his promise and be gone from this place in the morning.

Chapter 14
Message from the Grave

Where Dermot had lost the time he did not know, on the sortie to Arthur's old room or engrossed in his thoughts. Tidying himself as best he could, he remembered to pocket the envelope.

Dinner had begun. The disheveled new arrival held the floor, all eyes on him. Madame with Sophie beside her, and Simonne, he was glad to see.

Madame had not risen from her seat as the other Malenfer women had done. She lowered her spoon and glared at him the full length of the table.

"We're late," he said, redundantly.

"We?" said Arthur, shaking his head.

Sophie and Simonne retook their seats on either side of the table, a signal for their tardy guest to enter and join them. Dermot gave Simonne a little smile hello.

"Keep those birth certificates in your pocket." Arthur volunteered his advice. "Better to wait for them to ask you." Had Simonne cocked an ear at his whispers?

Madame motioned for dinner to continue.

A ruddy-faced woman bearing a cauldron of soup lumbered towards Dermot; she looked like the sort that could split firewood using only her bare hands. He guessed creamed potato with something green, judging from the plates of the others. The handles must have been hot to the touch – her chubby fingers gripped towels.

Dermot felt uncomfortable being served. In the army everyone stood in line with their Dixie cans held out. In Paris he'd eaten at laborers' cafés or out of tins up in his room. There seemed too much cutlery and an abundance of plates for one man having dinner.

Cook hovered by his chair with the big pot held aloft. Dermot was left to wonder how the soup would fill his plate. The assorted spoons confused him. Feeling embarrassed, he was about to ask when another servant approached him.

The man's limp and his gargoyle face repelled and drew him at once. Dermot stared openly at the scars that disfigured the man. They were gas burns, he decided, the kiss of a modern war. Every soldier dreaded the poison that blistered the eyes and mouth. Moist skin was its favorite target, which made the lungs so vulnerable. Dermot heard the man's rasping breath and knew that he was right. *Poor bastard.* He felt for the man. He thought of the hole at the end of the tunnel and the miners filling it in.

"Dichlorethylsulphide." It was Madame's crisp voice. "That's what the chemists call it. Isn't that right, Gustave?"

The footman endured Dermot's inspection without word or look of complaint. He presented a polished ladle and commenced to serve soup from Cook's copper cup.

"Yes, Madame. That's what they say. Mustard gas as to the rest of us." Dermot put the face to the voice he'd overheard outside Arthur's room.

"Start from the outside, work your way in." Arthur helped him out. Dermot settled on a spoon.

It was Sophie who opened the questioning. "Is your room to your satisfaction, Mr. Ward?"

"Wonderful, yes. Very well arranged." *What do you say to such a question?* "And I like the resident mammal very much. I think you should feed him a little more often and take him out for walks." He tried to make light. Simonne smiled.

"Do you like this dress, Mr. Ward?" Simonne asked the question.

"Simonne!" her mother chided. Dermot blushed despite himself.

Simonne sat forward in her chair to give him a better view. It was a lovely dress, but she could have worn anything.

"I recognize the style somewhat..." He waved his hand to summon the word but was never going to get it.

"It's a Jean Patou, Monsieur Ward. It was my Grandmother's. Wasn't it, Grand-mère?"

"It is mine, you've got that part right. But it's not a Patou, it's too old. Silly girl."

"It is! You're just being spiteful. Did you guess right, Mr. Ward? Is that what you were thinking? Do you *like* dresses, Mr. Ward, as much as you like books?"

He nodded. He didn't think he should be having this conversation.

"I found it in an old wardrobe upstairs that someone had locked and forgotten. Did I not find it, Grand-mère? You thought it had gone, didn't you? Despite the color, I like it."

Madame said nothing further but continued to eat, slowly, methodically, observing.

"Grand-mère has lots of pretty things," Simonne confided.

As is often the case between the generations, Simonne seemed to have an ease with her grandmother that Sophie could not manage. Simonne's mother looked horrified at her daughter's exhibition. Dermot tried to reconcile Simonne's humor with the agitated girl who'd fled the library. She'd either had a glass too many or was trying too hard to change his impression.

"I find all the secrets, don't I, Grand-mère?" Simonne boasted. "Nothing here is hidden from me long. Can you believe Grand-mère wore this thing, Mr. Ward? She must have been something! Were you something in your day, Grand-mère?" She looked now at her grandmother.

"In my day!" Half a smile slid out from under Madame's mask, the first Dermot had seen from her. "What cheek, young lady! And it's a Poiret, not a Patou, you silly girl, though I'm sure Mr. Ward doesn't care."

"It looks like one, at any rate. So it's a Patou if I say it is."

"That's quite enough. Please, Simonne." Sophie was uptight.

"When was it you were drafted, Mr. Ward?" Madame moved the conversation on.

"I wasn't, Madame. I enlisted."

"Oh, I remember, our Foreign Legion, you said. When was that, did you tell us?"

"July 2nd, 1914. I wanted to join up with France."

"And what would possess you to do such a thing? What was the matter with your own country? Were you running away from something?"

He didn't immediately answer. Dermot felt uncomfortable and clumsy. The impolite curiosity of his hostess was bad enough, but he caught the eye of the fey Simonne and it served to unsettle him further.

Yet there was something more. Something about the room itself that was making things more of a problem. Akin to the vexing scale of the house, it took him a moment to peg it. As a salvage party stumbles upon a broken ship, so Dermot felt himself amidst the debris of the Malenfers. It was a broken family, a family that once had been but was no more. Three women garbed in mourning gathered around a table too large for them. They were the flotsam of a dynasty that drew sustenance off its memories. The room conveyed a sense of the many who were absent and would never return.

"No," he answered Madame at last. "No, I wasn't running away from anything. Perhaps I was looking instead... looking for something that was missing."

"And did you find it, Mr. Ward?"

He considered the question. "No. No, Madame, I did not." If the ladies were hoping for him to expand, he seemed reconciled to their disappointment.

Dermot had scarcely touched his soup. "I think we are ready for the meat," Madame bellowed. "Tell Cook to bring it!"

"The meat, Madame?" The footman confirmed, appearing at her elbow.

"That's what I said. Have you all gone deaf? I'm ready to eat immediately."

The staff scurried about clearing dishes. The scarred Gustave whisked off Dermot's plate with a wheeze that might have been a chuckle.

Madame took a sip of wine. "Mr. Ward, you have come a great way to see us. You said you knew my son Arthur? When, may I ask, did you meet him?"

"Verdun-sur-Meuse." Arthur and Dermot both said it together. The town was as synonymous with the year, 1916, as it was with the infamous battle.

"It was said to have been horrible." Simonne spoke with a hushed voice of reverence.

"Verdun saved Paris," Madame pronounced.

Dermot looked at Simonne through eyes pained by history. "Our side and the Germans ground away at each other for around about a year. If we had lost, Paris would have fallen. Three hundred thousand dead and half a million wounded."

"You are counting the Germans too, Mr. Ward."

"As I recall, Madame, they were there." He continued to Simonne. "General Nivelle had command. He told us that 'They will not pass' and put us in the line."

"He kept his word."

"Yes, Madame. He did that, at least."

"And what did you do in the battle, Mr. Ward?" Simonne was clearly curious.

"I was a sapper, Mademoiselle. A *pionnier*. A digger, a tunneler," he explained. "My job involved blowing things up. My unit was assigned to a part of the line where your uncle happened to be stationed. We became close friends."

"We heard little from him," said Madame.

"I don't think he was much of a writer."

"What was he like, my uncle?" asked Simonne. "What did you think of him?"

Dermot did not look at Arthur as he spoke, but the words came from the heart. "He was a very brave man and he was very smart, and he looked out for his soldiers. His men respected him greatly, as did I, and in that place and at that time there was no greater compliment."

"And what of his death, Mr. Ward?" Madame Malenfer wanted more.

"I was with him at the last."

The answer froze Madame, who said nothing for a minute. Perhaps she thought of a little boy who had grown up and gone away, or perhaps she thought of a grown-up son lying struggling in pain. Perhaps she thought of nothing at all, and so was able to endure it the better. Whatever was going through her head, she eventually resolved it.

"How did he die, Mr. Ward? How did my son meet his end? Was he brave at the very last? Was it quick and painless?"

Arthur stood ashen-faced, as if dreading what would come next.

"He died like all the rest. What would you have me say, Madame? I hope the end brought him some peace."

They squared off. *If she thinks me evasive or impertinent, what of it? I've had enough of lies.*

"You leave me to think the worst."

"Is there a good way to die?"

"There is honor. And there is courage. And bravery."

"He had those. I hope they bring you comfort."

"Then he died doing his duty? It gives me solace to think so."

"Yes. Be assured on that."

"Not the worst then. You are embittered, Mr. Ward? Does it come from having no country of your own for which you were able to serve?"

"Forgive me, Madame, if my candor aggravates. Embittered, you ask? Yes. I admit as much, but it comes from seeing good men die for other fools' illusions."

"Well, I am surprised my son took you to heart. You have unconventional opinions, Mr. Ward."

"I arrive at them honestly enough."

"And you are tactless in their expression."

Dermot bit his tongue. *She's a grieving mother and widow.*

"You didn't know him very long, Mr. Ward, if you met him at Verdun."

"Time is relative in the trenches, Madame. I knew your son for a hundred years."

Madame did not seem to take his tone well; he wondered if he should care. She had started to annoy him, and he knew the reason why: She was the kind that treated loss like a commodity and wanted it all to herself.

"If you say so," she retorted. He knew he hadn't won a friend. "Then might I ask about the news that you wished to bring to my attention? Are you willing to talk about that now? What is the purpose behind your thoughtful visit and the pleasure of your company?"

She was riled, her feathers ruffled, but Dermot couldn't help that. Dermot looked over to Arthur and the big man slowly nodded.

"As you wish, Madame." Dermot put his hands on the table. "I can tell you now if you wish it."

"Speak plainly."

Her hospitality, it seemed to him, had almost reached its end.

"Very well."

The attention of all the Malenfer ladies were now fully settled upon him, their ears keened, their senses tuned, as were those of all the servants.

"I was entrusted by your son, Madame, with the care of some official documents."

"Indeed," she said. "And what, might I ask, is the nature of these documents of which you speak?"

"I obtained them only now. I have a confession to make. Until today I had only the word of your late son concerning their nature and purpose. I am ashamed to admit that I failed him in my belief as to their existence and their value. I doubted him, and I have been proved wrong. Everything he told me was true.

"He entrusted me with the documents' location and told me to give them to you. He told me that you would know their worth and that you would put things right for him. I survived my war, Madame, and I should have discharged my duty earlier. I am sorry that I did not, and I hope that somewhere he forgives me.

"I am late to dinner because I snuck life a thief in the night through your house. Only one hour ago I got entry into Arthur's old room. He had told where to look. I thought the documents fictitious, their existence unreal. But on that point I erred. I have read them, and I ask you now to do the same. Think no worse of me than I hold myself – I who doubted a friend."

Dermot produced the envelope without further explanation, its cover slightly stained by damp but otherwise undamaged.

Madame, at its sight, did not seem quite so sure of herself. "You said you got this from Arthur's room?"

"I did," he answered. "This very evening."

The footman limped forward, bearing a tray, and received the envelope from Dermot. He dragged himself behind a frozen Sophie and offered it up to his mistress. The exercise seemed entirely absurd, for she sat not five feet away. Madame received it in both her hands from off the tendered platter. She turned the envelope over, once, then lifted the flap at the back.

She read the contents, then read them through again. The cursive scrawl of officialdom had taken Dermot a while to decipher. The seals and stamps of bureaucratic pomp were evident to everyone. Simonne looked keenly interested; Sophie appeared pained.

"Mother?" Sophie inquired. Madame had paled. The elder Malenfer folded the papers up before dropping them onto the table.

"I apologize, Mr. Ward. It would appear that you are who you said. I will have to get these authenticated, but it makes sense in a number of ways."

"Arthur told me that his own father arranged for everything."

"Well. That might be so. I can't see how it might happen otherwise."

"He said he did it to keep them safe. Something about a family curse..."

"Do not speak of that here!" Madame was adamant and shrill. Sophie flinched visibly. Dermot checked his flow of words and spoke no further on it.

Madame's anger seemed to fade. She sat back in her chair and breathed deeply.

"Mother?" Sophie asked. "Might I?" In the absence of objection, Sophie picked up the papers and read. "Why, these are birth certificates, Mr. Ward! Birth certificates of Pierre and Émile. But why would Arthur have something like this hidden away in his things?"

"Oh, don't be dense, Sophie." Her mother was sharp.

"Good Lord! It states Arthur as their natural father. But how could this be the case?"

"The usual way, I suppose," Madame chided. "Try to exhibit some imagination."

Simonne looked quite amazed.

"If it's true," Madame went on, her mind seemingly flying through the connotations, "then the Malenfer name still lives on. And I have myself two new grandchildren."

"I hope the news is well received, Madame." Dermot sensed there was much here he was missing.

"I seem to have lost my appetite," Madame announced, though not without some cheer. She rose to her feet. "I'll take that back, please." She lifted the envelope and contents. "I am going to retire early. There is much here to consider."

The table rose to its feet and there was a stirring among the servants. *Their* ears would have heard everything. *Their* eyes recorded all. News had been promised, news was expected, but nothing like this had been foreseen. Madame hurried out and was gone.

Dermot felt somewhat foolish. "I hope I haven't upset anyone," he said, retaking his seat amidst all the hubbub.

"I've got two cousins!" said Simonne. "I can't wait to tell them!" She seemed innocent and gay.

"It might not be true, dear," cautioned Sophie.

But it was. Whatever the consequences might be.

Arthur stayed alone in the dining room, long after everyone had gone. His children would now find their place, of that he felt quite certain. Yet the sharing of his secret brought no hint of peace to him. Instead a dormant fear was stirred: *What if Father was right after all?*

Chapter 15
Downstairs

IN THE KITCHENS AT MALENFER MANOR, THE NEWS ARRIVED LIKE A spilled platter.

"Get down there, girl. Tell Cook." Gustave dispatched Alice the maid, who didn't need further encouragement. Alice was a local girl: fresh, cheerful, and dim. Cook was fit to throttling her for details she couldn't give.

"And who said that? The exact words again!"

"The new fella, Cook. You know 'im, yes you does. He's handsome too, leastways Mary says so, and I'm not mindful to disagree."

"The words, girl! The words!'"

"Birth certificates he had. Said it was Master Arthur in the war had told 'im where to find 'em. And he'd gone and opened the room – you know, that one that Madame had shut in and boarded. Gustave, I mean Mr. Durand, no disrespecting him. Mr. Durand says he's going to put a spike in it now. Shut it up proper, he says. He's been told to plaster it over too, cover it, though he might be making that up. Do you think? He says that anyone so much as thinks of going in for a peek best pack up their bags before trying. Done and gone, that's what he says, and I believe him when he's angry."

"Yes, yes!" Cook shook poor Alice; her prodigious strength rattled the girl. "Forget about that. But what did Madame say about the boys? Tell me this very instant."

"'It makes sense in a number of ways,' that's what she said when she read it. 'It makes sense in a number of ways.' Then she gets up and goes."

"Blessed saints, can you believe it? Madame's for believing it's true!" Cook was turned over. The idea pushed her conception of credulity and set her world to spin. Alice's bruised arm was let go.

"You'd better start believing it. It's happened!" Gustave's voice boomed. The footman hadn't waited long. He'd stayed till he was sure there was nothing else to learn and then had come downstairs sharp.

Word had spread; they were funneling in, the kitchen their destination. The remarkable had happened at Malenfer.

"Fetch a bottle of wine!" Berthe was right behind him, struggling with her apron. "Dear oh dear, whatever next. Where are the boys at now?"

"Madame Marchand?" Alice addressed the housekeeper.

"What is it, girl?" said Berthe.

"Does this mean that Pierre and Émile will be moving upstairs right away?"

"Oh, bless you dear. I can't say. I have no idea what's to happen. Can you imagine such a thing? To think of their poor mother."

"I can say what's to happen, you damned fool girl. It means a damn sight more than a change of bedroom – this changes everything. It means their mother was a whore, and that they were lied to, and that they got nothing but toil as reward."

"Gustave, you can't say that!" Berthe was scandalized.

"Why not the truth? Out with the truth, I say. Upstairs pulled the wool over their eyes, but today it's going to change."

"What's going on? What's happened?" Émile appeared, fetched by Mary, his jacket undone in his hurry. He feared that someone was hurt, given the commotion – the maid had said nothing beyond her summons. He saw them all here, the regular staff, those that had the running of Malenfer: Gustave and Berthe, Mary and Alice, Cook and Pierre his brother. Where was his brother?

"Pierre! Where is Pierre? Is he hurt? Has something happened?"

"Oh, something's happened all right, my boy. Prepare yourself for a shock."

Pierre walked in, to Émile's relief. "What's going on in here?" he asked. "A regular conspiracy by the looks of it. What are you all up to now?" Pierre looked like he might have been sleeping. He smelled of drink, his clothes were ruffled, his eyes were bloodshot and swollen.

"Madame Marchand," Émile addressed Berthe, "Would you explain what's going on?"

"Boys, it's about your mother…"

"More about your father," Gustave imposed.

"… it's about your mother, and how you were raised, and what happened to your father."

The kitchen, so often a place of warmth, took on a chilly air.

"What about our father? What business is that of yours?" Pierre, perhaps with the grape in him, was caustic with his words.

"Mind your bloody manners. Just because you're a Malenfer bastard, don't make you better than us."

"What did you say?"

"You heard me."

"No, Gustave! Pierre, calm down."

"Why is he saying that, Berthe?"

"Because it's true, you selfish mongrel. Your whore mother passed it around."

Pierre's punch would have landed hard if Émile hadn't stopped his arm.

"You shut your mouth, you twisted old sod. I won't hold back from beating a cripple, even one as pathetic as you." He tried to push his brother away but couldn't shake him off.

"Don't fight. No! Please leave him."

"What's he on about, Berthe?"

"Upstairs... Madame... Boys, they have what they think is your birth certificates, and Arthur Malenfer is listed as your father."

There was a moment when the kitchen fell silent but for the noise of a body at rest: the gentle sputter of a kettle of soup; the popping of wood in the stove belly.

"It can't be true."

Gustave snorted.

"It must be very hard to accept, boys, but Madame believes it herself. Don't go thinking the worst of her. Madame didn't know herself." Berthe was near tears, and Émile broke from Pierre to console her.

"How is that possible?" Pierre challenged.

"It's true, Pierre, I heard it. That visitor had the news."

"The Colonel it was who fixed things up between Arthur and your mother, that's how he told it," spoke Alice. She'd taken her time collecting all the plates, and had overheard Dermot speaking to Sophie.

"And the Colonel arranged for all this?" Émile was stunned.

"Arthur went along with it. The idea was to keep the both of you safe."

"To hide us and keep his shame a secret! I think that's what you mean." Pierre was dark with aggression.

"To protect you from..." Berthe interrupted. "Well, you know."

"From what?"

"The Curse."

"Alice!"

"Well, he said as much, Madame Marchand, begging your pardon, you knows you did. He knew. It was his words, honest, the stranger's words. I didn't make 'im say it. I swear."

"So what are you waiting for, you little Lords? Shall I fetch your new silk pajamas and go and run you a bath? Perhaps you might ring and I'll bring you a brandy before wiping the pair of your arses," Gustave baited.

"You watch your mouth, I've warned you already! Any more of that talk from out of your mouth and I'll give you a nice broken lip."

"You see?" Gustave played to the room. "You see why they were hidden away? A whore of a mother and this is what you get. Can you imagine this one running the place?" Pierre hit him hard on the mouth. The Malenfer footman landed on his backside.

"You had that coming!"

Berthe was wailing. The maids jumped in to stop it; Cook wrung her aprons to end it. Nothing rougher took place, however, for the wounded Gustave did not rise to defend himself. He smirked and wiped his wound, a red smear over the back of his hand.

"Yes, Pierre Malenfer, this place has been ruled before by those as brutish as you, but none of them, from what I know, were ever quite as stupid. For the sake of the estate, and for all of us downstairs, I hope you never inherit. I trust Madame will see your quality and leave you as her rent collector. You're barely fit for that. Now get out of my way." He rose to his feet. "The little people have a dinner to clear up."

Gustave made his way to his room at the end of the servants' hallway. His leg had been giving him pains all week, and he was fearful of worsening arthritis. His lip had swollen – little bastard – he touched it and it proved tender. He'd give it a wash in salted water before he turned to bed.

Gustave worried about Madame. She had taken to her room after dinner was interrupted and she had neither asked nor sent for anything. He had paid a call from curiosity, bearing warm milk, but even that overture Madame had spurned.

"No, Gustave. Leave me be. I want peace for the rest of the day."

After the 'to do' in the kitchen earlier, he'd finished up the last of his duties. He'd dug out old clothes that Berthe was looking for, and then he'd waited for upstairs to retire. He was on his way to his rooms, and was almost at his door.

"There you are. About time too. I've been waiting for you, dog."

Pierre. Pierre Malenfer. Sodden with drink. A nearly empty wine bottle dangled from his hand; the blowhard could barely stand erect. Gustave decided that if the pup swung now, he'd give him a beating to remember.

"What do you want?" he grumbled. "Are you worried we haven't made you a room upstairs yet, or are you scared that the curse will get you? Get out my way, you unworthy drunk. I'm going to my bed."

Pierre blocked him with an arm.

"Steady, boy," warned Gustave.

"Shut up, old man. I want you to listen to what I've been thinking."

"Can't take long then. What is it?"

Pierre missed or ignored the insult. "I'm a Malenfer. Do you hear me, old man? Today I've become a Malenfer. Madame and everyone knows it now, and I have more rights than her daughter to the title. *I am the son of her first-born son, which means I am going to inherit.*" He toasted the long-serving servant.

"You've got a brother, bastard, or have you forgotten that with your manners too?"

"And when I run this place," Pierre carried on, "when I run this place, and I'm in charge, I just want you to understand something. You think you're Madame's pet, but you are no friend of mine, old man. I'm going to throw you out on your ear, I want you to know that now. No pension. No home. No nothing. Out you go like the bad dog you are. How much have you got in your savings?" Pierre laughed. "How do you think you'll find work elsewhere? A broken and crippled old man. That's all. I just wanted you to know that, to think about that, so you can sleep all the better for knowing. Things will change soon, and I'm sick of your face. Now run along, dog, to your kennel."

Pierre staggered off.

Gustave waited alone for a moment and then slowly made his way to his room.

The wine was talking, he knew as much, but there was far too much truth mixed in with it. Gustave bathed his broken lip in the stinging solution; if he'd had a wife she might have done better. The Malenfers were all he had. He had served them all his days.

Gustave didn't know it, but he wasn't alone in finding sleep difficult that night.

Chapter 16
Lay of the Land

ON MOST NIGHTS SLEEP CAME FLEETINGLY TO DERMOT, AND WHEN IT came he would dream, and when he dreamed his war returned – there were no other dreams for him. The scenes would vary at the start; happy days and boring days and fearsome days between. But no matter how his dreams began, they would always end the same. And then he'd be back, beside that hole, for all his dreams led there.

He would see it in the black and white of a clicking newsreel that he watched alone from the second row. Sometimes he'd scream and sometimes he'd plead, but mostly he'd watch it and tremble. The man that worked the projector never gave him a care – he played the same reel again. Over and over, the chattering film would tick by once again. Dermot would watch as down he went, back inside that hole. Down once more into that tunnel, down into the void below.

Dermot jolted awake. He was feverish, breathing hard. He could feel his heart still battering, trying to escape his chest. He was grateful to be pulled back out but was shattered with fatigue. Every night it happened, every night the same, evicted from the earth's dark womb to gasp his breaths awake. Reborn, he rose from the couch, the long lonely hours still ahead.

Arthur was settled in the long chair, smoking his pipe contentedly.

"What are you thinking about?" Dermot bothered him.

"This is my first morning back home, Irlandais. I'm thinking about that a little. But mostly I wonder about Pierre and Émile. My boys have been occupying my thoughts."

"They're handsome fine boys. Not at all like their pa."

"This is their first morning too. They'll know by now. The house will be alive with it. They'll have gone to sleep knowing. *What do they think of me now? What kind of father was I to them? Will they ever forgive me?* These are the selfish things I ponder. I'm a selfish man, Dermot. I know it."

"Get away. You've done all right."

Arthur continued. "Do you know, I half thought that by doing this I might end up moving on."

"Moving on?" Dermot was muddy with sleep, but he had half an ear open. "What are you on about?"

"I had to do this, I knew I did. I had to let my boys know. But now what? Is it done for me? Yet I don't see any change from yesterday; everything continues as before." Arthur's pipe had gone out. He cleaned out the bowl with a short-bladed knife and refilled it before he continued. "I thought this would resolve things, Dermot, for me as well as them. It sounds crazy, but I thought this one act would fix everything. Does that sound like crazy talk to you? I don't know. Perhaps it is. But what is stranger is the reality I am left with. Tell me, Dermot, what should I do?"

Not getting an answer, Arthur looked over, but Dermot had nodded off.

Dermot woke up, stiff on the couch.

The day had broken, cloudy and wet. Arthur was gone. Dermot wasn't worried; a housemaid must have come because a fire was set, and Dermot assumed that he'd slid out the door. He had family to see, after all. There was a bowl of water set out for shaving, barely warmer than the cold from the tap. It would have been hot an hour earlier, but Dermot didn't object.

Dermot's proposal that he leave in the morning had been refused out of hand last night. On the matter, Sophie and Simonne had been adamant: Dermot was simply the messenger, and as a friend of Arthur's he must oblige them and stay, and do them the honor of his company. A few days at least, they had insisted, anything less would be rude. Dermot would see the estate – horseback was suggested – and he raised no further objections. "Some of the Colonel's old riding gear," was the answer to the question. He saw it now, stacked and folded, waiting for him on a chair. Along with the change of clothes had come a tray of breakfast things: coffee – real coffee, not chicory – warm bread, and raspberry preserves. Was that a bar of chocolate wrapped in paper? *Chocolate!* Dermot ate voraciously, licking jam off his fingers. He rubbed his stubble chin. A razor had been furnished with the water. A little smoother and much fuller, he turned to the matter of dress.

His shirt went over a muscled chest that banded him like iron, a knotted strength that peacetime and rationing hadn't managed to soften. The tweed jacket he'd been loaned proved tight – he left it unbuttoned – but the pants fit well enough. The late Colonel Malenfer,

Madame's husband, had been almost exactly his size. The Colonel had been fuller around the middle than Dermot was right now, but Dermot didn't judge. He knew that with a few quiet years he would struggle to get them on.

Daylight changed Malenfer. It was no longer a groaning, drafty stack of stones. Above the ground floor it was full of windows – the fields ran up to its walls. It was airy, open, and full of sky despite the grayness of the clouds. *Imagine this place when the sun is out. Imagine calling this home.*

Below him, in the courtyard, Dermot could see Émile. Arthur's son, whatever had happened last night, was still playing at Malenfer groom. He was brushing down a spirited animal, a spritely chestnut mare. Dermot watched him unclip her halter from the cross-ties before leading her back to her stall. He had a comfort with the animal, an assured command, that Dermot respected and admired. Émile came back out and spread a blanket over a waiting horse's back, then lifted her leg with a trusting hand to check for any stones lodged in her hoof. The young man went about his daily work with a serious expression. If Émile had heard the news at all, he seemed stoic and resilient.

Simonne emerged from the house directly below him. She was masculinely dressed for a wet day's riding: a green twill jacket with a scarf at her neck, a hat and a crop in her hand. She wore high polished boots with a dull spur, and bore a cape or a blanket over her arm. For all the cloth that covered her up there was no escaping the woman beneath; her coat was tailored, her pants fit snugly, and her braids bounced with each step. Dermot watched with false detachment until she disappeared into the stable. He shook his head clear, like the chestnut mare, when the spell of her passing was broken.

Simonne; Émile; the horses; the family; the house; the farm; and the land. It was all so alive, Dermot mused, all so knitted together. He was glad he had stayed, he had to admit, he was glad that he'd agreed to come.

When Dermot got outside it was to join a small crowd, all in evident good cheer. Sophie raised a hand in greeting. "Good morning," she welcomed him.

"I'm sorry. I hope I'm not late again."

"Is it a habit of yours, Mr. Ward? Did they let you sleep-in in the army?" Around her bonnet was a wide silk ribbon of respectful mourning black.

"We never fought anyone till after ten. It was very civilized that way."

Simonne was already mounted, happy as a lark. She chatted to a young man who could only be Pierre. The brothers were both colored dark from a life spent out of doors. Pierre's horse tossed its head playfully, mimicking the rider it bore. The boys weren't as big as their father, but their hair certainly carried his curl.

"Good morning," Dermot hailed the assembly.

A chorus of "good mornings" returned.

"You slept well?" Simonne asked.

"Like a log. I haven't slept that way in months." No one liked a whiner. "I almost missed our outing, you know."

"Oh, we'd have sent someone to kick you out of bed sooner rather than later," she smiled. He liked her hair that way.

The housekeeper appeared with a basket.

"I'll take that, Berthe. Thank you." Simonne took it from her arm.

"But Mademoiselle?"

"It's all right, Berthe, I talked to Alice. I told her she won't be needed this morning. I told her to stay at home. I'll bring the lunch and set things out. No need to drag her out."

"Simonne, really.," Sophie clucked, but there wasn't a hint of fight.

"Bread, cheese, pâté, sausages, and wine." Simonne inventoried the contents. "Will that be good enough, Mr. Ward, or is there something particular you desire?"

"It all sounds mouth-watering." *She's something else*, he thought. Then, as an afterthought, "Is Madame coming?" Not seeing the elder Malenfer anywhere, he was starting to get his hopes up.

"I'm afraid Grand-mère has declined us the pleasure of her company today," Sophie passed on the reply. She held a dappled gray by the reins, the nose of which she rubbed. Émile was tightening the girth on it, and adjusting the occasional buckle.

"These days the old dear hardly sets a foot outside the walls." It was Pierre who piped up. "Too wet, too cold, too windy! Always some excuse." He had a denigrating voice that Dermot found grating.

"Show some respect." It was his brother, Émile.

Pierre gave his twin an annoyed look that Dermot observed but that his brother did not; Émile had moved on to adjusting the leaping horn that showed Sophie would be riding sidesaddle.

"We're going to head up to the abbey," Sophie told him. "What about you, Pierre?"

"I'd like to join you," answered the athletic youth, "but I have six overdues. They'll take me all over the estate."

Pierre was the Malenfer's factor, as Dermot had heard the night before. A factor liaised with the tenants on the estate, and was responsible for collecting their rents.

"We had a quarantine here until recently, Mr. Ward. You might have heard? Got all the schedules behind. You don't know how much you miss your freedom till somebody takes it away."

"Well, if you get through them early, Pierre, please come find us up that way."

"I don't see it as likely," he answered, "but I can't say no to that."

Dermot moved about the stables until he found what he thought was his horse. It was the only animal left in the stalls, and the reason for that was obvious – the old plug was a massive slobbering beast, and had clearly seen better days.

"He doesn't get ridden much, not since his youth." Émile apologized.

Dermot reached out a hand.

"Cyclone's his name," said Émile to introduce them.

Dermot recoiled in horror.

"Don't let that worry you, though," the groom reassured him, as he saddled and bridled the imposing mount with a quiet confidence. "He hasn't thrown anyone in years." Émile gave Dermot a leg up. "First time?" he asked, cocking an eyebrow.

Dermot shook his head. "Might as well be, though."

"Well, take him slow at first. He's usually friendly, it just takes a while to know him."

Dermot was not entirely comforted. *God almighty*, he thought to himself, *this is someone's idea of a joke*. But there was no backing out for him now. Simonne and everyone were watching him. He'd have to make the best of the show.

In his lifetime, Dermot had been on a horse a handful of times. He'd worked with the ponies at the colliery, but they were not for riding. He carried the suspicion of the ill-acquainted which the animal sensed immediately. Finding himself up on Cyclone's back he seemed suddenly very far from the ground. Dermot started to have his doubts, and the animal seemed to share them. He struggled to turn it to face the courtyard, and then it walked out by itself.

Arthur was there. He fell in beside him as Dermot wandered out into the square. "Do you think they know yet?" the big man asked him, nodding towards his boys. "The pair of them haven't said a thing. I've been watching them most of the morning."

Dermot was conscious of the group, and couldn't risk drawing attention. He answered Arthur with a shrug while wondering where the animal was taking him.

"No one's mentioned a damn thing, Dermot, and it's starting to annoy me. Here are my boys, going about their jobs as normal. It's not quite right. Is it?"

"Whoa, girl. Whoa."

"She's a boy horse, Dermot. Just show the creature who's boss. But the twins. Has really no one told them yet? I can't believe they don't know. What do you think we should do?"

Dermot had given up on the twins – his attention was all on his animal. The damn horse simply didn't obey and seemed to have little intention of stopping.

"Sophie. Simonne. None of them have breathed a word of it from what I've managed to hear or gather. But someone must have set them wise. Just ask them, Dermot, will you?"

"Ask them what?" Dermot was flustered. He didn't need other distractions right now, and Arthur certainly wasn't helping. The beast continued to walk on by itself, and Dermot was wandering with it.

"Sorry?" said Sophie, thinking he'd said something to her.

"Nothing," called Dermot, mumbling equestrian obscenities continuously under his breath.

"Firm with the reins," she said helpfully.

"Ask them!" Arthur was adamant as he followed beside the stirrup. "What do you have to lose?"

It was too much for Dermot.

"Hey, Émile," he called to the nearer of the twins. He felt closer to Émile somehow. The boy seemed more genuine, or it was his care for the animals, or it might have been he'd just known him longer.

"Monsieur?" The groom came over.

"Can you give us a hand here, mate?"

"Of course, Monsieur." Émile brought the horse to a halt.

"Oh, please!" Arthur berated him. "Where's your mettle, Irlandais?"

Seeing no one was looking, Dermot whispered a reply. "And what am I meant to say?" he told Arthur off. "'Émile, my friend, any guesses this morning on who your daddy might be?' You want me to get my head punched in? Is that what you want from me now?"

"Are you all right, Mr. Ward?" It was Sophie again, who seemed slightly concerned.

"No, no! Got it sorted!" He put a heel to the flank of his horse and left Arthur behind.

Soon after, all mounted and ready at last, the riders moved off. Dermot took one look back. There he saw the tall figure of Arthur standing by himself. He watched till they moved out of view and then wondered if he'd seen him at all. No sooner had they departed the gate than Pierre broke away by himself. He turned his horse west, towards the small bridge, and coaxed her into a trot. Pierre gave them a wave and in a minute, no more, he too was out of sight and gone.

Sophie, Simonne, and Dermot followed the road for a hundred yards before cutting off down to the right. The path here rounded behind the farmhouse, passed through a copse of willow that hugged a stream, and then emerged into the fields beyond. From here the ground rose gradually and left them more exposed. Luckily the wind had let off for the time, though it left a soft drizzle of rain.

"Are you taking the ridge route, mother?" Simonne inquired. Their destination was the abbey, just as Sophie had said.

"No, dear," her mother corrected. "I thought we'd keep to the lower woods and come at it from around the other side."

"It takes longer," Simonne pointed out.

"Yes, dear, but it isn't a race, and the trees provide some shelter."

Simonne didn't seem disappointed. She rode close by Dermot's side.

The path they followed wound back and forth as it traced the contour of the valley, and the rising land on their right hand side pushed them steadily over. If the valley floor looked tamed and kept, the hillside, in comparison, was wild; it had been turned over to grazing sheep, the scattered inhabitants visible in clusters. From up ahead, though out of sight, came the distant low of cattle.

The path for the moment was wide enough for three to ride abreast. Dermot took the middle spot with Sophie on his left. The ladies were polite hosts. They avoided the state of the local clergy and trivial neighborhood gossip, and generally eschewed topics that they felt Dermot was unfit for. They were charmed to find him in a curious mind, inquisitive about things in general, and he asked them a great many questions about their family in particular. He willfully acknowledged his ignorance on the subject of rural matters, and they happily spent an amusing hour filling his ears with details: lambing and contracted labor, grain tariffs and harvest schedules, the basic points of viniculture, and the perils of staff succession. Dermot learned the myriad details that are the workings of an estate. He was filled in on matters that had encapsulated rural life since back in feudal days. With half a lifetime spent underground, he amused the ladies with his questions. They laughed, just as Persephone might, at his blunders and amazement.

They passed alongside a vegetable garden overseen by a mossy glasshouse. There were stacks of pots and empty crates and bundles of tied-up cane.

"And that one?" he asked.

"It's a potato plant, or it will be, come the spring."

"But how do you know?"

"Now you *are* teasing me, surely?" When Simonne said it, he reddened.

He knew he'd taken a shine to her, and that she bore a certain charm. But what he couldn't fathom was the way *he* was behaving. She was seven years his junior, and they'd only recently met, so why did he feel like a blushing schoolboy whenever she was around? *I clearly need to think about this more.*

"Please, Mr. Ward." Sophie was inquisitive. "I am interested to know why you remained here in France, once the war was over. Are you not married?"

It seemed to Dermot that the small talk was over. "No, no. I have never had that particular pleasure myself."

"No family at all, then?" she continued.

"Siblings. I had a brother. And my mother. They're all doing well enough without me. I left home a long time ago." He didn't wish to expand.

"Well, even without a family to support, wouldn't events in your native Ireland have called for your attention?"

The comment earned Sophie a measure of Dermot's respect. The subject was unexpected out here in the French backwoods, but it was clear that Sophie had an ear to the ground for international events. Simonne looked confused.

"Oh, they have. Indeed they have. I follow developments with some interest." He elucidated for Simonne's benefit. "There's a growing independence movement in my own country, Mademoiselle. The party that champions that cause, Sinn Féin being their name, they recently won the election there, taking the majority of Irish seats."

"Sinn Féin?" The word sounded alien on Mademoiselle's tongue.

"Politics, Mademoiselle. A party made by Irishmen who want their own free country. *We ourselves* is what it means. Right now London rules all the land, and they're having nothing to do with it. So those Irishmen have refused to go to England to take the seats they won."

"You're not disinterested then," Sophie observed.

"No, I don't suppose I am. The British have ruled in Ireland for going on 800 years. Right now it looks as though things are about to change. Them that won the people's vote have met for an Irish assembly. It's the first of its kind, it is. They're calling it the Dail Eireann.

Their leader won't be there to see it, though, he's in a British jail. Éamon de Valera. That's the fellow's name."

"And what did he do to get himself in jail?" Simonne asked.

"Oh, they've had it in for him, you know, for quite a while already. There was a revolution in Ireland while the war was going on. Back in 1916, most of it in Dublin. He was a part of that. The Easter Rising it was called, and the British army put it down. A lot of men were executed for treason to the crown. De Valera only missed a firing squad because he was an American – born in New York City, he was, as Providence would have it.

"Anyway, as your mother was saying, Ireland right now is in flux, and an Irishman of any heart has an opinion either way. Right now in Paris, they're petitioning the Peace Conference for independence. Not that they'll get it, Britain won't have that, but still... at least they're trying."

"Yet you stay here with us? Happy to be here in France?" Sophie pressed him.

"I imagine that I'll return one day, maybe even soon." He'd answered her question honestly. "But for the moment I'm sorting myself out, and doing my duty to friends."

Sophie seemed to consider this and didn't pursue him any further. He used the opportunity to shift the conversation.

"And what about *you*, Mademoiselle? What are you interested in? What amuses Simonne?"

"Interested in? Why, lots of things." She seemed unfamiliar with talking about herself. "My future, I suppose."

"And what is there in Mademoiselle's future that interests her the most? If you don't mind my asking, of course."

Simonne wasn't shy to talk at all; she leapt at the opportunity. "It's a simple thing I covet, a small thing, Mr. Ward. Easier to say than it is to do."

"Certainly sounds intriguing. And what might that be, then?" Dermot noticed that Sophie too was paying keen attention.

"I want to make my own choices; I want my freedom. My freedom is what I want, Mr. Ward. I told you it was a small thing."

"A noble aspiration," he pronounced. He looked across at her; she seemed very serious, even tensing for a fight. "And what will you do with it when you get it, Mademoiselle?"

"You don't doubt me then?" She seemed surprised. "Or are you making fun?"

"Not in the least. Why should I? I asked the question."

"You think I'll get my way?"

"I see Mademoiselle getting whatever it is she sets her mind to do." She seemed pleased, flattered even, and she relaxed her defenses a little. "But supposing that you get your wish, what choices will you make? What life will Mademoiselle decide to live when she has the freedom that she wishes?"

She laughed then. "I don't know which I like the most: your impudence or your honesty." Their eyes met again. "But I like your questions, Mr. Ward, so I think that I will answer." Simonne drew up tall in the saddle before she spoke, and when she did she was animated and flushed with obvious excitement, as if this were a game they might be playing of make-believe and fancy. "I'm going to see the world, for one thing," she began. "I've only been to Paris, and it's very fine for sure, but I want to go to London and to see America too."

"Simonne!" her mother despaired, but her daughter paid no notice.

"I want to go where things are happening," she continued, "which isn't here."

"I wouldn't be so hard on this place," Dermot defended.

"Have you traveled, Mr. Ward?"

"I've been to London, at any rate."

"You've been?" She was excited to hear it.

"Worth a visit. But it's still a city like any other, I imagine."

"Then I think your imagination needs stretching." Once constructed, she wouldn't allow any mark on the picture she'd painted.

"You could be right," he conceded. "Full of shops and parks, and galleries and museums. Oh, it was fine, don't get me wrong, but I've always fancied the countryside."

"For raising a family in, Mr. Ward?" Sophie put in from over her shoulder.

"Well, eh… there are lots of advantages…" but Simonne saved him.

"I don't want to live here ever!" she announced. "And who mentioned anything about a family? We were talking about me, mother, and what I get with *my* choices. Now please leave poor Mr. Ward be."

He was grateful for her intervention and found her gentle teasing funny. "Very well. So Mademoiselle's going to see the world and enjoy her newly won freedom. All the finest cities in Europe, then America over the sea. What comes after that?"

"After?"

"You can have anything you want, Mademoiselle." And now it was her turn to redden.

"Robert's good fun," her mother interrupted. "Perhaps your fiancé will take you somewhere nice after the pair of you are married.

Why don't you ask *him* if he'll take you to America for your honeymoon? Would you like that, darling?"

"Robert!" Simonne spoke it like a rash. Nothing Dermot had heard to this point had pleased him more to hear.

"I want to be in charge of *my* life!" Simonne said. "I want to make my own decisions." She spoke it to the trees. Dermot read the subtext; this was a familiar appeal and one her mother was not happy hearing.

"Thing is," Dermot put in, trying to mollify them, "that a lot of advice folk hand out is often well meant. An experience shared is twice learned, and all that sort of thing."

"If you're trying to kiss up to my mother, Mr. Ward, you best save your breath and efforts," Simonne called him out. "Grand-mère signs the diktats here and maman follows orders. Just like everyone else." She spoke the last words wistfully.

Dermot couldn't see Sophie's face but felt embarrassed for both of them.

"I'm engaged to a man who loves me, Mr. Ward, and whom I find quite pleasant. My family encourages me in the match; I'm an animal at market. They worry at the price I'll fetch because I don't meet their conventions. They think I'm odd – a little strange – but I'm only what they made me." She brought her horse to a stop, and Dermot's halted also. Sophie's still walked on, away, lengthening their distance. "What should I do then, Mr. Ward? What do you think of my choices?"

Dermot didn't know what to say; his heart was in his throat. He found her vivacious and contagious and she scared him half to death. He couldn't help himself, he only knew he cared. He wondered if she had spoken the truth about her fiancé, and what she could mean by revealing it.

"Love as you please, Mademoiselle," he spoke from his soul, "and marry as your heart advises. I don't think anyone else has the right to decide your happiness." He blushed as he said it despite himself. He felt suddenly like he'd shown a hand of cards he should have better guarded.

"Well, exactly, Mr. Ward! Do you hear that, maman?" she shouted out ahead, and Sophie turned to listen. "Mr. Ward is a true French romantic, despite his awful accent!"

They passed loose stone walls and tight briar hedges that ran sporadically to their trail, and the scaffolding of vineyard turned to fields of plowed brown earth. Fallow ground awaited seed it would not see for months.

They followed the course of an angry stream with wood on either side, water churning as it drained the higher ground. Diluvial aggression taunted them and challenged them to cross.

They now reached a point where the bank sank down, and the river slowed and fell. The ladies coaxed their horses in, though Dermot could not see the gravel bed. Simonne stayed back and with her help, he won the other side.

Eventually the trees started thinning. They had gone half the circumference of the hill and were on its other side. They emerged into a glade. Within the clearing stood a grand oak tree, a solitary sentinel. Beyond it, Dermot made out the washed bones of a once impressive building – the remains of the Abbey of Saint D., as Simonne and Sophie had promised.

They had arrived.

Chapter 17
The Malenfer Curse

THE OAK WAS VENERABLE, A TWISTED MUSCLE OF LIMB AND TRUNK THAT thrust up from the grass. In leaf its canopy might have consumed the sky, but today its branches were bare. The tree was dormant – brittle and utterly dark. As they drew closer, Dermot saw the illusion for what it was. The tree was dead. It would not leaf again. It was too stubborn to lie down gracefully and admit its fate.

They dismounted at the tree's base, standing beneath the skeletal boughs, the Abbey in the distance. The blackened branches dripped with moss; the thick bark was peeled or fallen. The trunk was scaled with lichen and choking ivy had taken hold. The undergrowth, held back for generations, was fast reclaiming ground.

"You heard about our curse, Mr. Ward?" Sophie asked the question. "You alluded to it last night."

Dermot thought she was joking until he caught her look. Her mouth was tight, which spread wrinkles around her eyes.

"Your mother didn't wish to talk about it. Does that mean she thinks it's true?"

Sophie walked on, a little deep in thought, as if wondering where to begin. She didn't reply at once.

Dermot looked to Simonne, who remained quiet, close-lipped, and unmoving. She did not seem too happy.

"Do you spy that branch up there?" Sophie said finally, pointing up to a spot high above Dermot's head, where a thick limb was prominent, forked like a serpent's tongue. "Where you stand now, Mr. Ward, a young girl was once hanged; she was about an age with my Simonne. The horse that she had been lifted onto was pulled from under her. She swung. The rope drew tight around her neck. They did a poor job of it – that's what I was told. Her neck didn't snap, so she choked instead and thrashed for almost a minute. Almost a minute till it was done, when her brain was starved of air. I sometimes wonder how that felt for her and what she was thinking about."

"It doesn't sound like a nice way to go." He couldn't help looking up.

"The rope was tied to that very branch," she pointed, confirming his view. Sophie lowered her hand and continued to walk on slowly.

"A girl?" he said, "Why did they hang a girl?" Dermot moved a bit off to the side, away from under that fateful spot.

"A *witch* is what they called her, their excuse for what was done. She was a young woman, a Roma by birth, that's how the story goes. Sold as a servant to a wealthy family on a neighboring estate; she was very likely ignorant and almost certainly poor."

Dermot fought the urge to genuflect. He followed Sophie around.

"And is this where your curse came from? But what nonsense is that! What did she do to deserve her fate, this gypsy girl that was hanged?"

Sophie had approached the tree. She removed a glove and put her fingers up against the bark. She didn't immediately reply.

"You might have heard, Mr. Ward," Sophie said, resuming her story, "how the first years of our Republic were very difficult ones?"

Dermot nodded; he remembered his history from the army and the stories men told. It was a time when France was at war with its neighbors, but mainly at war with itself. The Reign of Terror with its short-spun trials and the busy guillotine.

"It was a troubled age," Sophie went on, "unstable, like our own. And there was much distrust throughout society... even among friends.

"You see the abbey in ruins?" she continued. Its chalky stone shell was clear from where they stood. "There was an accident there, a terrible fire. A dreadful accident that happened over a hundred years ago. Until that day there had been a handful of estates nearby, ownership all scattered about. Worried landowners, all of them, fearful of the new regime. But after that night there was only ours, the Malenfer Estate alone. All were consumed, except for our own, and our family prospered by it."

"What exactly are you saying?" Dermot read into her tone.

"On the night of the fire, it was said, you could hear the screams of the trapped from as far away as Chevecheix. I don't believe it, yet the wind has been known to carry a noise. Who knows if that was true?" Sophie put her glove back on and looked back into the branches. She moved away from the trunk once more and circled again around it. Dermot stood nearby, captivated. Simonne had scarcely moved.

"Can you imagine it, Mr. Ward? Please try. All the families gathered together in the abbey for a baptism, all except our own. Can you picture it? Just over there," she pointed again. "I was told that the leaves on this very tree – the living leaves, Mr. Ward! – they curled with the heat from that fire. They said that afterwards you couldn't lay a hand on the stones for a day, they were so hot. And that when the rains came the rocks cracked and the abbey fell in ruin."

A scene of desperation and wild panic filled Dermot's mind, people falling over each other, unable to escape their end. Such a noise might carry far, even through the centuries.

"Eighty-six people, Mr. Ward," Sophie continued, "twenty-two of them children. Then the Malenfer estate buying everything up afterwards. Our lands grew six-fold within a month of the tragedy of that fire."

"This really happened?" he said.

"We have the deeds," she replied. "They sold."

Dermot shook his head. "What of the witch? I mean, the girl you said was hanged."

"Élise Beauvais was her name, the unfortunate servant girl. She took her surname from her reputable family, the ones who had held the baptism. She watched them all die that day. She was there to watch them go."

"But why was she hanged?" He didn't understand. "Did she do it?" The thought seemed inconceivable; the whole thing didn't make sense.

Sophie took a minute before answering, as if carefully choosing her words. "We all have things we aren't proud of, Mr. Ward. Isn't that true of us all?"

Dermot flinched to hear her say it, and he thought again of the hole. *Can she know?* But there was no accusation forthcoming, only the lingering taste of his guilt.

"I had a relative who was head of our household just after the revolution; we were *noblesse militaire* back in those days: nobility from rank. Remember, Mr. Ward – we have always served.

"Understand that time!" she appealed. "Understand that we lived in some fear! There was a new order in France, and great danger in not conforming to its twisted notions of patriotism."

Dermot stood patiently as Sophie's passion grew.

"The servant girl calls him out. That's what she did. Old Malenfer stands under this very tree, this very tree!" Sophie seemed incredulous, amazed that such events might happen. "He's watching the abbey burn to the sky, and Élise Beauvais calls him out.

"'*Le Diable!*' she cries, and throws it in his face. She accuses him in front of everyone of setting the torch himself. She says that the pyre in which her family roasts is all of his handiwork: a murderous bonfire to Malenfer greed and to further Malenfer ambition.

"There is a crowd gathered here, helpless to do anything but watch. Can you see the immolation? And on sacred ground! The crowd stands and listens to the howling of those poor terrified souls, the damned that were trapped inside."

"Dear God," Dermot muttered, the thought of the poor trapped children, their frantic mothers by their side.

"Élise Beauvais calls Old Malenfer the Devil! Not *a* devil, you understand. *Le Diable!* She says he arranged for it all himself. That sort of talk wouldn't do, not back then. From a servant? Can you imagine? What would people say to such a thing? He couldn't let it go by.

"So he calls her a witch, says it is *she* that did it, that she is guilty of black magic against the very family that has taken her under its wing. Says they gave her good Christian care, but they brought a viper into their home. And then he demands a rope, and so a rope is found.

"He has her hanged for a witch, Mr. Ward. Right here on this spot. And all the while the flames of the abbey still cook the sky above."

"The good old days," said Dermot.

Sophie's voice dropped, the magnitude of the event free to speak for itself. "And a legend was born," she continued, "with the rope around her neck. Just before she passes to shadow, Elise Beauvais speaks.

"'*A curse on you, Malenfer!*' she cries out. '*A curse that is born in blood! Know that your name will shrivel and die, that your brood shall know no rest. The Devil always takes his own, and you were spawned from between his legs!*'"

"She said that?" Dermot was impressed.

"So legend goes."

"Well, you can see why she'd be upset."

He was affected by the dreadful tragedy and disturbed by the likely murder, but curses? Is that what Sophie really believed? *Superstitious nonsense!* Yet he remembered his strange night in Le Jardin des Cygnes. A night when his own belief in the world took a sudden dramatic swing.

A man who shares a train with a ghost but cannot believe in curses?

He felt the fingers of possibility creep inside his head, just as he had only the day before when he stood looking from that bridge. And as he conceded to the doubt, he suddenly felt cold within. The hair on Dermot's neck rose up and he looked into the branches.

"Malenfer ordered her body left hanging," Sophie continued. "She was denied a Christian burial and rotted where she swung. The animals eventually took her. That's the story that's been handed down."

Dermot turned to Simonne and watched her watching him. She had not said a word through it all, letting her mother talk on. Perhaps she'd listened to the legend retold countless times before?

"Don't be upset, Simonne." Dermot tried to cheer her, for she looked saddened by the tale. "If it did happen, it was all a long time ago." Simonne smiled at his kindness, but said nothing in return.

"Oh, it happened Mr. Ward," Sophie put him right, "but that's not quite the end. Our family has lived under that curse for over one hundred years. The Curse of that Beauvais witch girl. And her word has been good to form, for none of the Malenfer brood *has* known rest, just as she called down. Since that night there has not been one of our family who has died of honest old age – all of us have been taken early, and most in violent ways." She paused to let the words sink in.

"Ours *is* a cursed family, Mr. Ward, of that you can be sure. And when Michel passed away, so young, the last of our line passed with him. *Your name will shrivel and die,*" she echoed the witch's words.

"Except Émile and Pierre are Malenfers too," he pointed out.

"Indeed," Sophie replied. "You brought them that gift. And how do you think they feel about that?"

Dermot did not know what to say.

"Mixed blessings, Mr. Ward? You said last night my father had the children's identities hidden. Was he worried? I left the farm myself."

"But you came back," he said needlessly.

"What choice had I? We are fated, we Malenfers; it's what we are."

"You think the Colonel hid the twins to save them from a curse? You don't think his own reputation or that of his son had anything to do with it?"

"Your skepticism can be unkind," she bit back. "You don't think it's true? Over a hundred years, Mr. Ward! One hundred years. And all of us die early. Think of those boys now, think of the twins. Is that a trade worth making? A fortune they can lay their hands on in exchange for an early grave?" Sophie had gone full circle now around the once-great tree. She came slowly back to her horse and mounted in one fluid motion.

"*The Devil takes his own!* Do you think they thought about that last night? That was quite the news you brought with you, although how were you to know?"

She pushed her mare to a slow walk and turned her towards the abbey. Simonne made sure that Dermot was fine, and then they fell in together following. They parted to either side of the trunk and left the dead tree behind them.

They skirted the wreck of the abbey that stood up from the invading grasses, its broken walls a wind break for sheep that came inside to forage. Dermot could scarcely believe it had been standing a century before – the place seemed broken from antiquity, as if Frankish kings had warred there.

How fleeting, he thought, *is our mark on this world.* But the notion gave him comfort, for were not some things better forgotten? Their memory lost in history? Perhaps the abbey was one such place, and the curse that had sprung from its passing.

He cast around, half expecting to see the spirit of Élise Beauvais, her dark reproachful eyes watching somewhere from among the stones.

"Simonne!" Sophie called out, and Dermot was just quick enough to stop her fall from her saddle.

"Are you all right? What happened?" He strained to keep her up. Simonne jerked and shook, as if snapping awake, and once more regained her balance. She turned to look at him, her braids sent spinning.

"Don't you feel her?" her smooth lips asked, but he didn't understand.

She was pale. She blinked to clear her eyes as if she'd just been crying. He had a hand on her arm, but she pulled it away from him.

"I thought you had it too?" She sounded hurt.

"What's the matter, Simonne?" Sophie was at her side. "Are you ill? What happened?"

Simonne sat quiet and steady once more and looked only ahead down the road. Then she opened her mouth and spoke clearly and slowly, with a paucity of emotion. "The witch girl is here, mother; she's come back again. Another Malenfer will die soon, just like our Michel."

"Goodness, Simonne! Don't say such things!"

"Let's go home. Let's leave this place. Please, mother. I'm sorry we brought you, Mr. Ward. We'll have to forego our picnic."

They left the abbey behind them with the wind suddenly rising. Dermot caught a faint scent in the breeze: the bitter smell of burning.

Chapter 18
The New Malenfer

ON THEIR RETURN, THEY FOUND THE HOUSE IN AN ANXIOUS STATE OF confusion. They could see the front doors open and there was shouting from without and within.

"What's going on, Émile?" Sophie asked. The young man ran to meet them as they drew their horses up. Something was clearly wrong: His arms pumped like pistons as he crossed the cobbled square.

"Have you seen my brother?" He couldn't ask them quickly enough.

"No, not since this morning," she relayed. "What's happened? Is there trouble?"

"Pierre's horse came back, not half an hour ago." He took the reins from her as she dismounted.

"His horse?" Simonne questioned. "Then where's Pierre?"

Émile shook his head. "The horse came back riderless. I hoped he was with you."

"He never joined us, but there could be a hundred explanations," Sophie replied sympathetically, yet Dermot saw the fear on her face. Both were reminded of Simonne's chilling words when she'd had her 'turn' at the abbey.

Dermot could imagine a number of reasons why rider and steed had become separated, though none of them were good. As if thinking the same thing, the group of them looked to the small winter sun that was hiding low in the west. The light wasn't good and would soon be gone entirely. The sky was shrouded in the ashen cloud that had drizzled on them all day, and the estate was a vast area over which to look for one lone man. If Pierre was badly hurt or even knocked unconscious... this was no night to spend outdoors, injured or otherwise.

Their arrival galvanized the household. Gustave was just leaving, dispatched to raise assistance from the tenants who lived close by. Dermot resolved to join Émile. Arthur's son planned to retrace the route his brother had taken that morning, hoping that if Pierre had fallen, it would be somewhere along the way.

"What are you doing?" Dermot asked Arthur. He had seen the ghost emerge from the house and come across to join them. But as he watched him climb onto the horse he'd just left, he felt the need to inquire.

"What does it look like? That's my son out there!"

"You can't come with me! Where are you going to sit? On the back? You're barely going to fit!" Dermot, for the moment, was in no danger of being overheard. The ladies had gone inside, while Émile was busy swapping Sophie's tack, apparently intent on taking her horse for himself.

"I don't weigh a damned thing," Arthur said tersely. "What the hell's the problem? You've got plenty of room. If I could actually hold the reins, I'd be out there already. Come on. We're wasting precious time." He was clearly set on going, and Dermot found to his surprise that he was pleased for the company. He managed to relax. Having Arthur's ghost with him was a comfort he'd not have thought possible.

"I'm sure everything's all right." Dermot tried to console the anxious father. He didn't mention Simonne's recent vision. What, after all, could be helped by that? *Another Malenfer will die soon.*

Madame provided a list of the rents so they knew whom Pierre had been visiting. Simonne ran it out to give it to the men, with the housekeeper close at her heels.

"You had better not refuse my basket of food, sir!" And indeed Dermot did not.

Émile took the list from Simonne and looked at the names on the paper. He nodded. "It's what I thought."

"I know them all," Arthur said, looking over Émile's shoulder as he sat up on the horse. "They're miles out, though."

Beyond this intelligence they had nothing to go on for the moment, but it was the best plan they had for the present. They hoped to find out where he'd been sighted last and narrow the search from there. Arthur grabbed Dermot around his waist; it felt like being draped in a blanket.

"We'll be back as soon as we can." Dermot assured Simonne. "Take care, Mademoiselle."

Simonne laid a hand on Dermot's leg, looking up as he returned her salute.

"You too," she added as they started off, and she stood there watching the riders till they'd passed from sight.

Their plans did not work out as well as they'd hoped. By seven that evening it was completely black out, very difficult conditions for the twenty people the Malenfers had raised in the search. By nine at night the number had doubled; almost fifty now combed the roads and ditches despite the rains coming on even worse and the temperatures falling.

Everyone out there knew Pierre by sight. Knew the boy who had grown up there. Knew the man he had become. He was one of them, whether they liked him or not. Few needed convincing of the urgency in their hunt. It went unspoken, but everyone was thinking of the perils of a fall. Pierre coming off his horse and breaking his leg, or Pierre taking a blow to his head not paying attention to a branch, his horse bolting then wandering off, leaving him on the ground. The worry was the weather and the danger it posed. A man outside who had no shelter was a man in mortal peril. Dermot had found soldiers in craters during the war. Wet, cold, and tired, they had finally gone to sleep never to awaken again. The race tonight was against time, and they had precious little of it left.

Eventually they managed to establish his last sighting, and for a short while their hopes were buoyed. At two o'clock that afternoon Pierre had visited and collected from the final "overdue" on his books. This croft was only two miles from the Manor, but after that there was no further trace. The bad news was he could have gone anywhere if he hadn't gone straight home, and all that was hours ago.

The searchers worked in groups, spreading out in a thinly spaced line, calling out and ringing bells to signal to each other, scouring with their lanterns as they combed the byways and chased the shortcuts between the various farms. But of Pierre there was no sign. It was as if he'd simply vanished.

At eleven in the evening Madame called the search off, to resume once more at daybreak. It was common sense; the volunteers were tired and wet, and there was the danger of missing him in the darkness. In the morning they would all be fresh, and yet the order felt like failure. Émile refused to accept it and Dermot's support was resolute. Dismissive of the fatigue and the cold, the two of them and Arthur pressed on.

They found Pierre a few hours after midnight. Persistence has its own rewards, but theirs was a bitter victory. They were on a road they had been down already, but for some reason this time they turned off it. They followed a track back into the trees, a shortcut over a stream. They could tell before they reached him that there was no more need for urgency.

"This isn't good, Dermot." Arthur slid from the horse, the first man down.

Pierre lay on his chest in the middle of a clearing. He might have passed for a rock in the dark except that his hands and face, gleamy with rainwater, reflected the glare from their lantern. The body threw a vulgar shadow in a game of sickening charades. Like a broken reflection from a dropped mirror, it was twisted to unnatural shapes.

"Émile, stay here," Dermot told the twin in his stiff sergeant's voice. "No," he changed his mind quickly. "Go back. Ride for help! You know this place – tell the others. Find someone and then come back here, but stay away for now. Don't, Émile! No!"

The plea from Dermot was futile because Émile would take no instruction. He'd seen his brother down and hurt, still and unresponsive. He ignored Dermot's well-intentioned words and crossed the open ground.

"Pierre!" he choked out, dropping to his knees beside his motionless kin. "Pierre!" Émile howled again in impotent frustration.

"Let him grieve, Dermot," said Arthur, who stood over his sons. "Leave the boy be."

Émile touched his brother's cold cheek before he turned him over. Moving him was a desecration that none of them anticipated.

Dermot tried to avert his eyes. He lifted his scarf to his mouth and drew long breaths of air. Émile saw the mess beneath his brother and emptied out his stomach. He crawled away two feet to the side and vomited in horror.

"Mother of God!" Arthur crossed himself. "What did this to my boy?"

Poor Pierre, thought Dermot, daring to look, still breathing hard. Poor unfortunate bastard.

Pierre it was. Pierre it had been.

His once strong face was now pulled long, stretched and white and frozen. It bore a look of understanding at the horror that was happening.

Arthur and Dermot, now the first shock was gone, could do nothing now but gape at him. Pierre the brother had been clearly shot; Pierre the son had been gutted.

Émile wretched uncontrollably. His twin lay open like a fish. Dermot cast their lantern around the clearing; it looked like a butcher's shop.

"Can you come with me? Can you get up?" He steadied Émile's shoulders then took his arm and lifted him up gently. "You'll be all right, come back with me. There's nothing you can do here."

Dermot led him carefully back to the horses, away from the dreadful sight. Émile was white, trembling in shock. Dermot wasn't sure if Émile was taking in what he was saying.

"Just sit here, you sit here. You'll be all right." He didn't want him riding; he was in no shape to do anything. Dermot felt his own legs trembling and fought to steady himself.

"I'm not going far," he comforted Émile. "I saw a house not too far back there. I'm just going to get some help and then I'll be right back, OK? Don't you move!" Dermot remounted.

"Keep an eye on him!" he shouted to Arthur, useless though that was, and then Dermot sped off for aid. Whatever had happened here had taken place hours ago, so he wasn't afraid of immediate danger. True to his word, he was back soon. "Help will be along in a minute."

He consoled Émile, who sat speechless and shivering exactly where he'd left him. Arthur hadn't left Pierre; Dermot found him mourning over the body.

"Arthur. Are you all right? Arthur?"

The ghost of Arthur stretched up slow and heaved a soulful sigh. "I brought this on him, Dermot. I did this to my child."

"No. No, Arthur. There's no curse here. There's just the hand of man."

"Don't tell me what there is or isn't!" Dermot backed off in the face of his fury. He had never seen Arthur's anger, since his death or before, but Arthur was seething and spitting spite and was terrible to behold. "If I'd not brought you to here to the Manor, do you think this would have happened?"

Dermot didn't reply to the blasting wraith; both of them knew that answer.

"We should see if there's anything here. Something that can help us." Dermot tried to be practical.

"Dermot! When we find who did this. Do you hear me? When we find who did this, I want you to kill them."

"Arthur, it's a crime. We'll get the police..."

"Listen to me!"

The Irishman stopped in the midst of his speech and looked again at the specter, at his friend's once whole, now marked face, his skin like colored ice.

"You helped me once." The ghost reached out, and in his eye a tear? "I beg now openly for your aid... I am helpless to avenge! What sins must I atone for that the heavens now punish me so? I search my heart to list them and I only come up short. This, this here" – he gestured at the body – "this was my child... my little boy! I only wished to help him... Oh, dear God, what have I done? Why did you let this happen?" He raged at the elements above.

Dermot, his heart in his throat, could not deny his friend's plea for a father's justice. "I'll help, Arthur, I'll get who did it. We'll get the bastard together."

He promised it and he meant it, though it might mean his very soul. The comrades stood resolved beneath a blackened rain, sharing the misery, the mud, and the pain.

"Arthur, I'm going to have a look at Pierre and see what I can learn. You might want to go back over and check on your Émile."

"No," Arthur refused. "I'll stay and help you if I can. I can't do anything for Émile."

Dermot gave Arthur a knowing nod. "As you wish." Then he got down to business. He knelt beside the prone Pierre, and opened the dead boy's jacket. "It's a bad business, Lieutenant. Look at this."

The forests of Haute-Marne harbored creatures that would scavenge off a body, but the skin that Arthur pointed out was cut open cleanly and smooth – not torn by teeth or mauled by claw to broach the inner cavity.

"And I think there's another bullet wound in here too." Dermot poked his finger in as far as he could get. It fitted tight and was hard to pull free. Following his line of thought, Dermot lifted Pierre's arm up. He pulled back his shirt. A second grievous wound was revealed under the boy's right armpit.

"You're right," Arthur confirmed. "Shot at least twice, then cut open. Jesus Christ. They will suffer!"

"Why cut him open?" Dermot remained incredulous.

"Why shoot him?" the ghost asked back.

"Look back here."

Dermot, holding the lantern low, retraced the scene as he saw it. A wounded boy, crawling away, his guts caught up on the thorny underbrush. Snags and twigs had hooked in him, and he'd unwound himself as he crawled away and bled out on the ground.

Dermot, consumed by these thoughts, did not notice the new arrivals.

"Dermot," Arthur said, bringing his attention round. "We have company."

"Someone take care of Émile, please!" Dermot shouted. "The rest of you please stay back!" He didn't see any of the family here yet; he was glad at least for that.

Dermot crawled in the mud of dark reddish earth and searched for other wounds or evidence. His arms were stained with blackish blood that marked him to his elbows. He went through Pierre's coat and pockets, checked his fingers for missing rings, he went over the ground on his hands and his knees from the body back to the lane. Satisfied that he'd covered everything, he returned to the body again.

Dermot pressed Pierre's face, and gently closed his eyes. He lifted the screaming lifeless jaw until the boy looked silent. Dermot's blood-ied fingers had marked Pierre; the boy looked like an Indian brave. He closed the boy's jacket out of respect, covering the offense from view. Dermot removed his own coat and draped it over Pierre, but the stains on the ground told their story.

More people were arriving; the word had gotten out. Dermot talk-ed to the first of them but could not keep control for long. Emotions were taking over and he felt his own exhaustion.

"I'm going to have Émile taken home," he told Arthur. In the darkness and noise of the gathering crowd, Dermot didn't worry who heard him. "I think I saw Berthe arrive."

Dermot enlisted the housekeeper's assistance. She did her job with a quiet resolve and took care of the wretched Émile. He needed space, peace, and comfort, none of which he would ever find near that desecrated glade.

How do you recover from the murder of a brother? Dermot asked the question. He watched Émile being led away through the gathering crowd. He knew the answer. Connor Ward would always be fourteen, just as on that last day that he'd seen him. *How do you recover from the murder of a brother?* That was easy. *You don't.* There is only a hole you can never fill, and the anger that boils out of it.

"I'll help, Arthur, I'll get who did this. We'll get the bastard together."

Half-facts and speculation. Grist to the mill for gossips. Pierre Mal-enfer was brought back home, laid out like Michel before him.

The factor's bag that carried the rents had yet to be recovered, and the talk around the estate quickly turned to robbery and bandits, of army deserters living rough, or German spies, or anarchists. While such inventions spun on people's lips, the hushed tones spoke of tor-ture, of defilement, human sacrifice, and even demon worship. Half-truths were sanctified that day and elevated to gospel.

The news of Pierre's real father emerged and was relayed for miles around, and quickly enough his death was ascribed to the workings of the curse. Dermot felt hostile eyes on him as if *he'd* laid the hex.

A gendarme was brought to the farm and pressed to keep good order, for the common people gathered there wished vengeance for the murder. Pierre was viewed as one of their own, and he carried all their sympathy. A crime so heinous needed a reply. Fear's child was always hate.

Chapter 19
The Mill

MADAME TOOK CHARGE.

She loomed large on the staircase, aloof and imperious, as quiet fell over the crowd. They bore Pierre into the Manor wrapped in a bloody sheet. In that heavy hall grief was tinged with anger, respect melded to solidarity, and ferocity and anguish married.

"My grandson is returned to me."

Madame, the Malenfers, the land, and its people – to Dermot, alone on the periphery, the bond was tangible below.

"Gustave." Madame summoned her footman. "Did I not hear stories of strangers around these parts?" When she spoke, they were tools for her bidding. All ears were tuned to her.

"As you say, Madame, there has been recent talk of outsiders."

"Clochards, Madame!" "Vagrants and vagabonds!" Nameless voices from the assembly confirmed the footman's report.

"Up by the old mill they were, the one back of the village."

"Deserters more like!" another chimed in, "and hiding out, I'll warrant!"

The denouncement was met with popular agreement, and each testimony birthed another. The workers proved they were keen to the task, tenants bidding up their knowledge. Madame nodded her approval as if swayed by their wisdoms. Resolution seemed close at hand.

"Send warning!" she ordered so that everyone could hear. "Send warning to all who dwell nearby that thieves and murderers roam our lands. All must look to the care of their own and the protection of their families. None of us are safe while such men roam loose. You see what they did to Pierre?" The chorus was in favor and a baying aggression ensued. Dermot wondered where it would spill, for it had the makings of a riot. Madame didn't wait long to tell them. "I ask for your help! Let all able-bodied lend aid to our efforts, and we'll run these beasts to ground!"

"Yes!" the people shouted; the air was full of fealty to the cause. "Yes, we will, Madame!"

"Have the arsenal unlocked," she ordered. "Gustave, issue arms. Those amongst you who do not bear rifles must ensure you protect yourselves." Gustave nodded his head, acknowledging her popular instruction. Dermot had managed to press in closer so he heard Madame while the shouting went on. "And Gustave, I wish to know of anyone that balks at volunteering."

"As you say," Gustave confirmed. "It will be done, Madame."

"Hear me now, and hear me well. Know that I want justice! They spill our blood and think to gain? They'll rue the day they came here!" The cheering rose in temper till it matched her own conviction. Dermot saw it – everyone had – there was no mercy for her quarry. Madame bore the eye of an executioner, and it spurred the gathered troop.

Woe to the one whom fate sends begging for compassion from that face.

The armed host sallied forth from the Malenfer courtyard. Dermot watched them go. In truth he welcomed the reprieve. Ne'er-do-wells, squatters, tramps, deserters, outsiders of any hue – guilt would cover them as naturally as sleet upon the field. There was a clannish passion to the mob and Dermot knew he did not belong. But he watched them leave with reservation, for they looked like a hunting party.

He would have bartered his boots for a few hours sleep. A day in the saddle and the search for Pierre had drained him more than he would have admitted. He looked longingly at the staircase. Rest must wait – the stakes were too high – and first he had to check on Émile. Dermot needed reassurance that the boy was safe, and Arthur mirrored his concern.

"He's as well as to be expected." Berthe stood guard over Émile's door and grumbled about giving admission. "Give him peace and rest; let the boy be. Don't be disturbing him needlessly."

"He's in safe hands," Arthur conceded after Dermot was rebuffed and bullied. "She's more of a family to him than I ever was. Oh, that I could make up for all my mistakes!"

"What of these men at the mill?"

"It has to be them, Dermot. You heard."

"If they're still here, then I don't think so, Arthur. Your grief's clouding your better judgment."

"They could have done it. Dark hearts. Who knows?"

"You saw a bit of the world, Arthur. You know what locals think everywhere – that outsiders are capable of anything. But be sensible, man. The factor's bag went missing. If they had Pierre's money and his blood on their hands, why not flee the minute it happened? You'd be crazy to stay any longer."

"Why not flee, you ask? Complacency is why! Or they're stupid, or they're greedy..." Arthur countered. "Did you never known men in the army like that? Of course you did, there were plenty. It could be them, Dermot. It could be."

"Then why not take Pierre's horse too? Why let it get away and raise alarm if they lay in wait and ambushed him? And no one yesterday during our search mentioned seeing a group of strange men."

"Maybe they did, though."

"And didn't say so? No. It would have been the first thing they'd have said. No. If it was such men, then they're long out of here. And if it wasn't, then I fear for these ones now."

Dermot rattled off his objections, having trouble keeping up with them, they arrived so fast to his head. He thought back to the small road and the track from it to where they'd found Pierre. It told the tale of an ambushed man, robbed and sickeningly assaulted. A wounded man who tried to escape and bled out from his wounds. Would deserters be desperate and ignorant enough to do something like that and stay locally? He had a great respect for the stupidity of man, but the gutting felt more intimate. There was a sickness behind that sort of violence that Dermot could not reconcile to chance.

"You overthink it, Dermot, it's simple enough. The horse likely bolted, running before they could stop it. Or maybe not all of their group took part in the attack. Who knows? Maybe they had to stay the night because they don't know their way in these parts. Perhaps they'd planned to leave at first light but we got the jump on them. Have you thought about that?"

"Most unlikely."

"What does it matter, Dermot, anyway, so long as the culprits are found?"

"What type of men are they?" Dermot asked. "Do you know they're deserters for sure?" He hoisted his jacket.

"A rough lot – you heard it." Arthur seemed placated, perhaps thinking he had won the point. "They've definitely served. One of them was in the store last week and admitted as much when paying. That means they're deserters, likely as not. Maybe they're desperate, fearful of discovery, and they saw Pierre as authority."

"There's no proof of anything." Dermot dismissed it. "I'm worried, Arthur; you should know better. Madame has got the countryside stirred up. Is this really going to help Pierre?"

"They could be the ones." Arthur wasn't apologetic.

"Yes, I suppose they could. Are we going to get the chance to ask them?"

"I want the truth, Dermot."

"Well, forgive me, but your family doesn't strike me as the forgiving sort. Where is this mill exactly?"

"Past the village. I know where it is," said Arthur.

The Irishman's brain ground away once more, turning and calculating. He formulated and measured the situation but was missing too many pieces.

"I need my trunk."

Dermot's statement brought a lifted eyebrow to Arthur's sulky face. The Lieutenant was intrigued, at least.

"And what, Irlandais, is so important in your trunk that it needs your attention at this moment?"

"Come upstairs and see."

Dermot dragged the steamer trunk to the center of his room. It had arrived the day before, delivered from the station by an unhappy straining fellow. With the assistance of the Malenfer staff, Dermot had gotten it up the stairs. "Careful now," was all he'd told them as he watched them puff and sweat.

Dermot turned the key, threw the lock, and drew the bolt aside. The stout lid gave a groan.

Arthur peered in.

First on view was a tray of shirts and a folded army uniform: a Kepi hat and epaulets to distract the casual observer.

"Why do you have a ski-pole?" Arthur was curious.

"Long story."

The tray was lifted out.

"Bloody hell, Ward!" Arthur exclaimed.

Sapper, soldier, military engineer – through five years of service in the war, Chief Sergeant Pioneer Ward had been a collector.

"Bloody hell!" Arthur seemed to feel the need to repeat himself.

Dermot was tooled up for battle.

Three pistols – a French Lebel Modèle 1892 standard issue, an English Webley Mark IV revolver, and a P08 Luger, each cleaned, polished, and immaculate – were pegged onto the back wall of the trunk. In the middle, suspended like a rib cage, were three rifles on fitted racks: a French Berthier, a German Mauser (alone amongst its companions this was fitted with a sniper's scope), and a British short magazine Lee-Enfield. But this wasn't what occasioned Arthur's remarks; in fact he had barely noticed these fire sticks.

"How the hell did you steal that?" Arthur asked of Dermot.

The gleaming Lewis gun, though partly dissembled, was distinctive by its drum-pan magazine. Weighing thirty pounds and capable of five hundred rounds a minute, it could summon a monsoon of fire. The gun was stowed snuggly at the bottom of the trunk between ambitious boxes of ammunition.

"You're probably not allowed to have that." Arthur peered in.

The Irishman grinned with the pride of a magpie. "No, but that's not what'll get me arrested. They would be much more concerned about this."

Pyromaniacs might get it – the feel from a freshly struck match. Dermot reached inside the trunk with the tingle of anticipation. He gingerly removed a small box. "Got to be careful with this one."

Safely out, he opened it up.

"Bloody bloody hell!" Arthur was out of words.

There are other tools besides picks and shovels for those who play beneath the earth. The detonators, fuse wires, and triggers in the box were clearly bad enough, but Dermot knew that Arthur had recognized the contents of the bottles. The Lieutenant had seen enough of these things to know what they could do.

"You brought that on the train with me? You let the servants drag that up the stairs?" Arthur was going apoplectic.

"It was heavy!" Dermot said defensively. "I needed help. And what are you worried about, anyway? You're well dead already."

"This is my family here! You could have blown this whole house up!"

"Hypothetically" – Dermot was slipping a few things into his pockets, the bottles and the revolver among them – "but not if you're a careful fellow." He looked longways at Arthur, a little mischief in his eye. "And *I* am always careful." He reached for a stale bread roll.

The Lewis gun went into a drawstring bag. Dermot added a second magazine and then slung the whole lot over his back. Satisfied he had everything he might need, the Irishman closed the trunk.

"It's only a few wild men, Dermot."

"Easy enough to say when you're dead."

Chapter 20
Deserters' Desserts

DESERTERS.

Men pushed beyond their limits weighed two futures in despair, their minds worn raw by madmen's tactics that threw flesh in front of steel. Detestable cowards who gave succor to their nation's enemies, or desperate men without the fare demanded of them by others? Back in the trenches the closest of friends might speak of such things in hushed voices, for a firing squad awaited those who strayed and were discovered.

Dermot had seen it happen. He always believed that unless you'd been there, you should not be hasty to judge. The men holed up in the mill had been soldiers just like him once. They were clochards now, wandering tramps, and today they had run out of options. The outcome of a court martial would look bleak by any comparison, so it came as no surprise that these rough men had parleyed with their rifles.

Dermot arrived to a confused scene. Crouched groups of armed farmers were scattered behind cover, and in the distance the squat old mill, her stone walls and tile roof intact. An aging peasant braved a dash across the road to meet him. The gun he held might have been as venerable as he was.

"Monsieur!" the plowman hailed him.

"What's happening? What's going on here?"

"It's not good. Things have gone all out of plan!" he puffed.

"Just calm down and tell me."

The farmer took his advice to heart. After a few deep breaths he went on. "There were a lot of us to start," he began. "You saw us at the Manor?" He didn't wait for Dermot's answer. "I followed the main group up here and more joined in as we came. We were quite the brigade and brave in our numbers! We knew where the murderers were hiding." He relayed his tale with enthusiasm and not the slightest hint of doubt.

"They were camped out there" – he indicated – "The old mill. You can still see what's left of the waterwheel from around the other side."

"And what happened when you got here?" Dermot put the same question again.

"They heard us coming, they must have. We were stirred up and excited, a few of the others a little scared too, perhaps? You understand? There were a lot of angry words. Some of the younger ones…"

"So they didn't give themselves up quietly?" The answer was obvious.

"No, Monsieur, they did not. They shot first, I'm almost sure of it. We hadn't even asked for their surrender and they shot at us, the brigands! I don't know what happened next… everyone scattered and took shelter, then they ran, and then more shooting."

"They ran?"

"Like rabbits they did. The scoundrels fled, but one of them was hit. I saw it myself with my own eyes, he took a bullet but was helped up by a friend. His cries were terrible, Monsieur."

"But then what happened?" Dermot was frustrated. "Who are you laying siege to here?"

"They fell back, they knew it was hopeless, but that's when the worst of it happened. Some of our own, keen in pursuit, were caught when the scoundrels retreated. They have some of ours prisoner, sir, and that's where we are now."

"What are you saying, man? They've taken hostages?"

"They're barricaded inside, Monsieur! They've threatened to kill them unless they can go free!"

"Jesus, Mary, and Joseph. How many of your men are in there?"

"Three, they have. They won't give up, and we don't dare go near them. No one knows what to do."

"All right. Stay calm. Who's doing the talking? What have they done with their prisoners?"

"One of them is a woman."

"The deserters?"

"No, Monsieur, one of ours. They took her, she came from the big house. They showed her at the window."

"Why would a maid come up here?"

"No, monsieur. Not a maid. Madame's granddaughter. Oh, you know her, Monsieur?"

Dermot ordered the farmer to stay and keep his head down, and he seemed happy to oblige. Dermot crossed the road with Arthur and asked him to scout the mill. Indeed, it was as the farmer had said. Dermot chanced a peek around the corner. The mill sat atop a banked slope not one hundred yards away. Broken or shuttered windows were visible and one big front door, firmly shut.

It wasn't long before Arthur was back. "The windows are broken – it was easy enough to get inside," the ghost related. "She's shaken up, but she looks unhurt. They're keeping her in the corner near the front door. Not the spot you'd want to be in if we try to force an entrance."

"Or if they try to leave in a fight."

Would they take hostages with them? he wondered. *Would they simply let them go?*

"There's a loft in the place too. One of them's up there, sniping, so watch out where you go. Small window, second floor."

Dermot peeked. "I see it."

"Keep your head down. The other prisoners are on the main floor with Simonne. I remember one from the tabac in the village; it looks like he's taken the butt of a rifle and isn't in the greatest of shape. The other man I don't recognize, but he's holding up OK. They've been placed so they can keep an eye on them all and shoot them if they move."

Dermot had been thinking. "They won't take them all when they leave. I wouldn't. Slow them down. Too easy to be found out or given away, dragging others around."

"If they go."

The thought was sobering.

"The injured man has died of his wounds. He either wasn't a smoker or his friends took his cigarettes." Dermot didn't ask. "They're not a happy bunch. The one in charge is a big fellow, completely bald, a bit of a hot head. He's the one that was firing..." As Arthur said it, another shot went off from near the mill and set off a flurry of gunfire in response. After a couple of seconds of quiet, Dermot got up from the ground.

"Jesus Christ!" he hollered around the wall. "Hold your fire! We've got people in there!" He turned his attention back to Arthur, who stood out for a better view. "How's their ammunition?" Dermot chased a hope.

"They'll hold up well till Christmas." Arthur quashed it. "Fine for food as well, but your thinking is right if I guess it, Sergeant – they'll have to make a break for it soon. They can't afford to wait for real policemen or soldiers to show up, and now their injured friend is dead, he's not around to slow them down."

"Bloody hell, Arthur." Dermot shook his head, dismayed at the turn of events. "And then what happens? They get a packed lunch and just hoof it? Simonne is stuck in the middle of this. We need to let them go."

"Well, Irlandais, you'll need to convince twenty armed strangers surrounding the place, and then win the trust of the mill."

Dermot remembered Pierre again, face down in the clearing, and a scene from Simonne's dark hallway painting, the one with the little people – a rabble of beetle vigilantes armed with sticks and hooks and scythes, a mob tearing vengeance on their quarry, hacking it into gory chunks.

"Is there anyone in charge?"

"Over there – see that house? In there. Crevel is his name."

"Why does that sound familiar?"

"Why? It should be familiar to you, Dermot, the man is practically family. It's his son Robert who's engaged to marry my niece, our young Simonne. Crevel dithers because his future daughter-in-law is trapped inside that mill."

There had been a knot in Dermot's stomach since the news of Simonne's great plight, and it twisted like an ulcer at this reminder of her fate.

"Monsieur Crevel?"

"Who are you?" The man continued to study his drawings and did not look up.

"Ward is my name."

"Well, you're lucky no one has shot you, Monsieur, mistaking you for a deserter."

Crevel held court at a splintered table in the ruin across from the mill; half of the roof was open to the rain and half of the wall to the air. The man was well-dressed in a dark three-piece suit that looked out of place in the country, but with his neatly combed hair and his calm steady voice he seemed unruffled despite all the violence. On the hand-drawn map in front of him sat a pistol and a wine glass, its rim wet as if recently used, with a bottle open beside it. Crevel sat with one leg up, claiming both the chairs in the room. He rubbed his knee as if it gave him some pain.

"We need to let them go, Monsieur."

"Them?" Crevel still gave him his back.

"The suspects," Dermot said tersely. He could feel himself getting annoyed.

Crevel seemed to find this somewhat amusing. "Maybe you *are* one of them after all. Are you sure you're not a deserter, Monsieur

Ward, whoever you are, a stranger who comes late to the show?"

Dermot restrained the urge to kick the chair from under him. "They have hostages, as you very well know, and there's no way to get them out safely."

"They'll give up."

"Don't be stupid." Dermot cut him down coldly.

Crevel put aside the sketches and shifted his reptilian attention. His head pivoted on his stock frame till it faced the new arrival.

"You're the Malenfer's charity case." Crevel spoke with a cold objectivity. "I heard of your arrival. What on earth do you think you're doing here? Whatever it is, I suggest that you reconsider. This is no concern of yours. Please crawl away home, Mr. Ward, if you can in fact remember where you came from."

If Dermot hadn't understood the French, its tone would have told him everything. He stared in mounting rage, but Crevel was coolly placid; he'd renewed his attention to map and leg as if the appointment was completed.

"Robert!" Crevel barked suddenly, cutting short Dermot's retort. Coming into the pregnant silence his voice rang unexpectedly. A movement from the corner revealed a man who had stood unobserved. "Robert, go and ready the men. We attack at the top of the hour."

"Monsieur, this is madness!" Dermot stepped forward. Nothing was more dangerous to Simonne's chances than what he had just heard.

"We'll attack in force from the south and distract them from your fiancée. We'll get her out, and when we do we'll finish all the others." His words were spoken to Robert, but he was loud enough for the audience.

"You'd risk her life, Monsieur, in an act of desperate folly? And what of the men you have? What risk to them? They'll be mowed down in the open!"

"We have the numbers and the advantage of surprise."

"Let the men in the mill leave instead. Allow them to go free. Risk no one!"

Crevel turned on him. The clay mask had been dropped for a look of unguarded hate. "Monsieur Ward" – he almost spat the words – "they are going nowhere."

A cool head restrained Dermot's hand. "Twenty minutes!" he pressed. "That's all I want. Twenty minutes, and then do what you want."

Crevel seemed surprised at the suggestion, but he quickly recovered his poise.

"What do you mean?" he said suspiciously. "What idea do you have?" Crevel consulted a pocket watch that he fished from his waistcoat by its chain. "What are you going to do that you think might make a difference in such a time?" His eyes narrowed distrustfully.

"You'll get a signal," Dermot told him.

"What signal?" Crevel demanded.

"You'll know it when you get it," Dermot told him confidently, sensing the opportunity was open.

"And then what?" The mayor let the conversation linger, conceding his own uncertainty. It was an admission in itself that they were in a pickle and that the situation was desperate.

"Storm the building. On the signal, rush it. Take the men in the mill alive, unless they offer resistance."

"I see." Crevel nodded as if that was the first thing he'd heard of sense. "Twenty minutes is all you get," he consented, "and then we'll finish this job properly. Robert?"

"Yes, father?"

"See the men are ready for action... and Mr. Ward?"

"Monsieur?"

He flicked the watch case open and took a long lazy look at the cold physics within. "I am counting."

Arthur and Dermot were on the grass verge, halfway down the riverbank.

"Just what in the hell *are* you planning to do?" Arthur asked, now that they were alone once again.

"You said those men were at the front windows?"

"That's right."

"Then the river is out of their sight."

"We're going up there, then?" Arthur asked, but it wasn't really a question.

Moving quickly and quietly, crouched over and screening himself behind the riverbank's vegetation, Dermot drew closer to the mill, Arthur right behind him. There was a stairway at the back of the place, but it fell short and was in ruinous condition. The windows here could not be reached without the help of a ladder. With luck, Dermot thought, the men's attentions would remain focused out the front.

He reached the base of the mill. Here the grass path narrowed and then pinched at the river's bank. A waterfall thirty feet away spilled down into a rocky pool – the sound of the water made it hard to hear but served to cover his own noise. The spray began to soak him. The once-great wheel still stood, though lurched, propped against the side of the building. It looked like a drunken man chasing balance, broken and rotten in poverty. The stream from above had once powered it to turn the grindstone within.

"You're going to blow her up, aren't you? We aren't here to bag flour."

"The thought might have crossed my mind." Dermot spoke matter-of-factly; he was busy in a professional appraisal of the stonework in the embankment. "Unless you've got another suggestion?"

Arthur did not. "Simonne's in there," was all he said. Neither of them needed reminding.

It's best to end this as quickly as possible, Dermot reasoned. Men under rubble would be easier to overcome, *providing they're all still alive.* He measured carefully. There was no chance for a surprise raid with a barricaded door, but remove a wall or open the floor and the odds might shift a little. Simonne was at the front – that was the key to this adventure. *And if they'd moved their prisoners back?* The prospect was unthinkable.

Dermot went about his business, assessing the retaining wall and the posts and their foundations, the bowl of the riverbank with its curving bank, the forces and blast radius.

"What's that you've got there?" Arthur asked. "You're like a squirrel hiding nuts for the winter." Dermot was crouched down by the foundation wall, rolling something between his fingers.

"You wouldn't want to bite hard on this nut."

"Dermot." Arthur spoke it low.

Dermot turned, fearful of discovery. He saw Arthur staring across the river, but there was no apparent danger.

"Mmmmmmm?" he answered him back, a firing cap between his teeth.

"Dermot, there's a girl over there. She's watching what you're doing."

"Hmm hmmmmm?" he repeated. What the hell was a girl doing there? She'd be out in the open, a clear straight shot! He looked over but saw nothing.

"You see her? On the far bank, directly across from the wheel?"

"Where?" Dermot had freed up his mouth. "Where'd she go? The place is about to go up – she's got to clear off pronto!" He spoke to be heard above the sound of the river, which passed a few feet from where he crouched working.

"She's coming across!" Arthur cried, pointing. "Go back, girl, don't come any closer!"

Dermot looked to the side and back up the shore and scanned the short scrub that ran to the river. *What the hell's he on about?* There was no one there at all.

"Look," he said, distracted, his mind consumed by a ticking watch. "If she comes back let me know, but I've got to finish this." Dermot returned to playing out the blasting cord out as he finished his last few touches.

"Stay away, girl, do you hear me? Why do you say such things?" There was fear in Arthur's voice.

What the hell's the matter with him? Dermot set the last of the charges and double-checked his wiring. *How much time?* Four minutes before Crevel's deadline! Would it be enough?

Arthur was shouting. Dermot looked up and saw the Lieutenant back away from the river – no girl, no woman, no voices.

"What do you mean?" Arthur was trembling. "Come no closer! I can guess your name. I'll strike you, girl, I swear it!" Arthur's eyes were bulged, his jaw was set, and he held his hands out ready.

"I'm lighting it, Arthur. I'm getting Simonne out now. Let's go!" Dermot struck the fuse, warning him as he did so.

Arthur, oblivious, clawed the air, swinging his arms like a wild man.

"It's lit! Let's go!" Dermot got in his face, and the spell that held him seemed broken.

"The girl," he mumbled, looking around. "She was here, Dermot. She was right there."

"It's lit, Arthur!" Dermot pushed him.

"She was here, Dermot. She was here, I tell you. She told me what she wanted." Arthur's voice was trembling.

"She's gone now, Arthur, and I'll be gone too if we don't make it back to cover! It's coming down, the lot of it. Get the hell away from here!" Dermot ran back the way he'd come, with the smell of cordite in his nostrils. His legs pumped hard as he made for a rock he'd picked out earlier for shelter.

They'd just dropped behind the boulder when the sky lit up around them. The noise and the punch of the air hit next like a boxer's combination. When the falling debris had subsided enough, Dermot risked a look behind.

The mill had been built into the hillside, and Dermot had taken its footings. The force of the explosion was directed down the riverbank to spare those on the street above it. As the dust cleared a new horizon was revealed. The once-proud slumbering water wheel spun in a final death rattle. It rose and fell like labored breath as it teetered on its axle, and then, like a tossed coin, it gave up its answer and finally went quiet. The mill was gone. A pile of rubble filled the gully beneath where it had stood; tumbled timbers and threshed masonry were visible through the dust. All that had once been the mill was a ruin of a ruin, and in it there were people.

Dermot sprang up and set off like a deer, leaping through the air full forward. He rushed the site, now sprinting ahead, no more shrinking from sight behind cover. As he went he removed the bag that had hung across his shoulders, and drew from it the Lewis gun and leveled its maw at the wreckage.

"*Jetez les armes!*" he shouted – drop your guns – his strides eating up the distance. "*Capitulez!*" Surrender.

Something moved in the rubble through the cloud of dusty air. He reached the blasted piles of stones and started to climb over them.

"Simonne!" he shouted, looking around, and then, at last, he saw her. She trembled and staggered, but managed to her feet and held out her arms towards him. But to her left a man rose up, half visible behind broken beams – a faceless form, unreadable, ensconced in a black balaclava.

Dermot raised the muzzle of his terrible gun and trained it on the fellow. "Surrender!" he shouted and fingered the trigger. "Show your hands right now!"

The man stumbled and pushed the wreckage aside and swung his rifle to bear, and as he did so Dermot paused and thought of what Arthur had seen. Was it a vision? Had the Beauvais witch come back again? Was she the girl by the river? Was another Malenfer to die so soon, after Michel and Pierre had been taken?

"Put the rifle down!"

The gun came around another inch. Simonne would be in the way.

Dermot never wavered. Dermot didn't hesitate. Dermot didn't close his eyes; he only closed the trigger.

For three long seconds thunder roared and split the air asunder. The Lewis hammered, back and back, and bruised and punched his shoulder. Empty casings thrown around, confetti at a wedding – the balaclava danced a jig to Charon's steady rhythm. Then everything was quiet at last. Dermot lowered his weapon.

"I'm sorry you had to see that," he thought he told her, practically deaf as he was.

Simonne stood still, unharmed and unhurt, though the air was singed about her, but at the sound of his comforting voice she ran forward into his arms. Her warm cheek pressed his chest and a sob broke from her mouth. "You came for me," was all she could manage, and he almost didn't hear her. She trembled against him.

"You're safe," he said, and held her.

Simonne sobbed and hugged him tighter. He didn't want to let go. He held her close, her hair in his hand, and then he forced himself to release her. "What are we going to do about you?" He pushed her hair back out of her eyes. "You're all right. It's over."

Somehow it had become more important to him than anything else in the world.

Other people were crawling on the wreckage.

"Robert!" Crevel interrupted. He was close by. "Mademoiselle appears unhurt – bring her away at once! You had best escort your fiancée back safely to her family."

"Yes, father," Robert called back, picking his way across the mound of loose stones. "Of course. Simonne, you're safe!"

"Monsieur," Crevel now addressed Ward, his voice direct and flinty. "This is not perhaps the best place for a lady, as I'm sure you will appreciate." He gestured to the man Dermot had killed and the stones that were stacked behind him, bloody and scattered with brain and splinters of shattered blasted bone. "Best she be home."

"He's right." Dermot released Simonne's hand to the waiting Robert. "If I can check up on you later?" he added.

She said nothing immediately, but then leaned forward and laid a kiss on his bristled cheek. She turned and left him standing without another look his way.

Dermot stood with his hand to his face where the warmth of her lips still lingered. He watched her go, with young Robert trailing close behind her. Dermot's heart beat faster than it had in the previous minutes. "Don't start," he said to Arthur, but he thought he sounded pleading. And then he looked around because there was no sarcastic reply. Arthur wasn't anywhere – he wasn't close to the wreckage site. Dermot had seen him taking cover at the rock but nothing after that. Where could Arthur have gone?

Crevel was ordering his men to trawl and search the ruins. Dermot caught his eye.

"You could have killed them all," the mayor chided. "You were rash in the extreme."

"You would have killed them all," Dermot replied. "And by the way, you're welcome." Crevel meant nothing to him; he was just one of those old men. He tried to sound less bitter, but the adrenaline talked for him.

Dermot pulled the balaclava off the man he had shot. It came away in pieces. *Twenty-one or twenty-two. Just about Pierre's age.* Where was Arthur?

He watched the couple recede down the road, Simonne now wrapped under Robert's coat. Around him others dug through the wreckage, till all were accounted for.

Two other bodies they uncovered: the wounded man who had succumbed before the attack and the sniper from the upstairs loft – the fall sustained when the building dropped proved too great to survive. The remaining hostages were both alive and would recover from their wounds. A shout went up when the bald man was found alive beneath a heavy beam. He was a prize, not just for his information but as a trophy for Madame. The search continued through the day as each brick was turned over afresh, but though they sifted every stone, no rent bag was recovered.

Arthur did not return.

Perhaps he went back already, alone. But then why wouldn't he have told him? Dermot had walked both sides of the river but had come away with nothing.

What had happened down there?

"Come no closer. I can guess your name. What do you want from me?" Those were the words that Arthur had spoken, as best Dermot could remember them.

The girl by the river. And Simonne's vision at the abbey.

I can guess your name, Élise Beauvais. Dermot was afraid for his missing friend.

When he got back to the Malenfer house the sun was once more setting, and its rooftops threw a serrated shadow far across the fields. Lights appeared as faerie fire twinkling in its windows, while animals, somehow disturbed, called madly to the heavens. The Manor had given sober welcome under the shroud of ill fortune, but to Dermot it seemed alive this night as if glutted on the violence, and an unnatural sound carried to his ears – the wild peels of merry laughter.

Chapter 21
Last Night

IT TOOK A HARD WASH TO GET DERMOT CLEAN FROM THE DIRT AND the mud and the blood. Arthur was not to be found. Dermot wondered at that while he shaved and changed clothes before joining the company. They were in the parlor: Simonne and her mother, both the Crevels, and what Dermot assumed was the Monsignor – a priest he hadn't seen before.

"Mr. Ward, this is Father Meslier." Sophie made the introduction. "He comes to us in our hour of need, to provide comfort to us all." Meslier was busy with his glass, but eventually gave Dermot a clammy hand. He looked like a man nourished on the grape as much as the word of God. "I am told you met Monsieur Crevel earlier?"

Crevel the elder bore an intoxicated glow. His glass of brandy looked undiluted. "I had that singular pleasure," confirmed the mayor – his voice suggesting it was one too many.

Simonne shared the sofa with her mother. She rested her head on Sophie's shoulder as an invalid might do. Dermot was concerned, but the opportunity did not immediately present itself to inquire after her health; indeed Mademoiselle dropped her eyes from him when he managed to catch her gaze. There was an obvious reason – Simonne's fiancé wore a scowl as he circumnavigated the room.

Crevel's boy seemed distracted, like a man in conversation with himself. He almost bumped into Dermot. Robert paused, his brow furrowed, but he nodded acknowledgment, whether in apology, thanks, or recognition, and moved on his way again. *Odd fellow.*

The mayor and the priest were celebratory. The excitement of these men in their snifter glasses was occasioned by another's fate.

"An eye for an eye!"

"Bald-headed bugger. He was never going to get away."

"You put yourself at too much risk, Crevel. But you got each and every one of them."

"He was a damnable murderer, like all the rest. They all deserved what they got."

The Father nodded his head judiciously. "Destined for the guillotine, I fear."

"Look at the state of the courts today. It's not like they haven't got bigger problems. Issues more worthy of their attentions."

"How right you are, Monsieur Crevel, how 'to the point,' as always."

"We've spared the citizenry the expense of a trial and the thievery of conniving lawyers."

"The profiteering from sin of that forked-tongue fraternity is a blight upon our challenged times." The Monsignor grew frothy as he grew righteous.

"What would the army have done with them, I ask?"

"Their fate was entirely their own."

"The outcome of a court-martial was certain." Crevel inspected his glass. "No doubt, I tell you. No doubt."

"The Lord will be their judge, Monsieur Mayor. As he judges us all." A fat finger was wagged at the room.

"Good work done, and Madame's wish..."

"Why, Monsieur Mayor, I couldn't put it better myself." Both cleared their glasses to underline the veracity of his point.

Dermot was somewhat mystified. He'd seen the bald man only hours before, but though injured he had looked well enough. "He died of his wounds?" he broke in.

"Lord, no!" Crevel burst out laughing. "He won't get off that easy!"

Dermot didn't understand.

"He'll be executed." It was Robert who told him. The young man looked uncomfortable.

"The villain will be hanged," Crevel clarified with relish. There was a slur to his smiling words. "And then his body will be displayed." Simonne looked pale. "It will be strung from meat hooks, through his torso: here... and here." Crevel demonstrated the anatomical violations for Dermot's edification. He rose from his seat and mimed a charade of a worm spitted out for bait.

"Good God," Dermot exclaimed. Sophie covered her mouth.

"An eye for an eye, isn't that right, Father?"

"An eye for an eye!" the priest reiterated.

"Isn't he a sensitive little egg?" Crevel laughed from his chair. He unwrapped a large cigar to balance the drink in his hand.

"And what of the gendarme?" Dermot asked.

"He'll file his report when it's over. These are guilty men, Mr. Ward! He'll get a warrant for their arrest and then close it just as quickly."

"It's outrageous." Dermot felt nauseous.

Crevel chortled. "What's the matter with you? I thought you'd seen a thing or two in the war, Ward? Everything is sorted now. It will set an example for any others."

"Do not distress yourself, Monsieur," Father Meslier consoled. "All is well, don't worry. The old ways are sometimes difficult, but they are surely for the best. The theatrics are perhaps a bit overdone, but these men were fated for bad ends. Think of all the others who are safer now – we can all sleep easier in our beds."

"You know this isn't right," Dermot reiterated. "It's not right, what you propose." He remembered the bodies in the mill – the face of the young man he'd shot. He tried to push away the picture of what they intended to do.

"Who are you to speak of 'right,' Mr. Ward?" Crevel's spoke harshly. "You killed two of them yourself with your own impulsive actions! Don't preach sensibility to men such as us. The act is justice, and it will bring us peace! Isn't it peace we want?" Crevel looked affronted, and motioned for the rest of the company to share in the offense. "Well, Mr. Ward? What do you say? Didn't we lose a generation to this last war just for such an end? Didn't you lose close friends? What was it they died for, sir, if it wasn't freedom from fear?"

"The prisoner should be tried. It is justice, and the law."

"I expect to hear illusions from the mouths of babes and children, perhaps even my own son," – did Robert look bitter? – "but don't embarrass yourself by pretending that this world is other than it is."

"Quite right," toadied Father Meslier. "The shepherd puts down the wolf in service to the sheep."

"What about Madame?" Dermot demanded.

"What about Madame?" The door had opened, and all who were seated struggled quickly to their feet. Father Meslier shot up like a jack-in-the-box – his feet momentarily trod air.

Madame it was who entered the salon, accompanied by Émile. Émile acknowledged at last. Dermot hadn't seen him since they'd found Pierre together. It was an awkward reunion. This was Émile's first turn to be served upon; he had crossed that invisible line. If the thought had not occurred to Émile, it made no difference either way – he would never again sup below, and if he looked glum for it, who could blame him? He wore his brother's terrible loss on every part of his face.

Where has Arthur gone? Dermot's last idea was that he'd gone after his child, but he did not accompany Émile.

Having politely risen at the entrance of her grandmother, Simonne was suddenly standing beside him. Dermot felt choked, suffocated by her presence. His knee accidentally touched her leg as he turned to make space between them. The contact, brief, unintentional, sent a jolt through his thighs and up into his belly that tingled long after she'd moved.

"I distinctly heard my name being mentioned. Might I inquire what you're talking about?"

Madame seemed smaller than he remembered her, but as flinty as before. A heavy jade necklace rose and fell on her chest, a splash of color on her customary black.

Meslier was quick to mew his attentions with a puerile show of concern.

"I'm perfectly well enough, Father, and I was talking to my guest."

Meslier was indefatigable in rejection, as all good clerics are.

"I was inquiring whether it was possible, Madame?"

"Possible, Mr. Ward?"

"Concerning the man taken into custody after the incident at the mill."

"And what about him?"

"I expressed my disbelief that you knew of any such plan."

"He will hang, Mr. Ward."

"Then it's true."

"Damned insolence!" Crevel burst out.

"True, Mr. Ward? I don't understand. What else would you suggest?"

"The police. A court-martial. A trial."

"My grandson was gutted like a trophy deer. Might you remember that, Mr. Ward?"

"I was there, Madame," Dermot spoke frostily.

"Then where is your objection? Or does your abandonment of your own family preclude any empathy towards another?"

Dermot liked to think he had the makings of manners, but his patience was about used up. "I'd think *any* family would want to see justice for just such a crime, terrible thing that it was." He spoke these last words in almost hushed reverence, catching a glance at Émile. "Whether you're poor, honest, and hard-working, or rich, spoilt, and self-serving, justice isn't the preserve of the pocket book."

"You think my justice bought?"

"There is *no* justice here, Madame, that's what courts are for. It's loyalty and fear that you have at your command, nothing more than that." Perhaps he had overstepped himself a little, but in good conscience he figured the gloves were off when she had thrown the first blow.

Madame was clearly not used to being talked to in this way. She tightened like pulled rope.

"Respect," she said to him at last, her voice as clear as ice. "Respect is what the people have for the Malenfer ways. The people share our values. They *respect* that we value justice, that we don't let murderers go free." She was thin and sharp and precise with her words – a seamstress snipping cloth.

"Or maybe you're just another landlord," he interrupted her, "same as all the rest. Thing is, no one's got a right to do what you propose to do." He ran on now without pausing, sensing he might never have a word in again. "Even if you're correct, even if they are guilty men, no one has that right. No one does. And that is all I'm saying."

He was aware of all eyes turned upon him, but Simonne's most of all. In her look he saw an adoration that flustered him beyond Madame's glare.

"Your tone is insulting, Mr. Ward!" the Mayor put in, championing his hostess. "You repay your hospitality in cruel coin! The family here suffers enough without you bandying your blatant nonsense."

"Where is the evidence against them? They were not seen. They left no marks to betray themselves. They did not confess. Did they?" There was a silence. "Why, you haven't even recovered Pierre's rents, which would be their only motivation." Dermot threw out his words.

"Your hands were stained in their blood!" Crevel shot back.

"But only because *she* set the pack on them. They were always going to fight back."

"Mind your place, you mongrel dog." Crevel slapped his chair.

"You keep your mouth shut!" Dermot stood up to him, jabbing a finger at the older man with a head of steam in reply.

"Why?" Crevel squared off. "So you can spew your lies in your guttural French? So you can be alone to charm the pretty Mademoiselle that you look at with loose eyes?"

Dermot went red.

"You are a disgrace, sir! You take the food and roof of a gracious hostess, and how do you repay her? By slurring the memory of Pierre? By slandering Madame, who does everything to protect and avenge him? By sniffing around her granddaughter?" Simonne let out a gasp. "I saw you at the mill, sir, endangering us all! You're an animal without thought or conscience, you act on your passions alone! And the Mademoiselle is engaged, Monsieur, as if you didn't know."

Dermot could not reply; he was furious but embarrassed, not so much for himself but for Mademoiselle Simonne. He clenched his fists in frustration, wondering at the fallout if he pummeled the bastard right now.

"Yes! See?" Crevel pointed out Dermot's pent up fury to all the room to view. "The common soldier has little manners, no honor, and base desires! Perhaps he means us violence? I do not mean to disturb Madame" – he turned his speech to entreat her directly – "but I worry that your generosity of spirit has been taken advantage of. You offer your hospitality with a naïve liberality that recommends you while it exposes you, Madame. Certain disagreeable types of company will always overstep."

Sophie stood up. "I can not tolerate this!" she announced amidst the bedlam, and fled the company and the room.

"I'll check on her." Simonne followed her mother out with a more composed withdrawal. Father Meslier curled his lip in disapproval while Robert stood mouth agape. Seconds it took for the ladies to leave, and then Madame was left with five men: Meslier, Crevel, Crevel fils, Dermot, and her new grandson, Émile. The lady was imperial, a caesar in state, attended by a querulous rabble of petitioners.

"I was telling you about respect, Mr. Ward." Madame did not miss a beat. "You came here at the invitation of my late son to whose memory you are, quite frankly, a disgrace. I don't care a jot what Bolshevik opinions you hold, or false grievances you nurture against God's natural order, but I *do* care about my family.

"You put my granddaughter in a great deal of danger today, Mr. Ward, and I don't take lightly to *that*. I will take your word for it that you will leave us in the morning. You will be good to it and spare me the duty of throwing you out on your ear."

In Madame's departure there was a vacuum. The train of her mourning dress sucked the air from the room as she took her leave.

"Party's over, Robert." Crevel straightened his jacket, his face flushed from the bottle and events. "Time we left."

"I think, Crevel, I'll join you?" Father Meslier scurried along as only the best of fawners know how.

The servants had scattered, keen to spread the news. Only two now remained.

"Mr. Ward?" Émile addressed the despondent Irishman. "I believe you, what you said. I too worry that these men... that they did not kill my brother."

He had not said a word all night.

"I'm sorry, Émile," Dermot said gently, "I don't mean to worry you, but I think you should be careful."

"You think the curse will get me too?" He asked it simply.

"Oh, Émile, I just don't know." And why again, Dermot felt, was it *he* who was at the center of this whirlpool, fielding questions he didn't understand? He who was seeing glimpses of another world beyond the understanding of a rational man? "I don't know if there is a curse, Émile, but those men at the mill had no part in this. I'm almost certain of that."

"You believe that whoever killed my brother still walks free, then?"

Dermot laid a consoling hand on the twin's arm. "I'm sorry," he said. "Yes, I do."

Dermot got up. He left Émile alone on the twin's first night as family in the Malenfer Manor. He had his own bag to pack. It seemed that this was to be Dermot's last night in that mysterious old house, just when his heart was telling him to stay. Just when he was growing fond of it. And he still had not found Arthur.

Chapter 22
Sleepwalkers

SOME TIME LATER, WHEN MOST OF THE HOUSE LAY DEEP IN SLUMBER, at an hour when no honest person willingly labors, two rough fellows approached Malenfer Manor en route to a summons. They came without the benefit of lantern or torch, invisible to the wariest of sentries under that dark and tousled sky, the ill weather and the hour both befitting their trade.

"Are you sure this is the right way, boss? Wasn't that a path we passed back there?" The man that spoke was rake-like thin, and his teeth chattered out the words. A soft down beard of first-growth fluff showed him but a lad.

"Keep moving," replied his walrus companion, impervious to the cold, "we're late enough already." Water rolled off his pate and jowls – he had no neck to speak of. "Stop your whining and pick up your feet. This is the way, I tell you."

Experience spoke true. Shortly thereafter the men took shelter beneath the eaves of the barn.

"Can't we go in?" asked the lanky fellow, nodding towards the house. He pulled his overcoat tightly around him and huddled against the stone.

"*Can't we go in?*" his compatriot mimicked, aiming a cuff to the back of his head. "Her place? Really? The Malenfer house? What are you thinking, Stéphane?" The brute warmed the boy with his boozy breath, but his abuse did not lack for affection –, he might have been the other's father if they weren't born of different species.

With faces knotted against the wind, they peeked around the corner, and clouds lit up like ashen lanterns above the manor's leering towers. Sunken windows cast bright reflections in puddles across the courtyard; they glinted like a score of eyes, predatory and watchful.

"You're late." A low voice spoke, unheralded, from behind them. The watchful pair shrieked in reply.

"You old troll!" The bald man recovered. "What are you doing sneaking up on us like that?"

"Is that a joke?" stuttered the younger twig, angry in his embarrassment. "Well, it isn't bloody funny."

The Malenfer footman chuckled. "A pair of little girls, the both of you. Are you sure that you're quite capable?" Gustave eyed them skeptically now that the thought had come to him. "Well, follow me, the pair of you."

Gustave led them a short distance off. The bald man lay beaten in a stall, separate from the pigs. He groaned awake and rolled to his knees as Gustave applied the boot.

"Get up. It's time."

The bald man struggled a bit when he saw the rope draped from the rafters. He was persuaded to take his place on the stage. He didn't want for assistance.

"What's he done again?"

"What does it matter?"

"I'm just asking. He's a big one."

"Shut up, the pair of you."

Gustave saw her shrouded in the corner, her face covered by a veil. He wondered if Madame ever had her doubts. Second thoughts never seemed to plague her. Did she know something? Had she guessed? Then why this change of plan? He wished for light to pierce the shadows that he might read what she was thinking.

He waited for his Mistress's pleasure.

The veil gave the briefest of nods.

Stéphane chanced a rogue glance back as they pushed their parcel in the cart, and woe that he did, for what he saw almost froze his beanpole heart. Not since Lot's wife had a look behind been so ill-timed – there were two seconds of light from the thunderstorm before all was turned to black.

It *had* been there, above the glass, above the highest windows; it had scurried, bent and animal-like, across the wet slate rooftops. A girl it was, or had the shape, her dress long and clinging, yet small and dark, on hand and foot, it moved too fast for nature. Insect-like she had scuttled to the garret window, probing the house for admission, but lit up in that briefest moment her face had crooked around to see him. Unlucky eye that he had! *Oh, Stéphane why did you do it?* Her gaze had sought him truly before the darkness returned and claimed her, leaving him with a sickness of heart.

Stéphane heard the fat man's biting curses as he pumped his legs and passed him. The prospect of pay for this dark night's business was cold consolation now. It was a long while yet, and much road covered, before he risked another look back, and some sixty years later, with his last dying breath, he asked his confessor to save him from her.

"You're up late, Berthe. Couldn't sleep well?"

"I was worrying about Émile."

"Any chance of a glass of wine? How's he doing anyway?"

"Not great. I don't think he's got over it at all. I think he's getting worse. There you go. There's still some soup. The pot's still warm. Can I fetch you up a bowl? No? It won't take a minute to heat, I promise. What gets you up at this hour?"

"Nothing much. Something I had to take care of. You raised those boys like they were your own. I don't wonder that you're anxious. It seems to me that you were more a mother than anyone else they knowed."

"I tried, Gustave. Oh, I did try. You know how it was. I'd have liked my own, once upon a time. But things were what they were. All the same, I wasn't ready for this, none of what's happened. I'm not."

"You did well by them, Berthe. By Émile."

"I don't know where I'm at."

"Don't distress yourself, girl. Oh, thank you, just a splash. You'll make sure the boy comes through it. I know that you will."

The old retainers took a sip of their respective glasses.

"Gustave."

"Yes, Berthe?"

"Can I ask you something?"

"Of course. We've got no secrets."

"You and Pierre. You never saw eye to eye. I know that he could be difficult."

"He was young and wild. We were guilty of that in our time."

"Maybe, I suppose. But you do miss him, don't you? You miss Pierre? I just worry."

Gustave said nothing for a bit, and then: "It's late, and I'm tired. Good night, Berthe. I think I'll retire. Get some rest yourself. God give us the strength to change that which we can, and the sense to accept what we can not."

Midnight had come and gone and the fire had burned down low, but Arthur's ghost had yet to return, and Dermot found his absence troubling. He made a decision. There was no sleep to be had; too much going on in his head. He opened the door to go look for him and fill the time productively.

He crept down the hall to Arthur's old room. It was the closest place he thought of, but he found the door nailed shut with a plank, all pretense at disguise discarded. Arthur couldn't get through that, he knew. He'd have to look elsewhere instead. Watching him was the painting of the cavalier, still gloating above his kill. "You don't know which way he went?" he asked. "Not much help, are you, mate?" Dermot moved away. There was one whole floor that he still hadn't seen, and he made his way there now.

All houses possess intelligence, and some, like people, grow cranky with their years. The Malenfer Manor knew Dermot wished stealth, and so it amused itself by denying him. It creaked loudly with each feathered stride, the softest tread scorned by a groan.

It was a pained Dermot that mounted the third floor, relieved to remain undiscovered. At the top of the stairs he stood stock still, not risking another murmur. His dark sight was attuned by now (for there was no lantern on this level), and he spied the stub of a candle on the table by the balcony. Dermot struck a match from his pocket and put it to the wick, and then he chose the passage to his right and wandered in that direction.

The rain drove across the windows, rapping against the panes. The cough of nearby thunder was close enough to shake him. The hallway twisted and dropped and rose, by little groups of steps. He protected the tiny flickering flame as he meandered further in. Dermot passed beneath the pointed rack of an enormous glass-eyed deer, and he wondered if he had not just seen its twin in the painting down beneath. Was this old Malenfer's quarry? Arthur was nowhere to be seen. He was thinking of calling it an evening when he saw a muted light. Its pulse grew stronger, dancing bright, and he heard a floorboard creak. Someone was coming towards him, and they were made of flesh and bone! Dermot did not wish discovery, but there was no time for escape. He fumbled for an explanation to account for his presence here.

"Hello? Who's there?" It was Simonne's voice. "Oh, Mr. Ward! You startled me!"

"Please excuse me. I hope I didn't frighten you." He couldn't fathom what she was doing up here so late.

"I'm fine. I got a little scared. I didn't know who it was. I'm glad it's you, Mr. Ward. Please, won't you take a seat?" She put herself down on the top tread of a step and patted the space to her left.

"Thank you. I'm fine." He regretted saying it; he rather wanted to sit down next to her now. Why on earth had he said 'no'? Had she taken offense?

Her dressing gown was the color of a Van Gogh night over a night-gown of white flannel. Her rich thick hair was pinned up behind her head, which struck Dermot as strange for bedtime. Being unfamiliar with the mysteries of women, he kept silent his curiosity.

"Shouldn't you be in bed by now?" he asked her instead.

"I think I might ask you the same question."

Dermot was pleased. She wasn't upset. He'd been worried about her all day. "I was looking for a friend." He said it without thinking.

"Well, you've found one," she said in reply.

For a moment he couldn't speak, and then he found his honest tongue. He couldn't help himself. "You look absolutely beautiful." And they both reddened a little in reply. "I'm sorry!" he blurted straight away. "I'm not really thinking. I didn't mean to embarrass you..." but she didn't seem offended. "I don't suppose I'm meant to say that sort of thing at all."

"No?" she quizzed him. "And why not? Why not say things if you think them true?"

He liked her dimples when she smiled like that.

"Well..." He hesitated, his thoughts a tumble. "I suppose, good manners? ... Say, what on earth finds you up here, anyway?" He'd been so surprised by her, expecting Arthur first and then assuming discovery by one of the staff, that it hadn't occurred to him to ask her.

"I was looking for someone too." She was evasive, not coy. "But she isn't here."

"How strange," he commented. "Say, if the offer is still open, might I take that seat after all?" It was and he did.

Dermot never took his eyes off her, watching her all the while. Her long slender fingers that would fit so well nestled between his own.

"I've been worried about you," he began, gravel in his throat. With the first words out there didn't seem to be anything he couldn't tell her, and he wanted to tell her it all. He stood up again suddenly, uncomfortable, straight and upright, trying to force the words out, finding the flickering candle in his hands and not knowing what to do with it.

"Of course you were worried, silly!" she chided him with good humor. "That's what's meant to happen." He wasn't sure what she meant. She explained. "You missed me and I missed you too, but everything's going to be all right." Dermot's chest burned. Her smile dropped for a moment. "You weren't really going to leave tomorrow, were you? You wouldn't leave me here all alone?"

"I didn't want to leave you..."

They were quiet together for a moment. Dermot struggled inside. *Should he explain?*

"How is your mother doing?" He needed to change the subject.

"Tolerably well. I left her in her room. All she talked about was you."

"I'm sorry about that."

"Pride doesn't come naturally to you, Mr. Ward. She's a fan."

He let that sink in. "And Grand-mère?" He used her familiar title, to Simonne's amusement.

"Even *Madame* too." He choked when he heard it. "Are you all right? I think she secretly admires someone who is willing to tell her off," she continued, "not that she'd actually say so."

"I don't know about that," he said, remembering. "You should have stuck around and heard her tonight after you left the room. She doesn't want me here. She made that very clear."

"I got the update. You're a guest. Be nice is all. See how it is in the morning."

"When is your wedding to Robert Crevel?"

Simonne's mood dropped. It was the first time Dermot had mentioned it, but eventually she spoke. "Do you remember when we went out riding together, Mr. Ward? Out to the old abbey and the tree?" Dermot nodded. *"It's your choice, Simonne, that's what you said. I may marry whomever I please. You said that when we went out riding together. Don't you remember that?"*

It was the veneer of a question, her heart gift-wrapped in a subtle appeal. She floated it delicately, launched it like a paper ship, conscious of the waves and winds that threatened it, but willing it to sea. This, of course, was what had consumed her, rendered her these past few days, the question she had to settle before all else came to be. Her chin lifted, her glossy eyes rose to meet his steady face, and with her heart laid out on the line she willed Dermot to speak.

Gentlemen dread such moments, insensitive beasts that they are – thick-skulled by nature, and blind to feminine subtlety. Dermot was no exception and was hampered by masculine incommodity. The best of men might recognize their deficiencies, a few tread water, and some even learn to swim. Dermot had ten years in coal mines and on battle-fields, a poor apprenticeship for games of the heart. He floundered in his uncertainty and missed the life ring she'd thrown. "That's what

I said. You do what you want." And he unwittingly broke her heart. Her paper ship slipped beneath the sea, and he knew that somehow he had hurt her.

Something had gone wrong. Something had changed. He didn't know what or why. It was a long time before the cold draft of the hallway blew the mood away.

"Why are you really here?" she asked eventually.

"Simonne," he said; he didn't want to lose her. "Will you listen if I tell you something strange?"

The men she had known who went to war did not often talk about their experiences, and never before had such things come like this, firsthand, into her own ear. She'd had crumbs only, secondhand wisdoms, occasionally the letters other women cared to share. In those redacted pages, things were always fine within the army: "Don't worry, we'll all be back soon," "I miss you lots," "I love you and the family." Platitudes, consoling words, and too much reassurance. But always there were whispers. Around men from the war she had felt like an intruder in a place she did not belong, but here with Dermot she was now his guest in a land she had scarcely imagined.

At first he had leaned back against the wall as he relayed his story, resting his arms across his chest. He blew out his candle lest all the light fade, and at some point he returned to sit beside her. Simonne squirreled in against him, her head lying on his shoulder, as she listened to the tale that emerged.

"That was how I met him, your uncle," Dermot said – he'd been talking for a while. "Of course, Arthur could be a pain in the ass, but I liked him very much. We got along. We ended up serving together over the next few months." Once more he fell silent and reflective, as was his pattern of speaking. "Then came the salient."

"The salient?" She didn't understand.

"The fronts hardly moved the whole time, but every now and again you'd get a bit of land that stuck out into 'their' bit, or God help you, the other way around. Holding a piece like that let you spot your guns better, let you snipe at their sides. If we had such a place, we'd pour men into it before an attack. It let you flank them or even cut them off... if you managed to hold onto it. That bit of land was called a salient, and it was highly prized on either side. We were digging out from one of these ahead of a big attack. That's when it happened."

She reached out a hand, a gesture of gratitude, and he took it willingly and warmly and with all his blunt, blind heart.

"You think I protected you, that I helped you, that I was looking after you and so perhaps I can be counted on?" But he wasn't asking her a question. "I... I care for you a lot, Simonne, more than any-one I've known. I truly do." Somehow now it was easier to say these things, and his words spilled out like water from a punctured can-teen. He squeezed her hand lightly. "Do you remember the library?" He smiled as she glowed brighter with every word. "Even then I knew something was... different." He still couldn't pin it. "Something had changed in me."

She remembered every moment, relived them now, but couldn't speak or acknowledge anything lest her heart give her away.

He risked a glance down at her, but she was silent and looked straight ahead. He wasn't sure if this was a good sign... still, when the charge is sounded and you go over the top, there is only one way forward. Dermot soldiered on.

"So I thought you were special, and I liked you a lot, and I hoped that you liked me..." He coughed, buying another moment. "Then with everything that happened... Pierre... the mill... the only thing that scared me was the thought of losing you. I already knew what I felt for you, Simonne, and I had to keep you safe.

"The thing is," he went on quickly, heading off the objections he was certain would come, "the thing is, I'm not very good at protecting people I care about. To those who need me..." She looked up at him now, hearing the change in his voice, the resignation and fear. "I'm not. You couldn't ever trust me, Simonne, and that was why I agreed to leave. One day I would fail you, just like I failed your uncle, and I couldn't let that happen." She was crying! "Oh, I'm sorry, Simonne! What is it I've done now?"

"I don't know what you're talking about!" His words had opened her and the happiness had spilled over, straining until she had thought she might burst. She squeezed his hand back, as he'd done to hers, and she knew in the core of her very being that they would never again be apart.

He did care for her, she knew it, and she loved him madly back; desperately, pleadingly, teasingly, helplessly. In her whole life she had never known anything like it, and she swore to herself that she'd nev-er let it leave and she would never give it up. Whatever he was talking about they'd sort out together. There was no other way.

She turned her chin up to look at him, her curls falling loose, her lips trembling, eager to feel his touch. But he was haunted. His smile was gone. "Dermot, my darling!" she pleaded with him. "Whatever is it that you mean?"

He composed himself. "I've never told this to anyone," he began. He had her undivided attention. Whatever would come now of it, she would forever know the truth. And so Simonne heard of the tunnel hole and the shell that went astray. Heard of the men that were trapped beneath the earth. Heard of the dead men below. Heard of Arthur and Dermot digging free from out of that grave. Heard of the escape that was met with disaster – of the guns and the clouds of gas. Of how her uncle was left bleeding and wounded. How Arthur sat wheezing the poisonous air while Dermot ran away.

"In the end we got him out, back down the tunnel and out the other end, but by then it was useless... The doctors wouldn't even treat him, the push had started you see, the place was littered with men.

"I got him in an ambulance that was heading further away, but there was nothing to be done for him. He died in terrible lingering pain, and that was how I lost my friend." He wiped his eyes, ashamed and embarrassed and, more than anything, terribly sad.

"Oh, Dermot!" Her words were wet with tears.

"I didn't help him. I'm sorry, Simonne. I didn't have the courage and I ran from it. I let him die, that's what I did."

"No, no!" She admonished him, kissing him, "You did your best!"

"Maybe I did," he agreed, fighting down the pain, "but that's just it. I think it *was* my best, and it wasn't nearly good enough." She shook her head, rejecting the notion. "No, Simonne," he refuted her. "I know. I didn't go because I was getting him help, I went because I wanted to... I went because I was scared. That's who I am, Simonne! Don't think I'm anything I'm not. Don't think I'll be able to protect you through thick and thin, because when the moment comes, when it's do or die, I leave my friends behind."

"No, no!" she insisted. "You tear yourself up for that?" She was riled, insistent, impassioned in her speech. "How many would have lasted half as long as you did? How many would have had the nerve and the fire to do everything that you did, to look on what you saw? You gave your all – your all! For your men and for my uncle. That is all anyone can ask, my love. That is all anyone can expect." She bruised him with the force of her convictions. Her lips were close to his.

"But it wasn't enough. I'll never be forgiven. Simonne, how can I trust myself to take care of you when I failed that test?"

"Pooh to that!" she said sharply. "I can take care of myself. And if it's forgiveness you want, Arthur would forgive you, I'm certain."

"No, he wouldn't." Dermot shook his head.

"So sure?" she said slyly. "Have you asked him, then?"

There was a turn to the corner of her mouth and a twinkling in her eye. Something that the night's emotions failed to explain away.

"I have something more to tell you. My last secret, I promise,

Simonne. You won't believe me, but it is true. He came back to me. Arthur did. He came back to me after the war. I can see him, Simonne. I saw him dying, and he came back. He asked me to come to the Manor with him, and I don't think that I'm mad."

"You can see him? You mean, entirely in the flesh?" It wasn't the reaction he had expected; she was curious, not incredulous in the least.

"Uh... well, he sort of glows in faded colors. And he doesn't walk through walls."

"That's amazing! And are there any others?"

"Others?"

"No others?" She gave him a very strange look. "That's OK," she said, "don't worry. We'll have lots of time to talk about it."

"Arthur's disappeared," he explained.

"They do that sometimes."

This didn't entirely reassure him. "I'm worried about him, that's why I came to look." A thought crossed his mind. "Who was it *you* were looking for up here?" He repeated his earlier question.

Simonne fidgeted and squirmed, hesitant to answer him, but then things were different now. This man who held her hand could really understand her, was someone who had risked his life for her, was someone who liked her for who she was, and needed her help too. Simonne was sick of making stories; she'd been lying all her life.

"I was looking for Élise Beauvais."

"The witch?" He shrank back. "Why on earth would you think she was here?"

"Because, Dermot... I followed her."

Chapter 23
Fall of the House of Malenfer

IT WAS MORNING. DERMOT WAS AVOIDING PACKING UP HIS THINGS. Running steps passed by his door, and raised voices conveyed alarm. Curiosity persuaded him out to the hallway where a squabble could be heard coming from the entry hall, two stories below. Dermot went to the staircase to look.

"No, it isn't so! It's a lie!" Was that Émile's voice? A scrum of men were pushing below, but Dermot was too high to see who. He took the stairs two at a time.

"Greedy bastard!" The warped figure of Gustave pointed violently. Dermot saw him lash out at the twin and strike the young man a blow. "How could you?" A second punch landed true while Émile was being held by others. "He did it!" someone shouted, and the maids were screaming now. Émile slipped and went down hard in the middle of the debacle.

Some tried to shield him. Others kicked him when he was down. Dermot, taking the stairs three at a time, was close, almost among it, and everyone was shouting. Berthe grabbed onto Gustave's arm to stop his rough abuse; she pulled him back, entreating him to do no more, but the Malenfer footman was raging.

"Stop it! Stop!" Dermot bellowed as he pushed into the milieu. He forced himself through the tightly packed group till he stood over Émile's bruised body.

"What is the meaning of this?" It was Madame's voice. "What is going on? Berthe?"

The fray divided like a playground fight at the sound of the school bell.

"Madame, your pardon. I don't know how, but it's true. It happened and it's true!"

"What are you wittering about, woman? What can have possibly happened to cause this unsightly... riot?" She looked most disapprovingly on the disorder. Men in the hall straightened their coats and passed fingers through out-of-place hair.

"We were cleaning this morning, Madame," Berthe pronounced, "and we were into Émile's room, begging your pardon, seeing as how it was the day we do those parts of the house. It's his brother's satchel is what we found, Madame, is what I'm saying. The rent bag! The one that was stolen. He had it!"

As proof to her words, the housekeeper lifted the leather traveling pouch. It was an old worn thing with a wide long strap; she brandished it like a trophy. At its sight a gasp went up, for there were few embroiled who knew. They had been drawn, like Dermot, by the disturbance but were not aware what they were spectators to. "Pierre's rent bag, Madame," she repeated. "We found it hidden in Émile's own room!"

Dermot recognized the bag; he recalled it strung across the youthful chest of the cockish young Pierre. He'd seen it last on that fateful morning as Pierre had ridden off. By now, and with Dermot's aid, Émile had gotten back onto his feet. He might have been Pierre returned but for the absent jaunty grin. *The rent bag in Émile's room?* Dermot didn't comprehend.

An enraged Gustave took up the cause just as Berthe had finished speaking. "He took Pierre's bag!" he accused, "and the money's in it still!" The footman dug out a fistful of notes to the general dismay of the room. "He had it hidden!" he riled, brandishing the money. "A thief and a murderer besides!" The accusation invoked shouts of dismay and anger in equal measure.

"Enough of this theater!" Madame shouted them quiet.

Dermot helped Émile to his feet. Simonne came to his side and volunteered her handkerchief; Émile was cut on the side of his cheek.

"Pierre's bag in your room, Émile? What is the explanation?"

"I don't know," the battered Émile managed to speak. "They say it was, but I don't know, it couldn't have been there!"

"The girls work together, Madame," Berthe clarified. "And I was right there behind them. We were doing all those rooms at that end of the house, it was just routine as always."

"I didn't know it was there!" Émile objected.

"None of us brought it in, Madame, none of them girls did – it was there when we got there, hidden it was! Oh, Émile, what have you done?"

"Nothing. I've done nothing. How could you think that of me?"

"Liar!" The ringside jury brewed up.

"I dread to think, Madame!"

"It couldn't be there," Émile repeated, but it seemed that he doubted himself.

"He wanted it all!" Gustave bellowed. "He's a black-heart villain! A lifetime in the stables, then a Malenfer overnight? How else does he come by the money? It's his brother's blood that's on that bag! Cain here coveted Abel!"

"No! Never!" Émile said desperately as the crowd again boiled around him.

"Mad with greed he must have been. He thought he'd become almighty!"

"No!"

"The desire for wealth proved too strong. He didn't want to share it!" Gustave lunged in to strike again, but this time Dermot blocked him.

Émile howled wildly at the room, pummeled by such accusations.

"It's nonsense!" Dermot shouted out, but the twin seemed sore afflicted.

"Take Émile up to the library and see he doesn't leave there. The rest of you get back to work. Berthe, I would speak privately."

The to-do broke up. Young Émile was shepherded off by two unsympathetic workmen. Berthe looked very unhappy. Madame now recognized her overdue guest as her staff dispersed around her. "Nobody goes home today until you've been given permission." She said it loudly enough for all to hear. "That means you too, Mr. Ward," she continued coldly. "Until we have this figured out, you will kindly delay your departure."

The house was quiet by the time the police arrived, but far from calm. Why Émile got the police while the men at the mill had not, Dermot wasn't told. Perhaps it was that Émile wasn't a stranger, or because he was family now. Perhaps Madame harbored doubts herself where before she had harbored none. Dermot didn't know any of it, and there was no explanation forthcoming. "Money makes people do the strangest things..." He heard it more than once.

Dermot was not immune to the sentiment's lure, yet he could not reconcile the Émile he knew, the man he had ridden with searching, searching through the night for his twin, with the man capable of this foul deed. The look on Émile's face, the shock of recognition when they'd discovered Pierre together – it *had* been real, Dermot knew it. Yet in the hours before the gendarme arrived the doubt began to creep in. Dermot sat alone with Simonne talking of nothing else. He began to second-guess his instinct. He saw things in different ways.

How was it, he wondered, that they had been able to find Pierre at all, when all the others had turned back for the night? How at that moment, at that very lane, in the middle of that dreadful night, had they picked that very place to look just a little closer off the road? Dermot couldn't even remember if he'd been the one riding forward or if he'd followed behind Émile. Was it luck at work or something more that had brought them to that spot?

And how came the money? Why was it there? The women were honest, weren't they? There was no conspiracy here. Three of them confirmed the story, two maids and the long-serving Berthe, that the bag had been hidden behind the dresser and could have remained undiscovered. Fate itself seemed to have revealed the pouch with its treasure still intact, fate and the diligence of hard-working folk doing their duty with a dustpan.

How else could Émile have gotten ahold of the bag? Émile hadn't even been fighting during the siege of the mill, so he couldn't have lifted it then. It didn't make sense. *Unless he'd had it earlier.* Dermot was wracked with doubt. It was clear that whatever had happened back then, Émile had some explaining to do.

What had Dermot seen on that terrible night? To this he kept returning. What had been written on Émile's honest face? Was it dismay or contrition? Could Dermot have mistaken the shock on his face for a soured conscience? He no longer quite knew.

Simonne sat beside him on a small leather couch, her skirts hugged in tight about her. Each lent comfort to the other just by being there. It was not spoken, but understood.

"Do you think he's going to be all right?" It was Simonne who asked.

Dermot wasn't sure what to say. "You've known him a long time, Simonne, haven't you?"

"I suppose." She was thinking. "Most of my life."

"Do *you* think he'll be all right?"

She considered it a while. "No. I don't," she finally answered. "I think he's been half-lost since Pierre went away, and now... to be accused of this. They're saying he killed him, oh, how could they, Dermot? There must be another reason."

Dermot took Simonne's hand. Her palm was so small in his, her skin pale and smooth, her thin fingers fitting snugly in between his own.

"Then you're on his side?"

"Of course!" She was unwavering.

Not shortly thereafter, the police finally arrived. The gendarme took statements from the staff while his superior talked to the family. Émile's room was inspected, the money was examined, checked again, and recounted. It tallied with the rents. Émile was taken into custody, with the suggestion of charges to follow. They led the twin away in handcuffs and put him in the back of their car. Dermot overheard Madame's instruction for Émile to have a lawyer. The police car drove away from the house. Émile did not look back.

And then it happened, though Dermot knew not from where it came. An idea that softly landed as he watched the police car recede. Perhaps it was the sight of Émile, stoic and rejected – the look of a man huddled in a trench ahead of a new offensive. The same look of disbelief that life had come to such a point. Dermot had been there: when you question your faith in an ordered universe and it is confirmed or it falls apart. Dermot decided at that very moment that Arthur's son was innocent.

"Simonne," – they had been inseparable – "what was it you said about Michel?"

"Michel?" In the preceding hours they had talked about a great many different things. "The flu, you mean?" Émile still wasn't out of sight. "Dermot, what do you want to know?"

"You said something about him being better, I'm sure that's what you said."

"I don't understand. Why does that matter now?"

"Please, tell me again. Tell me again about Michel."

"Well, he was. Getting better, I mean. I did say that, because he was." The police car moved out of sight. "I talked to his doctor myself." She turned to look at him. "His temperature had broken, and we thought him on the mend. That's why the others were so especially sad, because they'd just started to have hope. But I had seen the witch stalking us, and that could only mean one thing."

"His temperature had broken. Michel was getting better?" Dermot became excited, "But don't you see, that's it!" He pulled her close. Eyebrows were raised from those on the steps but Dermot was oblivious.

"See what?" Simonne didn't, but she was very aware of his arms about her.

"Come with me, somewhere quiet. I've got an idea I need to tell you."

He led her through the entrance hall between its crisp landscape paintings, past the beat of the grandfather clock still muffled under draping. He held her hand past the pitchfork battles that raged on her skillful canvas, and through the door beyond the empty fireplace colder than the outdoors.

"What's going on, Dermot? What is it?" They found seclusion in the cavernous hall beyond.

"I see it now," he began, growing excited. "Listen. Hear me through and then tell me what you think." She agreed. "We're looking for someone who killed Pierre, aren't we?" Simonne said yes. "And that's why they think Émile is guilty..."

"He's not!"

"But they think it. They do. Please don't argue just yet. He has the motive, he could have done it – for the power and money it might bring."

"What do you mean? How can you say that?"

"That's what they'll think. The Malenfer inheritance! Émile's motive was to improve his share of any inheritance."

"But he didn't do it!"

"I know. But they don't know that."

"He couldn't do it."

"But he could. Don't get mad. I'm not saying it. But please accept for a minute that they'll think it. Don't you see?" Dermot raced on, seeing Simonne upset. "We're looking in the wrong place. We're looking at the wrong murder! Émile didn't kill Pierre because he didn't kill Michel. When Michel died, Émile wasn't a Malenfer, so he didn't have a motive! Well..." Dermot stumbled, "*technically* he was a Malenfer, but he didn't know it yet." Dermot bubbled with energy – it fit so well. The jigsaw was coming together and the picture becoming clear.

"What are you saying, Dermot? You're saying Michel was murdered too?"

She seemed stricken at the thought and yet excited by it also. Dermot's enthusiasm was a mountain stream sweeping her along. She couldn't see the destination but was caught up in the current.

"Consider the facts that you told me: His temperature had broken; he's young and healthy. Why wouldn't he recover?" He didn't wait for an answer. "But let's say he was killed, let's just assume it. Let's say someone did do that – murder Michel. Why would they do that? What benefit would that bring?" He asked as one that already knew the answer.

"I don't know," she said.

"Oh, Simonne. I think you do."

"You mean money, don't you? You mean he's the last heir? Michel was the last of the Malenfer men." She was following his thoughts now, encouraged by the nodding of his animated head. "You mean after he's gone... I become an heiress!" Her mind rolled over and her alluring face turned sour. "You think I killed Michel?" Her voice changed pitch, making Dermot shudder.

"No no no!" he whispered, holding her arms in a hurry as she tried to take a swing. "Not you! Not you! No, of course not you! But if Michel *was* killed and you *did* inherit, who else stood to gain?" He let the thought sink in.

"You don't think..."

"Yes, I do. But then everything goes crazy at the Malenfer house because someone else appears. Who? Me. I show up, Dermot Ward, arriving out of the blue. I show up and spring the news that the inheritance isn't decided. It isn't guaranteed to be yours at all; in fact, you might get nothing, Simonne. Now there are two male heirs, bastards yes, but acknowledged as Malenfers through the dying words of their war-dead father. And that will surely change everything."

"My grandmother might have split it up?"

"She might have given you nothing at all. Who knows with Madame? The twins are men, remember Simonne, male Malenfer heirs of her first born. Who the hell knows what goes through Madame's mind with her feudal ideas? She might have given them nothing as bastards or made one of them sole heir. The point is that no one knew, perhaps not even Madame. Think of that. Now say someone had already killed Michel to settle all the money on you; do you think they'd stop now? Would they be happy to let chance intervene after doing what they'd done?"

"But all of this is conjecture, Dermot. We only know Pierre was killed. No one has tried to hurt Émile..." But she stopped as if seeing the flaw in that thought and the deviousness of the alternative.

"They didn't? But, my dearest, they hurt Émile more than anyone might bear. His brother's rent bag shows up in Émile's room and the blame falls squarely on him. Pierre's murder hangs over his head and the judge might be taken in. And even if he gets off, conjecture would follow him. Would Madame make him sole heir now? You know her better than I do.

"How much more harm can you do to a fellow? You kill his brother and then you pin the blame on him? Émile who has lost his twin could die an innocent man. Murdered with the guillotine and his memory cast in shame. And the beauty of the whole scheme is that no one is looking anymore. The real culprit will kill them both and is left above suspicion."

"And if that happens, I'm the sole heiress once more." She finished his reasoning for him.

"Yes, you are, my pretty girl. You were always the belle of the ball."

"You needn't seem so happy about it, Dermot."

"Unless things are settled on your mother."

"My mother!"

"I doubt it. I'm not worried right now. I don't think she's in any immediate danger unless she looks to marry again."

"Dermot, we've got to say something!" Simonne was shaking. The implications of what he was saying seemed to have sunk home.

"We will, we'll sort things out. It all makes sense, don't you see?"

"But where's the proof? There's no proof of any of this. The doctor signed a death certificate – he said Michel died of the Spanish Flu."

"He didn't know what he was looking for. And as for proof, I think I know how."

Dermot stepped back, but her hands still gripped his jacket, and he was glad because he didn't want her to let go. And then, because she was there, and because he had nothing else to hide, and because he knew, deep down in his core, that everything now, whatever else happened, would be all right, and because regardless of all else and any obstacles or objections that might arise – he knew he loved her, he did, and he would fight for her till his last dying breath. And fighting was something he did know.

He held her, his toughened arms slipping easily around her tiny waist, pulling her firmly towards him. Her urgent mouth reached to him willingly, her body molded against his. There was a passion in his kisses that Simonne reciprocated as his hands pushed the hair from her face. His eager lips lingered over hers. He kissed her down her neck. He wound his fingers through her hair and pulled her to his chest.

Dermot inhaled her floral scent.

Simonne laid her head to his heart and felt the beat of him against her cheek.

Chapter 24
Old Bones

By the old Chevecheix church was a graveyard, and in it the Malenfer tomb. Dermot paid the place a visit under the promiscuity of a full moon.

The cemetery was fenced by a low stone wall, its iron rails cut and taken, their metal gone to be smelted for guns, allowing the dead to assist the war effort. Dermot had no issue gaining admittance. Among the field of jutting stones the mausoleum stood out clearly – the other markers were short and worn, mere shards besides its presence.

The tomb looked Greek, yet if you squeezed past its Doric columns, at its heart it was something different. To lay a hand on its chiseled relief was to fondle its vulgar imagery. Angelic hosts and cherubim decorated it, the bric-a-brac of the faithful, but there were surprises found amidst its stonework that startled Dermot to witness: sprites and imps and daemon-kind, and other horned vulgarities, the fiends of hell all bent on war assembled on its surface.

"How did you find me, Dermot?"

"Your niece suggested I might check here. She's a very perceptive girl."

Arthur stood by the cemetery path. He seemed older when he stopped smiling, and now he looked wizened indeed. He knocked his boot against the tombstones, perhaps mocking them or from jealousy.

Dermot saw him as he had been, the Arthur before he had died. The profile of that leonine head so very familiar to him. His burn scars were hidden by the turn of his face; it might be that none of this had happened. For a moment he was again the Lieutenant he'd lived beside in the trenches.

"What the hell have you been doing down here?" Dermot asked the truant. "Do you know all that's been going on at the manor since you buggered off?"

"I hadn't meant to trouble you," Arthur explained. "I had to get away. The girl at the mill... I tried to tell you. Well, I needed some distance to think."

"Cheery place to come to."

Shaded from the moon and behind the pillars, the door to the tomb was in shadow. "Nobody ever came here much, and I find it rather peaceful."

Dermot hurt inside. He remembered the tunnel three years before. He remembered the last time he'd lost his friend and had returned to find him later.

"Are you a little sad?" Arthur read him. "You know, I'm told most people who can see ghosts are likely to go a bit cuckoo."

"Maybe I was a little insane to start with."

"Maybe you were, at that." Arthur seemed philosophical. He was fishing for his pipe. "You're not such a bad fellow, Dermot Ward, you've always been my friend. You helped me when I asked you to, and you're not to blame for Pierre." Dermot bowed his head. Arthur laid a hand upon his shoulder that Dermot couldn't feel. "Nor for Émile either... yes, I did hear about developments. I even saw him go by in their car." He had his Meerschaum pipe in hand now, knocking the bowl clean on the tomb. "And I'm glad you've made another friend. Good girl that you've got there." Arthur put the pipe to his mouth.

"Arthur..." Dermot stumbled now to say it, but all the truth needed telling and the time was overdue. "There's something I've wanted to explain to you for a while... Ever since you showed up in Paris, really. It's been playing on my mind quite a bit..."

"It's not about the tunnel, is it? And how I got out and all that?" Arthur struck a match first time.

"You know?"

Arthur inhaled strongly, drawing in the fragranced air to set the tobacco alight. He removed his glowing pipe to inspect his handiwork. "Like I said about my niece – damn fine girl you've got there. Be good to her. Grown up quite a bit lately too, wouldn't you agree?"

"Well." Dermot was a little lost for words. "I didn't know her before. I guess I wanted to say I'm sorry – I shouldn't have done what I did."

"Don't be a bloody idiot, Irlandais." And for the first time in a long time, the serious ghost looked pleased. "If you hadn't gone, we both know you'd be dead. Don't be so damned sentimental about it, there were a lot worse off than us. And let me tell you, while we're at it, that it's me who should apologize to you. All my life it seems fate was trying to do *me* some harm. I've had the curse over me since I was born, and then comes the bloody war. If I hadn't been down that tunnel with you, I doubt it would have caved in at all." Dermot looked doubtful. "Very few people looked out for me, Dermot, but you, my friend, were one."

"Well. I appreciate your words. But it doesn't feel right, and I don't know that it ever will."

"Bollocks, Irlande! Don't you bear a cross for me. And if you do, you should give it up and get on with the living. Listen, Dermot, you always did your best for me and you've always been my friend. I only wish I'd met you earlier, or at another time and place." Here he looked wistful, as wistful as a ghost can look, and one who is smoking besides. "You think of all the terrible things men have done to each other, all that needless harm... The only thing that gives me hope in the world is seeing people look out for each other. Like you did for me. Like you *always* did for me. Don't forget that. If you can do as much for my niece, then I know she's in safe hands."

Dermot was choked with sadness, shame, and grief. He missed his friend more than ever, and yet he seemed even further away. "Thank you," was all he managed.

"Don't be a daisy, Irlandais. Sergeants don't shed tears."

"It's grown dark," Dermot remarked, pulling himself together, and true enough, a solitary cloud had dammed the lunar grace.

"Will you open up the tomb for me?"

"You forget something in there?"

"There's something that I want to see. Come on, I'll show you how to get in."

It seemed rude to refuse the request. "Who was it that built this place?"

"You know him well enough, Dermot. You've even seen his likeness. It was commissioned by my illustrious predecessor, who hung our persistent witch. A bit grandiose, don't you think? I think he overcompensated for the doubt the girl had sown."

"Do you think he half-believed her, then, when she cursed him off to hell?"

"I think she scared him witless, and I happen to agree."

"For a grave it seems rather large. Was he planning for a dynasty, then?"

"He was hoping for one. And almost all of us are here. It looks big from the outside, but you'll see how tight it is. We stack the bones to make more room."

"Very cozy."

"I find the idea reassuring. A comfort, that's what it is. To be surrounded by the family." He smiled again, and this time Dermot saw him in profile but down his marked scarred face. "I've always liked graveyards, Dermot, even before I was dead. A couple of generations and you can barely read all the names, just like all these poor sods out here." He gestured with his pipe. "I find that very peaceful. Don't you?"

"You're a right cheery bugger, Arthur. OK. How the hell do we get in?"

"The key's up on the right side. Do you see that cherub there? Yes, that one. Up behind him."

"Hang on a minute." Dermot scrambled and hoisted himself two feet off the ground, his foot resting on the face of a frog prince worn smooth from the boot soles of the past. The frog was generous, un-complaining and solid, clearly used to such disrespect, a prince who had learned humility by serving others' needs. It was a reach to get the key – *God help a shorter man* – and then his fingertips closed on something thin and alien to the rock. "Got it!" he said, triumphant. The oiled lock smoothly turned. "After you." Arthur slipped through the door and Dermot closed it behind them. He didn't want unwel-come eyes asking what he was doing.

Dermot struck a paper match and fished for a candle stub.

The room was eerily familiar: The rows of coffins looked like bunks in the trenches, stacked high up to the roof. They were housed in slots, cut out from the wall, wide enough for a man to slip into. One fresh casket stood apart, perched on sawhorses right by the door – an elaborate box of polished wood with brass handles that reflected the flame.

"Michel Malenfer, my brother," Arthur pronounced, there being no plaque upon its surface. "They'll have to shift it for Pierre. I won-der if he'll get such a coffin? No telling with my mother."

"Young Michel, who died of the flu?"

"That's him that lies before us."

And so, by the light of a fading candle, Dermot told Arthur his story. He spoke of his suspicions and conjectures, just as he had to Simonne. The ghost's face darkened as he went further on, and he ground on the stem of his pipe. "It just seems so cold," he said at the conclusion after Dermot had told him everything.

"You'll help, then?"

Arthur laid a hand on Michel's coffin. "Of course I will. Any way I can. But you're wrong about the curse."

"How do you mean?"

"I've seen the witch, Dermot. I've seen her; I've heard her. She's very real, you know. She was the girl I saw at the mill, I understand that now. That's what I've been doing out here, trying to figure out what's to be done. She's not giving up, Dermot, and the curse of the Malenfers... it is real. It lives along with her."

"The dead can't hurt the living, Arthur. You're proof of that."

"No? You don't think I killed Pierre? I killed him as surely as firing the gun. His blood is on my hands. She means us harm, Élise Beauvais, she wants my family dead. She's twisted now, she hunts us down, she's human in form alone. Do you know the real reason you found me here, Dermot? Because I'm scared of her."

The Beauvais Witch, a harbinger of death. Was Simonne not a Malenfer too? "What are you suggesting, Arthur?"

"She must be stopped. Convinced to end her feud with us, one way or another."

"How the hell are you going to do that?"

"We've lived with the fear far too long. I've thought about this while hiding here, and there's something I want to try. I need two things: a little of your help – again – and a little bait."

Dermot had misgivings. "What do you mean by bait?"

Arthur told Dermot his plan.

The candle dimmed and died. In the pitch dark, the black of a mining tunnel, the darkness of a tomb, the smell of smoke and formaldehyde lingered amid the breath of man.

"The ghosting hour approaches," Ward spoke softly.

"How appropriate."

Arthur sat in the dressing chair from which Dermot had removed the dust sheet. The once-hidden door had been pried open according to his wishes, and the bolted window of his bedroom left open to the cold. Dermot had obliged in every particular in returning him to his old room. Arthur had then asked for solitude. "I must do this next part alone."

The specter that had once been Élise Beauvais had told him that she would find him. Arthur settled as best he could and waited for the fulfillment of her promise. He'd refused the well-meant offer of a lantern or a fire, but outside the snow had begun to fall, which lent the room a brightness. Arthur pulled up his collar, fished for his pipe and matches, and then nestled in with one ear cocked to await the ancient tormentor.

This was *his* place in which he sat – its stones had seen him through manhood – and not a room in the house knew Arthur better than these walls that cradled his presence. There was a comfort here, despite his goal, and with the passing hours his mind wandered.

There was a scratching.

Arthur sat bolt upright, his pipe long cold in his hand. There it was again! The rhythmic tapping of hardened nails or the burrowing of an animal; a rat, perhaps, clawing out a hole between the beams in the wall hollow. The sound was distinctive and clear, for the wind had now quit, and outside snow was still falling.

He looked to the doorway, open a crack, hinting of the passage-way beyond it, but the sound came from the open window – it was somewhere out in the night. Arthur rose and crept quietly towards it. Forward. Forward towards it. Forward till he held the edge of the frame and leaned out over the white world. And then the hush, the deafness of first snow. A smothering of nature, beautiful in its silence. Arthur stared down upon it. Not a soul, living or dead, wandered into view.

There was nothing there, the noise was gone, just tiers of shuttered windows; and then the shadow fell upon him – a darkness blocking the moon.

Arthur pulled back just in time as the witch lashed out with fury, yet she caught him with a glancing swipe that opened his cheek up deeply, a blow that bit his bloodless flesh but might have ripped his throat out.

Arthur backed away from the ledge but stumbled and fell on the carpet. Before him the spirit climbed through the window, her loose dress billowing about her. "No, girl! Don't!" he cried. She advanced unbidden on all fours, her feet and hands both gripping. He recoiled as he saw she was unshod of boot and that her feet bore toes like talons.

"Listen, please!" Arthur retreated on his elbows while the witch grew tall before him. It was no girl that bore over him, no young lady by the mill site; Arthur, so often indomitable, flinched before the un-natural creature.

The Beauvais witch had kept her pretty nose and a brow lined deep with sorrows, but her jaw was swollen full of teeth that were spiked and sharp and rotten. Before, her eyes had showed a human hate, but now they glowed with demonic fervor. An appetite for re-venge and death had stoked their juice with luster.

"Élise Beauvais!" Arthur bellowed her name, and at the mention she halted her progress. Arthur didn't stop to give it thought, but ran his words while he had the chance to. "Élise Beauvais, you have long been ill-treated and I, Arthur Malenfer, say so! I, eldest born, heir to the name, the family that wounded you, say so!"

Arthur had thought through his speech at the crypt, how he would try to reason with her, but the words that came in his desperation spilled out without rehearsal. As the girl paused, appearing to listen, he knew he had one chance to save himself. "I know what they did to you," he spluttered. "What *we* did to you... and I know what we did to your family! And it was wrong, and we knew it, yet we lived off the profits, and we'll answer to God for our actions. But end this! End your hate now, please. Let those that are left know solace.

"They're innocents," he implored, "the few that are left, the young who are left of this family. They love and they're loved, and why should they not? Put an end to your curse and your pain!"

He could see through the girl – she was a girl again – through to the still falling snow. His momentary reprieve gave him encouragement and he let his tongue run on.

"Is it fair that they pay for the wrong of another, in this century when all seem to suffer?" If she made reason of his words he could not tell; if she accepted his request he was no wiser.

"Élise Beauvais." When he spoke her name she seemed blown by a gust of memory. "I have but one son remaining, and he, like me, has known loss. Feed your grief with these children no longer! Blacken your heart no more! Leave us be and make your peace however you are able."

He saw Élise Beauvais as she once might have been: a fresh young woman with bows in her braids and a new spring dress for a baptism. A smiling young lady flush with good health and the warmth of friendship upon her. For a moment Arthur thought he'd touched her soul and calmed her troubled spirit.

But only for a moment.

Because the wrong and the hurt and the hatred of years in a life beyond life beyond meaning rose again inside Élise and with it the nightmare creature. Arthur cringed before the fiend and knew the entirety of his failure. "Dermot – help!" he managed to yell, and then the witch drove her hand through his belly.

Arthur's world exploded.

He looked to his stomach where he was coming apart, as if he had flesh and it was flayed from his body. Her fingernails cut and rent him inside like barbed wire tearing into a body. But it wasn't just his own pain which he felt that caused him to lose his mind. Her touch was like a shattered mirror, each shard a memory, every one of them poison and vile.

He didn't know what he was seeing at first; the vision shifted, and then came sharply to focus. He was standing in a bedroom: The chamber seemed familiar, and there was a man leaning over a bed. He felt the panic and the helpless trembling of the boy pinned beneath the pillow. Arthur tried to gasp for breath and found there was none coming.

Then the picture shifted, splintered and moved, and he was in one of the manor's staircases. There was an older man stumbling in the dark and the sensation of a sudden push. Down he slipped, over and over. Arthur felt each blow. His broken windpipe and shattered neck that lay at a crooked angle. His father's face looked up at him, just as the family had found him.

Again it changed, and Arthur was following a boy running along a glade. He didn't recognize the child who slipped and went down a wet bank into the river. He was underneath the water with him, watching him grasp desperately for tree roots, but a tug at the boy's ankle – it might have been the current – pulled them from his fingers. Arthur floated with the boy face down till the stones on the stream bed lost focus.

A boisterous man at a full Christmas table, slicing open a roasted hen. Arthur felt his hand slip as he was driving the knife, the edge of it slicing his hand. The skin flapped open wide at his wrist; it was the shock of it more than anything. It looked like nothing, the pain was numb, but the blood just wouldn't stop coming.

A rider not clearing a fence.

A boy on a wall, his arms wind-milling, reaching out to a hay fork for balance.

A woman up a tree, wild dogs down below, and the branch she was on giving way.

A young girl sliding down a rope into a well from which the mewing of a cat could be heard.

A powdered dandy being ridden by a whore whose discharge smelled of the clap.

A fusilier in burnished chest plate riding bravely towards the canons.

A mother in labor, squeezing out twins, feeling herself start to tear.

And then the last.

A tree. A single tree. The branches of a tree, turning slowly around. And in the sky a plume of smoke and the smell of sizzling hot pitch.

Arthur fought for breath.

He was pulled by a strength he thought only possessed by those who were still with the living. Beauvais dragged him by the guts towards the wide open window. "No! God, no!" he shrieked, clawing at the floor, but he was snared and barbed on her fingers. It was a hopeless pain, like in the back of the ambulance, which the dead should by rights be spared. He thought of Émile and then of his niece before sensation rent his reason. There was only the agony and the panic of hell into which he knew she was taking him.

"Help me, Dermot! Oh, please God no." The floor of his room slid beneath him. He'd been pulled half up onto the window ledge when Simonne burst in through the doorway.

Chapter 25
Entente

THE MAN APPROACHED THE TIERED STONE ARCHES WITH A SOFT AND stealthy step, a scarf tied high around his face and darkness covering the rest. He left a line of solitary footprints on the unbroken snow around him, down towards the railway bridge that spanned the broad Suize river.

The man paused. He stared ahead into the columns that rose up from the bank. At last he made out a small cloaked figure crouched beneath the viaduct, and when he did he retraced his steps and then circled back down lower.

"Hello, Simonne." The figure jerked upright, startled by his closeness. He stood behind her, only an arm's length away. "You didn't hear me coming?" He couldn't keep the smile from his voice; it gratified his ego. "I've come all alone, just the two of us, just as your message asked. Now what was it you wanted to talk to me about, all this way out in the snow?" Old Crevel spoke with a jackal's sneer. He restrained his lascivious hands.

The figure spun around to face him, and then cast back the deep hood.

"What? What's the meaning here?" Crevel stuttered, recognizing the man immediately. He staggered back as he collected his thoughts, thrown off balance but recovering.

"Surely you remember *me*, Mister Mayor?" Dermot rose to his full height now. His powerful shoulders rolled back, his hands ready at his sides. "I'm 'the common soldier,' the unwanted guest full of 'base desires' without a shred of honor. Didn't you say that? You remember that, don't you?" Crevel backed off a little further. "Do you know what else I am, Mister Mayor? I'm the spanner in the works, the fool that sentenced the twins to die. But I'm back to make amends."

Crevel stumbled in the snow, the temporary shelter of the elevated track no longer sheltering the ground. He held his hands defensively out in front of him. "What are you talking about? Spanners and twins!" His eyes beaded, black holes of malice, and his finger stretched out and pointed. "Why are you here to bother me, boy? Why haven't you left this place? You're nothing but a waster that Madame threw out with his tail between his legs!" He was puffed up with indignation now. "Are you after money, is that it? Have you sunk so low as that?" His voice grew in confidence and aggression as he recovered from his first shock. "What have you done with Simonne?" Crevel demanded to know.

Dermot the while had circled around so that Crevel's back was towards the bridge. "I'm sure Mademoiselle will be *very* pleased to hear of your concern for her health," he growled, "at least until she's married your spawn."

"What do you mean by that?" Crevel puffed. "Why did you bring me out here?" His political mind, suspicious and neurotic, whirled and parried. *Simonne.*

Simonne had talked to Robert that day, alone and by herself. She'd used his son to set up the meeting beneath the viaduct.

"Why?" Crevel had asked his boy, when he'd disturbed him with the request. "What does she mean, 'Come before dawn,' and what does she want with me there?" But Crevel had his suspicions, and was already working on how it should play.

"She wouldn't tell me, Father!" Robert had been adamant, his too-honest face devoid of sense or guile or hint of danger. "She just said to come alone."

"Don't worry," Crevel had said cheerily, calming his son, laying his concerns to rest. "It's bound to be some flutter of the heart she's had about the wedding. Some trivial detail she's turned into a burning wish of hers." He'd treated the summons as an elaborate fancy, reassuring his pliable boy. "She probably doesn't want you to know about it, something she's keeping as a surprise. I suspect it costs a little money, and her own mother has refused to comply. I'll take care of everything, don't worry about it at all." And when Crevel was alone at last, and he'd seen Robert off to bed, the cogs of his mind ground industrially away, reviewing scenarios of survival and danger.

There was only a murmur from the riverbanks below them belying the power that it channeled, and a faint distant whistle of a train engine carried, the sound trickling in through the quiet. These noises and the inconvenient Irishman were his only company here.

The old politician sized him up with his keen intelligent eye. "Why have you dragged me out here under pretense, Mr. Ward? I admit I am curious to that." He forced a smile upon his face and kept up his charade.

"You lied, Crevel," Dermot's voice was low and cold and flat; the time for platitudes was over. Unconsciously Ward leaned his shoulders in, but the older man did not rile.

Dermot wrestled down the impulse to cross the five yards between them. Much that was dear to him depended on his patience. Ward felt justice close at hand; it was time for retribution. "You lied," he said once more.

The Mayor paused, weighing his response. He had imagined such a conversation many times in many forms, though he hadn't known if or when or from whom it would come. It did not faze him now. "I am in politics, Mr. Ward, lying for me is a robe of office. You will have to be a little clearer if you have something you are trying to expound." He said it with all innocence, a smile of wax upon his face. "I tell you what. I'll give you the courtesy to speak to whatever fancy has entered your foreign head; and then I'll laugh it off, and then we'll go home out of the cold and back to our respective beds."

"No, Crevel. I think we both know that *that* is not going to happen here."

Dermot did not attempt to stem the loathing he poured on the man. Crevel backed slowly off.

"Forgive me, Ward, I'm a patient man, but I don't quite understand the point you are trying to make. I think I'll be leaving now."

"You don't understand?" Dermot was loud and aggressive and clear. "I think you know already, Crevel. I think you're lying again. I think that mind of yours is whirling around and you know exactly what I mean. *Does anyone else know? What has he told Madame or Simonne? How did he figure it out?* These are the questions you are asking yourself, Crevel, it's in your devious nature to do so.

"Can you buy a silence, you wonder, or is there another slippery way out? *Anything* but take responsibility, *anything* but accept the consequences for what you've already done. Parliaments and assemblies are full of people like you, Crevel, you're not so special, you're not alone. Belligerents strut, immune to the shells, and send good men towards the guns. But this time there's no escaping it. Today you pay your bill."

Ward saw steel behind Crevel's eyes, but he did not give a damn. Fleetingly he wondered if Michel or Pierre had seen that look as well – their last before they died.

Crevel laughed dismissively, but knew immediately he'd made a mistake. The Mayor was familiar with having an audience to play to, a crowd to convince, but he found himself alone. In this, a gallery of one, his pretense sounded hollow and wasn't believed by anyone. He knew it and he hated himself, and so he hated Dermot more.

This was no reconciliation, Crevel understood now. He thought to end it, fingering the service revolver he had in his pocket, but he wanted to hear out the Irishman; he needed to know more. What exactly *did* Dermot know? How far had it spread?

"Calm down, Ward." He backed off again, Dermot closing the distance to match. "Tell me, what is it you think I have done? I'll entertain that much."

"You murdered Michel Malenfer, that was a start, and then you shot and gutted Pierre!"

Crevel was taken aback by the outright accusation and the gale with which it was delivered.

"It was influenza, you fool!" But Dermot was paying him no heed.

"You fostered suspicion on innocent men to their ruin at the mill; then you planted evidence against Émile and aim to see him executed!"

Crevel shifted his step back once again, stumbling on a rock beneath the archways. The raised voice echoed disturbingly on the stonework; the sound of the train across the water was clear and growing louder as it drew nearer. Crevel fumbled in his pocket and cocked the hammer on the .38 pistol. He'd heard almost enough.

"You needed two things." Dermot looked like a bull before the Mayor, snorting and pawing the dirt. "The Malenfer inheritance had to fall to Simonne, and your son would have to marry her. That's what everything was always about, that's why you did everything that you did here."

"You rant, Irishman, I suggest you calm yourself." Crevel trained the hidden barrel on his adversary, ready to blow a hole in him.

"Rant?" Dermot seemed amused. "What else did you come here for, if not to hear someone speak and explain? I'll tell you how it went. First, Arthur died in service – I think that's when you hatched your wicked plan. It was only Michel who then stood in the way of Simonne inheriting everything, the entire Malenfer estate! Inheriting after her mother Sophie, the grieving faithful widow.

"But Simonne was still young back then. Too young to marry. And you couldn't risk Michel dead before any engagement could be made. No, no, don't shake your head! You know as well as I that people like the Malenfers wouldn't likely accept a common suit from a family such as yours – not if she was the heiress, not if she was all they had left." Crevel scowled at the insult but held his tongue. "Madame would not likely condescend to see her legacy weaseled away. You have no nobility, Monsieur Crevel, and not nearly enough money in hand to pretend it didn't matter. Madame might see you for what you are – a grasper on the make!

"Did you ruminate long over how or when to move Michel out of the way? I wonder, Crevel, did it linger in your mind for those two whole years after Arthur died in the war?" Dermot could see the mask begin to crack on Crevel's mannequin face, his eyebrows drawing together, his lips pressed tight and hard. "Do you want to hear what I've got to say, Mr. Mayor? Then listen closely and carefully.

"You played your cards well to win the engagement. Fate and circumstance seemed to be on your side. I imagine you took that as a sign from Providence that your scheme would work out fine. Robert has an aesthetic charm about him, and a perfume of sophistication. And he survived the war! Simonne, now of age, is ripe for marriage, and Madame approves as well. It's all coming together so nicely, and then Michel falls ill from the flu."

Dermot paced back and forth, consumed by the picture brought to life by his own narration.

"I see it now! You're standing there. I bet you're thinking that God is going to take care of everything. The hubris! The gall! To think with all the slaughter in France that He is looking out for you." Dermot laughed at him, irking Crevel, who suffered visibly at the Irishman's withering words. It is said of pride that a grain of truth is the seed that rubs it raw. "You did, didn't you?" Dermot continued. "You thought destiny had laid it out for you on a plate!

"Didn't turn out that way, though, and Michel broke the fever and started to get better. That couldn't happen, could it?" Crevel said nothing. The stones of the bridge now hummed softly with the approach of the locomotive. "But somehow the opportunity arose to be sure of Michel, and you took it! A pillow to his face? Medicine for him to drink? You played your hand and got away with it, and it looked as if you'd win.

"Only then did things start to go wrong for you; the Fates, it seemed, had turned. It was I, Crevel, I who arrived unbidden with the news of Arthur's twins. I who unwittingly marked them for your attention and ultimately their death." Dermot, who had been baiting and teasing Crevel, now found his firebox had been lit. "I arrived at the house and brought you Arthur Malenfer's confession. It was I who produced their birth certificates, I who had no caution. Careless and cavalier, I was, and I must carry that guilt with me always... It was I, Crevel, but how was I to know? How was I to know there was a snake in the nest already?

"Now what could you do? Would Madame divide the inheritance, or give it all to a bastard child? You didn't know, how could you? But it was a risk that couldn't be borne! You'd already murdered one man to stem chance, so what were a couple more? I think by that point you were not really a believer in Fate anymore. You were happier making your own choices, is that not so, Mr. Mayor?

"Did you meet the deserters beforehand, who were living at the mill? Did you tell them of Pierre, who would be traveling collecting rents? You know what I think, Crevel? I don't think you have the spine to do honest killing yourself; it takes a kind of mettle to fix a bayonet on a rifle, to stand up on the firing platform and wait to hear your orders. I don't think you have it in you to drive a blade straight through a ribcage, to watch a man cry bloody pleas as he falls upon his knee-caps. I don't think you have that in you because I've seen hundreds and hundreds tested, and after a while you learn about men and you can tell just what they're made of."

"Shut up, Irishman! You're a fool and you're done!" Crevel pulled out the gun. He trained the barrel square on Dermot, who froze before him, hands raised, palms forward in submission. "I shot the man! How hard is it to figure that out? I'm not going to confide in a pack of mongrel soldiers! Who do you think I am? It was easy enough to pin the blame; people around here are always suspicious of strangers from outside." The Mayor had had enough. Proof or not, Dermot was talking too much, saying things other people could never be allowed to hear. Ever.

"And I suppose you needed his satchel too, to be sure of getting Émile?" Crevel, a sneer of triumph on his face, didn't bother to reply. "But why did you gut the boy? Why knife him? Why defile... ?"

"They are sheep! That's why, Mr. Ward. People are sheep, easily distracted and led. Shoot a man and it's murder; gut a Malenfer and it's their stupid curse! Who will look deeper or think harder about anything when the supernatural is at work? Enough of this now. Keep your distance; we're going for a little walk."

"So you gutted Pierre!" Dermot spoke louder, moving around hands up, but still facing Crevel. "Pierre, who made the most of the life he'd been given, growing up without a father. Pierre, who might have enjoyed a little more. He threatened the coin in your pocket! You slaughtered him for avarice. You desecrated the boy!"

"Shut up. That's enough. Get going." He motioned with his gun.

"I've wondered about Sophie, though. What if she married again?"

"Who said I didn't ask her?" He regretted his admission.

"Aha! That's it, then! But she preferred a life of her mother's tongue than to sit and listen to yours. I had wondered... I suppose if another suitor showed up, she'd meet with a timely accident?"

"Keep walking."

Dermot moved slowly as directed, seemingly unfazed by the weapon. "You don't surprise me, Crevel," he continued after a moment. "I've lived beside evil for years. When we were in the trenches – not you, of course, you were too busy off doing important things – but when we were in the trenches we died in heaps beneath the guns. The pride of nations is an ordinary evil; king and country before man. It's so common we don't even give it its true name. I recognize evil, Crevel, and I see it alive in you. Do you know how Émile now suffers?"

"Shut up, Ward! He's getting what he needed, just like I'll take care of you!"

"Two more lives just to line your pocket?" Dermot waved his arms, excited. He had been poised in his trench waiting until now, goading his enemy to play. "But Simonne isn't going to marry your son. That's not happening, Crevel. Don't you see? You get nothing now!"

Crevel looked as if he could happily slit Dermot's throat.

"Changes things up, don't you think?" Ward grinned at him cheerily. "Mademoiselle doesn't want to marry into a family that's bent on finishing off her own – let's call it a case of bridal nerves," he taunted the mayor.

"She will marry him! She has to!"

"Not if she's marrying me."

Crevel raised his arm, his finger squeezing the trigger that would obliterate the man; the meddlesome Irishman that had descended upon him, ruining his plans. Michel had gone quietly, trusting, uncomprehending until the very last. Pierre had guessed at trouble but too late; when Crevel had stepped out and blocked his path there had been nowhere for the twin to run. Émile he hadn't had to watch; he'd been malleable and weak. But not this man, not the cretin Ward! He might already have ruined everything – but he would pay for stepping in.

A soldier doesn't often get to see the gun that kills him; he hugs the trench in front of him and waits to hear the signal. Forty meters above their heads the Paris night train hurtled. The earth it shook like cannon fire and its boilers blew the whistle. Dermot heard the call to charge and like a soldier he answered. The sergeant released and fell on Crevel like a hammer strikes an anvil.

"I... will... never... give in...!" The Mayor stuttered the words through foaming lips, both of his hands upon his gun. Dermot held it away from him with one hard and wiry arm.

Ward was cold and controlled, his voice level and low. "It ends, Crevel," he whispered gently to the struggling man, a tender terrible voice to hear. "It ends now."

"It's your word against mine, Mr. Ward. You haven't learned a bloody thing."

Ten years of tunnels, war mines and digging; ten years that had carved Dermot Ward. Crevel clawed against him, his foe less giving than the rock face from which he seemed hewn. Dermot reached behind him and took out his old bayonet. It was a stiletto blade of tempered steel that he'd strapped behind his back.

What had he promised Arthur as he cradled his dead son? How do you judge a man but that he keeps his word to a friend? *I'll help, Arthur, I'll get who did this. We'll get the bastard together.*

"This is for Pierre!" he said, and thrust forward into Crevel, who screeched as it pierced his belly. "For Michel!" Dermot thrust again, deeper this time, a fresh wound poked through his guts that came out the other side.

Crevel's shocked eyes looked up into his face, disbelieving. The gun fell at their side.

"For Émile and those innocent men!" Dermot bellowed and plunged into him a third time. Crevel's blood streamed out over his arm.

The Mayor's breath was now one long wheeze that rolled out of him like a snore. Crevel clung to Dermot's shoulders, fighting to hold himself up. His legs had gone beneath him as if he could not feel his feet.

Dermot shook with a frenzied passion. He pulled the bayonet from Crevel's abdomen and pushed the dying man down. Crevel bowed like a penitent before the cross, kneeling in the snow.

"And for what you would have done to Simonne!"

Dermot seized the villain by the hair and drove the dagger down. The blade tore into Crevel's collar only inches below his neck. Dermot buried it to its hilt. The bloody dagger was wedged in tight – it sprung free with a frothy jolt.

The last of Crevel spouted up and sprayed from that terrible wound. His body teetered a moment and then slumped slowly to one side, Crevel's head dropped down to his chest with his legs drawn up beneath him. His muscles gave a final spasm and sent his arms to tremble, as the pulsing blood slowed to a trickle and finally subsided. It leaked into a puddle dark against the clean crisp snow. It grew until it reached its limit and then it grew no more.

Dermot stood stock still, afloat for a moment in a serene calm. He had come through the battle, and come through unharmed. He had seen the gun that would have killed him and had come away victorious. He was distantly aware of noises – of mutterings and scrambling behind him, of the clatter of a train's wheels receding in the distance, of a cockerel crowing ahead of a dawn on a fresh new winter morning. A virgin land whose scars were covered, whose blemishes were hidden.

He saw figures help each other climb up the bank from beside the river. They emerged as trolls from beneath the bridge where they had spent the time well hidden. Dermot paid none of them heed as they gathered around him – Madame and Gustave and two other men: a beanpole and a barrel.

"You heard everything, then?" Dermot said matter-of-factly, his eyes still on Crevel.

"Unpleasant as it was." Madame spoke for them all. Dermot and Simonne had woken her in the middle of the night, and spent a rancorous half hour convincing her of their plan.

Madame dusted the earth from her skirts and straightened herself up. "It seems I've misjudged you, Mr. Ward. My family owes you a debt."

She looked past Ward, regarding the body of the slaughtered Crevel with the look of a scavenger crow. "Gustave!" she summoned.

"Yes, Madame?"

"Have your men remove this carrion. Dispose of it somewhere."

"As you wish, Madame." The bent scarred form of the Malenfer footman turned towards the two men.

"And there is likely to be a car somewhere up near the road. Have it driven off to a distant town and abandon it there."

"Of course, Madame. As you say."

"Mr. Ward?"

Dermot looked at her, the gravity of her voice was stronger than the pull of the dead Crevel. "Madame?"

"You have a Malenfer sense of justice in you." From the matriarch, it sounded like a compliment. "He got exactly what he deserved."

"I only did what needed doing. It was the only way she'd be safe."

Madame held his stare for a moment before she turned away. Was there a darkness, he wondered, that they shared? The guilt of past failures? Fear for those for whom you care? Or would he never understand her?

"Gustave!"

"Madame?" the twisted man had been putting the men to labor.

"Take me home, please, Gustave. And when we get there, inform Berthe that Mr. Ward will need his room for some while longer. I imagine for quite some time. And have her draw him a nice hot bath;

it looks as though he needs one."

"Of course, Madame."

"Well? What are you waiting for? Hurry up, man!"

Chapter 26
Laid to Rest

THE SUMMER OF 1919 WAS A WARM ONE. "UNBEARABLE," THEY SAID IN Paris. *How soon our sufferings change.*

The Peace Conference had finished not two months previously and everyone everywhere was upset. The American Congress couldn't ratify Wilson's peace and Chancellor Scheidemann had resigned. The press bashed Clemenceau for letting the Germans off easily, while the Brits thought they'd burned them to the ground. Ward saw all this as a good sign – perhaps after the months of wrangling they had gotten the best deal possible for the time. Germany was left intact, that was true, but the shelling was history for now. Across Europe the guns had stopped and long might it continue. Paris luxuriated in the torments of the sun, and the world around her moved on.

Malenfer Manor was a different animal in the glow of a summer's day. Where before the landscape had been charcoal drawn, Minerva had opened her paintbox. The funeral of Madame Malenfer proved to be a grand affair – she had succumbed to consumption in the springtime of that year. Crowds from the surrounding countryside flocked to see her off, united in curiosity but at odds over where she was headed. There were those who grieved from sentiment and those who attended to make certain, but consensus was reached on one thing: with her death an age was passing.

When Madame was born (it was only the very eldest who could remember her by any other name), Louis-Napoléon Bonaparte III sat upon the throne – he was the last king France had known. She'd been a child of the Third Republic in an age when empires ruled; progress for a continent, but under a gathering cloud. Hers was a time of colonial ambition that knew no moderation, of patriotic governments with feudal sensibilities. Disputes settled between gentlemen while the factories forged machine guns.

The people that came to watch her go shared a bond that went unspoken, for they had endured the darkest years and had lived to see the springtime. The mourners had borne privation and suffered plague and seen the fighting, had loved and lost or simply lost, and now they gathered to remember. Brutal times were behind them all, but what lay in the future? All they knew was that life for them would somehow forever be different, and so the living took heart in life and enjoyed the Malenfer spectacle. Madame's coffin trundled past, pulled by a team of horses, her casket draped in familiar black with lilies heaped high upon it. Malenfer Manor was opened to all and was a Wednesday long remembered.

Madame had lived long enough to see the wedding of her granddaughter. Madame Simonne Ward had been given away by her much approving mother. The private Mass was small and short but no less moving for it. Arthur wore a handsome new suit and no one asked him where he'd gotten it. The more solid Émile was entrusted by Dermot with the care of the wedding bands, and so it was that the bride's own cousin was best man to the groom.

The Malenfer twin was free on bail and the charges against him were thin; with a warrant out for Crevel's arrest, the case looked close to failure. Madame had sworn new written testimony against the absent Mayor, stating that he had confessed his deeds before threatening her life also. Madame had struck the prosecutor as a very convincing witness.

Crevel's car was recovered near a railway station some miles distant from Darmannes, while the man himself was not seen in weeks that turned into months. A warrant was issued for the Mayor in his absence at the summons, and his likeness still hangs on the wall of the local Chevecheix post office.

"Do you take this man to be your husband, to love and cherish for all of your days?"

"I do," Simonne told the young priest, while Father Meslier scowled on from a pew. Dermot kissed his radiant bride. They honeymooned in London and Ireland before sailing home to France.

Of Élise Beauvais there had been no further sign since the dark hour of the reckoning. Perhaps what humanity remained in Élise had accepted Arthur's challenge, and that forgiveness had finally brought her a peace that revenge could not provide. Whatever the case, her blighted presence had been absent since that night, when Simonne had closed the window on her and cast her from the Manor.

In the aftermath of that fateful dawn, Dermot had heard the tale. "She's gone?"

"I don't know for certain," Simonne had replied. "But I feel nothing of her now."

"What happened in Arthur's room? What did you see when you got there?"

"See?" Simonne thought for a moment. "It wasn't quite that way." Dermot knew not to rush her. "The children warned me she was coming. They were afraid, like they sometimes get, and I tried to calm them down. Then I heard him call. Arthur, that is. I felt his fear... his despair. It was terrible. When I got there, the window was open and the place was bitter cold. I hadn't been in that room for years. Do you know that was where Grand-mère put her babies? The ones she delivered stillborn. Why would she do something like that? Who would do such a thing?"

"I can't imagine, Simonne. Let's be generous and call her complicated. Perhaps she couldn't let go?"

"Well, when I got there, I felt a malice in the room. That's what it was. It filled the open window like a tactile darkness, and I thought it was trying to get in."

"You weren't scared?"

"I didn't even think, my love, I ran over and pushed it back through. I didn't want anything like that coming inside, being around people I care for. And then I saw her."

"Who?"

"Élise Beauvais. She was there. Just a young girl in a pretty dress, lying broken on the ground down below. Her arms were all twisted and bent at angles; I knew she had fallen somehow. She was staring blankly up at me from the snow-covered ground. But do you know the oddest part?"

"What's that?"

"I thought she looked quite peaceful."

Dermot thought about that. "There was nothing at all. There was no-one there. We went out afterwards and looked."

"I know. I know that. I can't explain it. But she was there. She was there. Lying like a broken doll. And the room was so cold that I closed the window. But I could see her through the frost on the panes."

"And you think she's finally gone?"

"Oh, I hope so, Dermot. I don't know for certain. But I've felt nothing of her since."

The crops had been sown, the weather improved, then summer arrived on cue; and when it did it found Dermot thinking more about his friend. He had seen less and less of Arthur over the last few months, though when he had come across him, his friend had always been content.

"Is there anything I can do for you?" Dermot had broached one day, catching Arthur in the library. "Is everything all right?"

"Just make sure Berthe keeps turning that book," Arthur replied gently. "She forgot one day last week."

The ritual of the book advancement was a mystery to the servants: Every day they flipped a page and never were the wiser. But this was no less peculiar than some of the other goings on. For one thing, under the new Master and Mistress, the tenants had been encouraged to buy their own land. The estate was giving out lease purchase agreements that the talk had labeled "generous." No one wished to ask or question, and the pages were dutifully turned.

"Arthur?" Dermot had been bucking up the nerve to talk about the subject.

"What can I do for you, Irlandais?" He mulled over the paper, his pipe clacking between his teeth.

He thought his friend had been different since the night the witch had left. "I was wondering..." Dermot continued, hesitantly, "would you like perhaps to..." He paused and then got it out. "Would you like if we had you exhumed? Your remains, I mean, Arthur. Would you prefer to be brought back to Chevecheix?" He'd been thinking about the tomb, the racks of Malenfer ancestors, Arthur's mother and father among them, old bones stacked like so many cairns of stones. "Would you like to be brought home?" He hoped he hadn't upset his friend by asking.

The spirit looked up at him, removing his pipe before he spoke. "It's a very nice thought, thank you, Dermot, and you know, I think I will accept. Why not?" He smiled. "I'm feeling quite... comfortable. I guess that's the word I'm looking for. Comfortable, and yet not quite settled. I believe I might be nearing... my rest?" He looked content, but a little distracted, a little preoccupied, as if the affairs of the living, their conversations and cares – including this one – were an abstraction to him now. A whisper he had to strain himself to hear.

Dermot said a few words more, but Arthur had returned to his newspaper. It was clear that he was immersed in it and was no longer listening. Dermot stopped trying to get through, feeling an unbidden tear in his eye. He knew it irretrievably now, that he was losing his friend once again.

One hot day in August, Dermot crossed the city square. He kept to the shade under the trees to avoid the direct heat, out of the way of the annoying cars that seemed at once to be everywhere.

"Four first class tickets to Épernay, please. Day returns, thank you."

They had set out together that morning: Dermot, his mother-in-law, Émile, and Simonne, newly expectant with child. The party lunched in Paris, where they bought their onward tickets, and found themselves in sleepy Épernay as the afternoon was fading. There was an evening train that would take them back, departing three hours later. They had no plans to stay the night. It was a long way to come for such a short visit, but for their purpose it was adequate.

The hospital at Épernay was in the process of being handed back. Dermot found he recognized little of it from the day, four years ago, when he'd driven up its gravel track. The rows of wounded, the efficient nurses, the stern-faced doctors all were gone. The sounds of pain, the cloud of fear, the smell of rot were nowhere to be found. It was a lovely house in mature gardens set far back from the road. They admired its form before entering and complimented its line. Inside they found it hollow, a few folding tables all that was left, and these stacked up in one room. There was a caretaker who met them; he got hold of an Army Corporal who looked fresh out of shorts. The boy was aware of the arrangements.

"Easiest if you go round the back, sir. Through the gardens, past a big tree. You can't miss it." He thrust his arms like semaphore to indicate the way. "There's a door in the wall at the back of the garden. I'll round them up and follow behind."

They trod the sod of the manicured lawn beneath the grand old maple's canopy. The grass was clear but for an occasional twig, while underfoot the crocus bulbs slept hidden.

The stout wooden door in the ivy brick wall was closed, but its lock bore a key and it worked. They walked single file through a small copse of woods on a trail that led them to a stream. They crossed the gully, with its trickle of water, and emerged at last to a field.

The crosses went on, row after row. There were hundreds of them, all neat and clean. So many of them, and yet almost none, for this was the hospital's own cemetery. Not like at Ypres, not like the Marne, not like at Verdun, not like the Somme. At a pallbearer's pace they went down the rows; Simonne reached for Dermot's hand. Almost all of the graves here had names – they were grateful – it wasn't like those other sites at all. Simonne paused by an exception and was joined by the others: *Here lies a soldier of the Great War, known only unto God.* Everyman. Her father perhaps. The somber party moved on.

Most of the men here were French. They shared the ground with the odd Belgian, and a dozen other nationalities: a Canadian, an American from their expedition only months before, an Italian, a Pole. Everyone a brother now beneath the verdant sod. Eventually they found what they had come for: *Lieutenant Arthur Malenfer* in the engraver's practiced hand. They stopped, gathered around it, and paid their respects silently, each in their own way, to the man who lay below: uncle, brother, father, friend. They had brought no wreath and they said no farewell, for they were taking Arthur home. The Corporal came with men bearing shovels; he didn't make them wait long.

Arthur reached the top of the staircase. He passed a short table on which sat the stump of a burned down candle. He turned south down the hallway, long with shadow from the afternoon sun, walking away from Simonne's and Dermot's rooms towards the sound of a distant shutter. He wound his way through the twisting passage, back towards the end of the house. Back towards the last of the rooms where the attic could be found.

Little stairs fell down in bundles and then rose in twos and threes. The hallway fingered a tortured path that led to the old nursery. The door gleamed bright in fresh cream paint and muted sunlight from the window. Arthur paused and checked himself, and then leaned up close against it. He could hear the voices now, little whispers stifling laughter.

"It's me!" he said. "Let me in!"

He saw the brass handle slowly turn and the door begin to swing. Arthur bucked up, and pulled out his pipe. He smiled and stepped within.

That's strange, he thought as the curtains fluttered in front of the dormer window, then he noticed that all the noise had stopped the moment he crossed the threshold. A draft pulled the door and threw it shut and rattled the hinges behind him, and only then did he catch the scent on the wind as it blew in off the hillside.

And something, somewhere, was burning.

THE END

Author's Notes

As in many works of fiction there is much based on real events. The battles of the Aisne and Verdun and the Spanish Flu occurred. The loss of life was not exaggerated. Paris, in 1919, did play host to the Peace Conference where the 'big four' divided up Europe – there is a marvelous book by Margaret MacMillan that should be standard reading.

You can see the Chaumont Viaduct to this day and ride across it by train, but other locales, Chevecheix being one of them, were borrowed in name alone. The maple tree on the grounds of the Épernay Infirmary is real, as are its hidden crocus bulbs, but they live 5000 miles away, here on the Canadian west coast.

I like to think that somewhere on the way to Montmartre there is a rue des Trois Frères. You won't find it on Google or on any maps, but if you stumble over it, and follow it trustingly, you will come to your garden of swans. Absinthe was banned in France in 1914, but was legalized once more in 1988, under a different name, and finally in 2011 as absinthe again. Names rise and fall in popularity: "Simonne" was common from the early 1900s until the 1930s, but these days has been almost entirely supplanted by the spelling "Simone."

Malenfer Manor itself is imagined: two parts historic, one cup familial, and more than a pinch of gothic literary. It is not entirely Warpole's Otranto, Du Maurier's Manderley, or Lovecraft's New England bizarre, but then again, it is not entirely not. If the characters bear resemblance to anyone you know, put it down to chance or fate. And what of the metaphysical? Curses, witches, and spirits? I leave their existence to the conscience of the reader, lest I intrude on a place none should meddle.

A historical novel set in a foreign country is a minefield for the unwary writer. My misunderstandings about issues culinary, automotive, socio-hierarchical, sartorial, equestrian, and colloquial were far greater than I imagined. In educating me, and correcting my blunders, I would like to thank the advance readers who graciously read and commented on early drafts. In particular, Caroline Pettinotti Strasmann provided invaluable information and insights into French culture and customs. Any remaining faux pas are mine and mine alone. My editor, Dorothy, deserves a warm thank you, not least for her grammatical wisdom. I accepted far more of those comment boxes than I ended up rejecting. The book would not be the same without the considered wisdom of many.

The majority of ink was put to paper during a fertile year in Ubud, Bali, Indonesia, where I sat at a desk in that tropical land with a towel over my head. It takes a special sort of understanding to go along with such an undertaking – snakes, spiders, and dengue fever aside, there is the matter of giving up a pay check. Without the unending support of my darling wife Adrienne the book would not have happened.

Made in the USA
Lexington, KY
21 October 2013